RETURN OF ANARCHY
The Fall of New Australia

King Everett Medlin
with Patrick Fiedler

BOOKS BY KING EVERETT MEDLIN

Rijel 12: The Rise of New Australia
Return of Anarchy: The Fall of New Australia

BOOKS BY CHANDRA PRESS

Fusion World
Shadow of the Demon
Rijel 12: The Rise of New Australia
Return of Anarachy: The Fall of New Australia
Thad Saves the Galaxy
Sworld: The Chronicles of Malick
Soteria: The Crisis Forge
Mirrors: The Shadow Conspiracy
The Moon Hunters
Edj of the Empire: Herrig's World

chandra

CONTENTS

CHAPTER ONE
THE PORTAL

"**M**r. Brilly, do we have confirmation yet?"

Admiral Slout Epididymus had just returned to the command bridge and was seated in his captain's chair onboard the Naustie flagship *Anarchy*. This had been specially made for him after the former freighter had been captured following the riot at New Australia Planetary Prison. Originally designed for humans, and with Admiral Snout being a Suidonji, it had to be altered to accommodate his form. He was addressing Ensign Frilbriliram who had been awaiting word as to whether the ship's science officer had given the green light.

His science team had been working nonstop for the past twenty hours. They'd studied the area and discovered conditions were right for the existence of a *wormhole*, a space anomaly that most considered theoretical at best. The idea of actually travelling through one had been routinely dismissed over the centuries. This concept of a 'space portal' was an old one; and to ship captains more legend than reality. A thousand years ago wormholes had been proposed by a revered scientist back on Earth. That being said, few outside the literary community or film industry ever imagined one being *traversed*.

That's precisely what had been argued by Science Officer Minggatu. He was an Earther and an astronomy professor once, or so he'd claimed. He was dead-set against the idea at first. He changed his mind once the admiral explained their situation to him in more visceral terms. Everyone on board knew they were being hunted by a superior foe and sooner or later the Interplanetary Fleet would catch up to them. It wasn't if, it was when, and time was running out. Eventually they would have to stop somewhere and take on provisions.

Changing direction wouldn't cut it. They were being tracked and had been for quite some time. Once within firing range they'd be obliterated. It was preferable to find some way to conceal their location for a time. Disappearing inside of a wormhole sounded immensely appealing right about now. Not that Minggatu didn't have a point.

True, the ship's spectrometer had picked up on the anomaly; but that shouldn't have seemed unusual. They'd been running for their lives for some time now; had activated their warheads in order to provide extra speed thus setting up a harmonic field which caused a subspace field to be generated. This had illuminated a corridor and the spectrometer had identified a passage parallel to the ship. Minggatu, who was a soft-spoken Mongolian, tried explaining this when it had first occurred. Admiral Slout only heard what he wanted to hear; especially when his first officer alerted him to the opportunity. Did they have the technology to "open the door" and thus "disappear" entirely? That's all he'd wanted to know. If successful and if they truly could burrow through the fabric of space and survive to the other side, the Interplanetary Fleet would have no idea where they'd gone. Minggatu thought it to be foolhardy. They'd met privately in Slout's cabin to discuss it.

"Admiral, you need to realize, or do you already know just how risky this would be? We won't have any idea what's on the other side, even if we *can* force it open, even if we *do* manage to keep it open long enough to pass through. You know this, right?"

He was trying not to sound insubordinate while being as honest as he possibly could.

"A wormhole, just so we're understanding each other, they're only theoretical; a passage through space-time that supposedly creates a shortcut between points in the universe. Yes, they're *predicted* by the theory of general relativity but nothing more. Predicted; not verified. And according to Einstein-Rosen theory there is serious danger of collapse, not to mention high radiation."

Slout did not interrupt. He'd learned when it came to subordinates expressing expert opinions that it was wiser just to let them speak their minds. If they rattled on long enough they'd often end up talking themselves into whatever was proposed. That was always best. Minggatu had plenty to say.

"The first problem is size, sir. You see, primordial wormholes are predicted to exist on microscopic levels mere centimeters wide at the most. I mean, sure, as the universe has evolved, it is possible, remotely possible mind you, that some may have grown. The universe is constantly expanding. But the main issue is stability. Even Einstein himself never considered them as a means of traveling from one galaxy to another because they collapse quickly. That is, we believe they do."

But that's where Slout had him. It was merely a matter of making the argument that the *Anarchy's* Alcubierre warp drive was predicated on the creation of non-baryonic matter. He too knew a thing or two about interstellar travel. Had to. He'd been a ship's captain for many years; was a smuggler before he was sent to prison. Offered a "deal" if he'd identify the mobsters he was working for, he'd wisely chosen ten years at New Australia Planetary Prison rather than cooperating with investigators. If he only would have, he might have gotten off with a commuted sentence but Slout was too smart. The mob would have killed him for doing something like that.

"Yes," the admiral replied, pretending to be ill-informed. "I've heard of this. We would need some form of exotic matter, I believe it's called, in order to hold it open long enough for us to pass through."

"That's right, Admiral. You were told correctly," Minggatu

observed. "And it's not clear whether such a thing exists in great enough quantity within the natural realm. True, it could work in keeping the portal open while traversing one end to the other, but..."

"But what?" said the old ship captain. He could sense that his science officer knew the answer. The trick was in getting him to admit it.

"Well, sir, it's just that such matter, exotic matter, has only been discovered while in certain vacuum states as part of quantum theory. Those experiments have only been conducted in a controlled laboratory environment."

Slout decided it was time to turn the screws. What had always been believed, though never attempted in space, was that exotic matter contained negative energy density and large negative pressure. If it could be "created" in a lab, why couldn't it be done now using the same technology they already had onboard?

"I see. And do we not have a laboratory onboard this ship?" asked Slout. "Do we not already have the necessary facilities to accomplish this?"

"Accomplish what, Admiral?" asked Minggatu, being extra careful not to sound flippant. The ship's commander wasn't just his superior officer; he was also a massive Suidonji, fully capable of snapping the man's neck if he wanted to. Still, he could sense what his commander was driving at and it made him terribly uneasy. Slout, for his part, was done playing cat and mouse with the former college professor. What the little fellow really needed was to see the bigger picture; and Slout was happy to enlighten him. After a pause he stood up from the small table they were seated at and snorted menacingly, placing his hooves on the surface and glaring at him.

"Perhaps it is me who should be doing the explaining. We're being chased, Minggatu, and by a force fully capable of not only destroying us, but every living soul living on New Australia. It is what it is, but you need to understand just what's at stake here. We've been running from the IPF for too long and to be honest, we may never see our home planet again. But if we can elude them just long enough, who knows what could happen? All we know is that we're alive today ... and you, my friend, can see to it we're still that way tomorrow."

He then grinned his typical grin. It looked more like a smirk. Not well-known for his humor he raised a thick eyebrow and waited for the science officer's response. Like any good leader he knew when he'd made his point; what's more he knew when to stop talking and let his subordinate process what had been said. Say too much and it allowed time for devising a comeback. Say just enough to make it clear what was required of the man. That's all he wished to do. Either way it was a direct order he was giving; whether implied or stated.

"Figure it out," he added, in order to remove all doubt what he was demanding. This he did while raising up and placing his hooves on his hips. Minggatu realized this meant it was the end of the meeting. Slout was done with him for now. He'd either produce the results they needed in order to escape through the wormhole or die right along with the rest of his fellow crewmen. Might be days, weeks, or hours later once the Interplanetary Fleet caught up with them; but they would.

"Yes Admiral," was all he said in reply.

True, the ship's warp drive could and did produce non-baryonic matter. This was necessary to create "waves" which propelled the ship through space at many times the speed of light. But could Minggatu and his science team produce a *surplus* of this in order to pry open the worm hole and shoot through it? Could they then "seed" the passageway with enough to artificially prop it open and keep it from closing in; crushing their space craft like an egg? If so they'd be accomplishing something no one ever had, at least not to anyone's knowledge. That is, no other ship's crew had ever attempted such a feat and returned to tell the tale.

"Yes, Admiral." answered Ensign Frilbriliram. "We have confirmation. The portal is open; our sensors are verifying this as we speak."

Excitement arose among fellow officers surrounding him at his console. Admiral Slout was cool as a cucumber, watching the massive display screen which occupied one full wall of the command bridge. All that could be seen was the blackness of space not that anyone would have had a clue what they were looking at. Eyes shifted back and forth from Brilly's console and the giant video screen. To their delight, Minggatu and his science team had come up with the solution to their problem. They could now proceed through, using coordinates they believed would aim the pirate ship into the mouth of the anomaly. After that, was going to be a mystery. No telling what would be on the other side of it not to mention how long it would take to cross it.

"Is the course plotted then, Mr. Brilly?" asked Slout in a commanding yet calm voice.

"Yes, Admiral," he replied. "On your command, sir?"

"Excellent." proclaimed the skipper. "Everyone return to your stations and hold on. Make no mistake; we don't know what this is going to do to the ship. Might crush us. Might come out the other end only to find ourselves at the center of a super nova... incinerated before we even know what's happening to us. Might emerge without a scratch. We don't really know. But we're about to find out. Execute, Mr. Brilly."

After punching through they saw a strange succession of images onscreen. The ship's cameras were transmitting pictures instantaneously which provided a constant view of their surroundings, but it didn't make sense. They saw what seemed to be star systems flashing by, smeared across the screen as though they were slipping into oblivion. No one spoke for a time; it was all too much to take in. Slout looked around at his crew. Faces frozen in fear. A few slowly returned his gaze, trying to call out to him over the noise created by the ship's hull. It sounded as if the craft's exterior might be expanding and contracting as they sped through the passage. And that wasn't all. It seemed like things were moving in slow motion for a time. Crewmembers covered their faces, shielding themselves from the light of the video screen, frightened by what they saw, their movements lethargic and strained.

In time things returned to normal and the noises subsided. Slout assumed this meant they'd survived. By that point he had no idea how long they'd been hurtling through the void. That's when the thought occurred to him they needed to reverse engines and come to a stop. He tried to speak but the words came out as though he were waking up from a deep sleep. He'd discover later on they'd been inside the wormhole for sixteen hours. It felt like only a minute.

"All stop, Mr. Brilly." he bellowed, only he drawled and slurred his words as though he were intoxicated. As he regained his composure he repeated the command in a calmer voice.

"All stop. Cut power to engines, please. Do you hear me, Ensign? All stop."

Brilly was unconscious, or appeared to be, prompting the admiral to override the helm and complete the task himself. He then engaged reverse thrusters in order to bring the ship to a halt. At this point it was crucial they assess any damage their journey had caused. And besides, protocol would be to reverse-figure their position and project their course out of known space, adding to the stellar map.

But what he discovered next astounded him. He barely had to add power to the reverse thrusters and the ship came to an almost immediate stop. Then there was silence. He looked up at the screen once more and it was now only a blank canvass. Stars began to appear, right along with yet another striking discovery.

Slout examined the view screen, scanning up and down and side to side. Others came to or arose from their stations to join him in doing so. They got up one by one and walked toward the screen, as did Slout, not daring to offer opinions as to what it was and they didn't need to.

It was a planet.

CHAPTER TWO
SEVENTEEN YEARS LATER

"Good morning, students," burbled the aging instructor, a creature by the name of Megalocyathus. He was a Slartigifijian. A Slart as citizens of New Australia called them; even though on their ancestral planet such a term would be deemed derogatory. Like all Slarts he was squid-like with enormous eyes and long tentacles used for grasping things plus a grouping of much smaller ones at the base of his head. These fluttered when he spoke causing his voice to vibrate soothingly, almost comically. However, to the young, wide-eyed candidates training to become junior officers in the planet's merchant marine, he was a legend.

Of the original Slart "planners" who'd contributed to the Naustie Rebellion back in those heady days when General Archibald Hicks and Pierre "Perry" L'Orange devised a daring plan to break out of the loading bay and seize the prison complex, Megalocyathus was one of the few of his kind to survive. It was not unusual for Slarts to live twice as long as humans; four times that of an Enoshi or Suidonji. However, the only Slarts to have lived through Earth's failed invasion attempt ten years prior were those who'd served aboard ships within the Naustie trade fleet. These had been ordered to flee at the very sight of Earth warships and told by Terminal Chief Solomon Mwanga not to venture back until hostilities had ended. Then and only then were they to return. This crucial decision had ensured the survival of New Australia and thus its rebirth.

"Good morning." replied the room full of students, practically in unison. Their instructor's specialty was mathematics and he was a master of mechanical engineering. Megalocyathus had been part of General Hicks' original team of planners and worked alongside his partner Perry in removing detonators from two nuclear warheads found onboard an Earth freighter called the *Unity*, later renamed by the victorious rebels. These had been used in blowing a massive hole in the enemy's defenses; a pivotal move in turning the tide of the rebellion. He'd then served onboard Naustie merchant ships as an advisor and aided in negotiations with black market traders.

"We have a special guest with us today," continued Megalocyathus, now gesturing with a tentacle toward a young Human seated in the classroom. She had piercing dark eyes and long jet-black hair to complement her olive skin. Round faced and Amerindian in appearance, her biological father had been an Earther and her birth mother a long-forgotten captive who'd been taken during a pirate raid only to die in childbirth. The class of candidates had been through six rigorous weeks of training by this point and educated as to every aspect, every nut and bolt, of a galactic freighter. They were overdue for a break. A celebrity guest certainly fit the bill.

"I'm sure you all know her name by now. She's the daughter of Felina Toyger and Solomon Mwonga, First Citizens of New Australia; she's here to discuss our upcoming Independence Day celebration as well as your role in the ceremonies. Please welcome Melody Estrella Esperanza Mwonga."

An enthusiastic round of applause erupted from the youngsters. Most of them were sixteen years old, the same as the day's guest speaker. And Megalocyathus was quite correct about them knowing her name. They'd been with her during the long march, up from the planet's depths, after explosions had destabilized the planetary core, unleashing hell's fury upon murderous invaders who'd arrived by the thousands bent on destroying them. They'd been young children at the time, offspring of the many former captive females and prisoners who'd sired them both in and out of wedlock; and to them she was larger than life, the adopted daughter to New Australia's two brilliant leaders Solomon and Felina. From the beginning she'd been raised to be sole heir to the legacy they hoped to leave behind, of wisdom and compassion toward all. No one still alive from those dark days only a decade earlier would dare to doubt what the couple had accomplished. That's why the Tribal Assembly had voted them "First Citizens". This gave them final veto power on resolutions passed by delegates. It had never *officially* been utilized of course; on the contrary their influence among the assorted tribal chieftains had been plenty to inspire sound public policy. Nausties of every station and gender now enjoyed freedom and equality. This had been enough to sway embarrassed policymakers within the Interplanetary Authority to grant them their independence and that's precisely what they were looking forward to celebrating in a few days. Young Nausties, who'd been born there and considered themselves "natives", referred to the event as VE Day: "Victory over Earth".

"Thank you, everyone," responded Estrella, humbled by the warm reception from her peers. She'd grown up with them and now she was destined to be their leader, most likely the next First Citizen of New Australia. She'd been trained and coached, taught and re-taught how to be regal and diplomatic. Plus, she'd been schooled by her foster parents to think two or three steps beyond any situation she faced, exercising caution in terms of the way she worded things whenever speaking in public. She dressed the same as any commoner would; never accentuating her looks which were in reality quite underwhelming as opposed to her mother, the Star Kitten. Felina Toyger was still a fetching beauty, even as she approached middle age. Estrella was by way of comparison rather average in appearance. One would never know how exceptional she was until she spoke. That's when her father's intellect and her mother's poise shone through.

"Tomorrow we begin preparations for our annual celebration, demonstrating devotion and loyalty to a cause which our ancestors fought to win and did so with both bravery and determination. It is to be a day of remembrance: For the fallen. For those who sacrificed everything, all they had to give, so that we might be free. Free of fear and the threat of war, free to live our lives and enjoy the rich bounty which our planet provides. Our warriors fought and died so that we could be here today in this classroom. And yet the struggle continues. Every day our parents and neighbors toil in the fields or in the mines below. Just like our warriors once did, they give their all. That is why the Tribal Confederation has set aside one day every year when we can all pause and reflect. One flag, one people, united."

This drew a smattering of applause.

"There are those among you who have never plowed a field, never swung a pickaxe. Your fathers are crewmen onboard our many merchant vessels; some of them officers and ship captains. One might consider such individuals to be the elite; thus many of you in this inaugural class might be deemed the children of the elite, and that is a big responsibility. But let us not forget the vital role that every citizen from miner to farmer, from equipment operator to transport driver, from boatswain to first officer plays in the success of our great society. Remember this when you march past the crowds during the festivities. They look to you, my friends, as tomorrow's leaders. You are the best and brightest; that's why you were selected. Join me in showing our citizenry how honored you truly are to accept this charge."

New Australia had seen a rapid transformation since those difficult days and weeks following Earth's defeat. There was little to celebrate when ten thousand initial survivors of the planet-wide debacle reached the old service tunnel network that was now a global highway system and made their way topside. Their surface facilities had been destroyed. The original prison dome complex, once headquarters to a prison administration which worked them to death in the mines, had been reduced to a skeleton of girders, beams, and the scorched remnants of support walls. The loading bay with its retractable dome, where the captured warden was tethered to a post and left to die miserably on the planet's forbidding surface, had been destroyed in a tremendous fireball which vaporized its roof and incinerated its lift mechanism. These had once been necessary in order to receive ships and bring them below to be loaded and offloaded. In a flash both were gone, along with the newly built service garage as well as the planet's first and last solar domed farm.

In a last-ditch effort to exterminate their attackers, Solomon and his planning staff devised a potentially deadly solution to their problem. They detonated warheads over the roof of a magma chamber deep within the bowels of New Australia; after sending billions of gallons of melted glacier water down volcanic shafts. When the "cap" was blown off the chamber, this ignited a storm of lava which surged upward and ripped through the Earth invasion force like a chainsaw. The invaders, what was left of them, got back on their ships and went home, leaving destruction and death in their wake.

But there was an unexpected benefit to this. The horrific blast which shot up from the magma chamber altered the atmosphere of the planet. Releasing a plethora of gases including colloidal carbon, plus billowing clouds of water vapor, caused almost immediate effects. Exploding planet-wide volcanoes compounded this, leading to the formation of storm clouds. The once barren surface now experienced something no one had ever seen. For the first time in recorded history *it rained*.

After rescue efforts brought up as many survivors as possible from among the Naustie Army still trapped below; New Australia was left with a predicament. All they had were their merchant ships which had scattered prior to the invasion. Other than that, there was little they could do to reestablish an economy. The mines were still there; yet the machinery and manpower had been either destroyed or seriously damaged.

Lacking the ability to produce mineral ore and perovskite crystals for deep space travel; and lacking the ability to trade for food, meant they faced starvation. Then the rains came, and an amazed population rejoiced to find they could walk out on the once-forbidding planet surface to experience a succession of showers which occurred off and on for nearly a week. Their faith and dedication had served them well.

In the months following, Solomon Mwonga negotiated lines of credit with the governments of Zorgolong and Suidonj. These former enemies seized upon the opportunity to bankroll the Naustie home world's rejuvenation. They needed the minerals; Nausties needed materials and equipment to rebuild. Alliances were established with both planets; meanwhile New Australia's hard-working citizens planted millions of acres of now-tenable farmland. Once the soil was workable, citizens of New Australia worked it 'til their hands bled. Fresh water no longer being an issue, they sowed the seeds for a miraculous recovery.

"You'll be marching in the parade we're planning through the district housing projects of the Schlpeeftkorkii, Why-O, Smilodon, and several other tribes. Once again, each of these have contributed floats they've constructed especially for the event, but this year they wanted to do something different. This year tribal elders will be riding on them, tossing trinkets to the crowd. It was an idea suggested by a member of the Templar Knights. It was something he said he'd seen done back on Earth when he was a boy in a place called New Orleans. It's going to be quite a party but we want the inaugural class of cadets to bring up the rear, as a reminder of what this celebration is all about. Everyone's heard of the new academy we've started; now they'll want to see the results. What do you say to that?"

Estrella was referring to the annual tradition of staging a seven-mile parade through the many neighborhoods created by the construction of housing centers which were self-contained multi-family monstrosities containing dwellings for the many workers who tended the fields of New Australia. Thousands more still lived below in communities dedicated to the mining industry. Each tribe controlled sections of those mining operations; or they controlled "farm districts" up on the surface; with land allocations commensurate to their tribal population.

Naturally this drew an enthusiastic round of applause from the young audience which was made up mostly of her peers from the social elite. Not all of course. A handful were offspring of commoners who'd tested and shown great aptitude for mathematics and science. It was a level playing field for the most part and Felina Toyger had seen to it. She'd instituted the testing program which had been utilized in selecting candidates for the new academy.

"Very good, then. I thank you all for the effort you've put forth. Megalocyathus has informed me this has been a very solid class of students. I have to say that I'm jealous of you, I really am."

A few snickers could be heard from among the students.

"But unfortunately, my duties keep me rather occupied as it is. On top of that we have the Independence Day preparations to deal with. Most of which, I'm afraid to say, have fallen to me. Somehow, and for some reason, they thought I could handle it."

Once again, humble and self-effacing. Just what her parents had taught her. Never reveal your true abilities until circumstances call for it. Let your opponents underestimate you all they want; then when the time comes, *deliver*.

"And oh, by the way, you'll be issued state of the art breather units for the march, so you won't have to use your own. These will be new ones we just received from Suidonj. Porkos are manufacturing them for us on one of their colonies. They took original designs from Slart scientists on New Australia and streamlined them. Now they're sleek and light. You'll hardly notice wearing them."

Porko was a Naustie term for Suidonji. It was never something one would hear on other planets. It was just a nickname left over from the days when human convicts poked fun at these swine-like creatures and eventually other prisoners adopted the term. What Estrella meant by breather units was that up on the surface it was necessary to wear devices which processed oxygen when outside of climate-controlled buildings. It was still broiling hot, even though they could now farm. But more importantly the air was too thin for prolonged exposure. It was bright too; though most creatures could adapt to that. Nevertheless, to work outside required an oxygen-generation unit worn on the back with an air tube strapped across the mouth.

Her audience was impressed. New breather units? State of the art? That would make things so much easier. To this they applauded once more, all one hundred seventy-eight of them. Seeing there wasn't much left to discuss, Estrella turned to their instructor and thanked him for letting her interrupt the day's lessons.

"Well then, Megalocyathus," she said in conclusion, "I believe I'll return these fine individuals to your capable tentacles."

Megaolcyathus fluttered his facial tentacles in response, which was a Slart's sole method of expressing emotion. Whether they were feeling joyful, indignant, thankful, confused, or excited, it didn't matter. To understand which was what required knowing the context. Estrella knew Slarts well enough by now.

"Thank you, Estrella," chortled the venerated old scientist. Teaching physics and engineering at the new academy was a dream come true for him. "Let's all show our appreciation, shall we?" he then said, prompting the class to applaud her once more.

Estrella demurred. The pleasure was all hers. A day off from traveling around with her parents? That was just what the doctor ordered. Planning for the Independence Day parade and reception following had offered her time away from being dragged along on their almost year-round diplomatic missions to meet with tribal chieftains. This visit to New Australia's new Merchant Marine Academy was practically a vacation. Her parents by way of comparison were about to travel deep below the planet's surface on yet another tour of tribal homelands. To Estrella, given all she'd studied about Earth history, it was more of a *campaign* they were conducting, filled with stump speeches, glad-handing, and when necessary, *propaganda*.

CHAPTER THREE

A GHOST FROM THE PAST

"*H*mmm that's been up there a while," muttered Solomon. He was staring at a large red banner with faded lettering adorning a wall which read "*RENEW*" in Galactic. It was a remnant of a public service campaign he and his wife had conducted some time ago. Felina, as always, was with him as he boarded a massive freight elevator which had been reconstructed after the war. "Are you thinking what I'm thinking?" he then asked. She was quick to correct him.

"Solomon, you know I can't do that. I've told you this before," reminded the elegant Enoshi. She was now in her thirties but still looked stunning despite being middle-age. Females from her species typically lived only sixty years. Males rarely lived past forty. "I cannot read your thoughts, no Empath can do that. We can only sense your feelings and react to them instinctively." Solomon recoiled.

"Oh yes, I know my dear. But what I was referring to is that banner over there. Don't you think that's a rather outdated message? I mean it's been years since we ran that campaign. That sign is so old the letters are barely readable."

Felina hummed softly while looking over at the sign. Soon the gate would be shutting and the giant lift mechanism would begin its descent. Her husband made a good point.

"Yes, I suppose you're right. I'll have Estrella get right on that once we get back. After the parade it'll give her something to do. She's growing tired of going on these diplomatic missions with us. I've sensed that in her lately."

Solomon chuckled. He didn't have to be an Empath to detect impatience in his teenage daughter. Any father possessed that ability. *Scout* is what he still lovingly called her; a nickname he'd come up with when they'd revived him years earlier inside a dusty mining tunnel. Attempting a desperate escape following the detonation of the magma chamber, he'd passed out from a lack of oxygen. He'd have surely died if she and her mother hadn't found him when they did.

"You have, have you?" he joked. Felina failed to see the humor. Sarcasm and irony were still somewhat confusing for her. Her species tended to take comments at face value. Even being an Empath, it was difficult to tell whenever her husband was kidding. She could only eye him suspiciously when he did so. That only added to her charm. Solomon wasn't about to provoke her; he wisely changed the subject.

"But I agree with you. Estrella needs things to do, definitely. She's been on enough of these missions to know all there is to know about our people. Besides, this trip wouldn't appeal to her. The Bandicoots are a peculiar lot. The environment down there is not terribly inviting for a young girl used to fresh air and sunshine. The odor, mainly. It's difficult even for me and I've lived here half my life. I'm glad she didn't come along with us this time."

Felina grinned knowingly.

Not that there was any danger. The Bandicoots were unwavering in their loyalty to Solomon; especially to his wife Felina. It had been she who'd met with their legendary Chief Murad years earlier and convinced him to change his ways. She'd charmed the beady-eyed creature; impressed him with her knowledge of Schpleefti culture and customs. Challenged him to treat his female captives with compassion and respect; offer them equality within tribal society. If he would, she'd assured him, it would demonstrate to other chieftains his generosity as well as his wisdom. He'd reacted sharply at first; but with Felina's tremendous talent for finding the right things to say in most any situation, he'd seen the logic in her words. The next day he'd gone out and freed every last one of them. Ordered his tribesmen to tear down their cages and share equally in their food and resources. He even married. Took several as wives, which he proudly displayed at Solomon's and Felina's wedding months later. His death while leading a squad of Spleef warriors on a raid during the war with Earth had only enhanced his reputation. Among the Bandicoots he was revered as both statesman and vaunted warrior. That, and a shrewd businessman ... something equally valuable among the Schpleeftii.

"Well, shall we?" Solomon asked, reaching over to engage the lift mechanism. Felina only nodded and sighed. Honest to a fault, just like all Enoshi, she wasn't about to feign enthusiasm. It was going to be a long day.

The journey would take over an hour. The Bandicoots controlled a section of the mining network which contained a series of caves where hydroponic farms used to exist. These had been devised years before by Slart scientists working for prison gangs. That was back in the days when guards rationed food to starving prisoners and to provide themselves with additional calories they secretly grew their own fruits and vegetables using cannibalized lighting equipment. After the rebellion these farms were expanded for a time, yielding fresh produce. After the planet was transformed following the war with Earth, they'd been abandoned. Now they were used in developing *topsoil*; and Schpleefti tribes held a global monopoly. Shipments of it ran daily up to the surface during planting season. Unfortunately, during the rest of the year that same freight elevator they were now riding on was used to transport manure.

"*Whew.* It sure reeks today, doesn't it?" declared Solomon. It had now been twenty minutes since they'd begun their descent. A group of passengers who'd joined them in the elevator several hundred feet down chuckled in response. *That was an understatement.* The stench was overwhelming. Solomon's wit brought a well-received dose of humor to their circumstances.

Of course, everyone knew Solomon and Felina. Recognized them instantly. They traveled freely between tribal homelands and no one gave it a passing thought. For years they'd done so; ever since they'd first met. Rarely needed bodyguards and in time had little use for them. Solomon had been a hero during the rebellion; afterward was Terminal Chief of the galaxy's most notorious pirate base. There he oversaw New Australia's emergence as a military power, then spearheaded its metamorphosis.

"It certainly does, Great Chief." responded one of the passengers. He was a Zorgolongian or *Zorg* as they'd been nicknamed since olden times, and he was part of a work detail heading down to the Lacertilia tribe's section of the mining network. Each tribe had its own original territory below the surface which had been allocated to them following a civil war many years ago. During those dangerous times it would have been impossible to travel between homelands without a flag of truce. Now it happened daily.

"Quite pungent." offered another. This time it was an Enoshi speaking, a member of the Smilodon tribe. These were cat-like beasts which stood six and a half feet tall; covered in brown, gray, or black fur. This particular specimen certainly wasn't the largest Solomon had ever seen. Luckily, he'd never had to do battle with one. Hard to believe that less than two decades ago his own tribe, the Schpleeftkorkii, had faced off against these monsters in combat. For the better part of a year they'd tried killing off their former allies from the Great Rebellion. No one talked about those bloody days anymore. Nausties had set aside their differences for the sake of the planet's survival. Their reward in doing so came in the form of a bold solution proposed by the very man standing across the platform. He turned them into marauding space pirates and they became stinking rich. This however was a different kind of stink.

"Always a bit stronger as we get further down, I've found. Wouldn't you agree?" quipped Solomon, endeavoring to keep the conversation going. Felina smiled toward the other passengers, sensing what he was trying to do. The oppressive smell was something she'd gotten used to over the years; best to try and ignore it, but right now her husband was *schmoozing*, as he liked to call it. Always the politician's wife, she jumped in to help.

"Yes, it sure does." she answered, encouraging further discussion.

This eventually led to the passengers joining in for a pleasant chat the rest of the way. It did well in passing the time; plus Felina got to know several of them a little better. These were not new acquaintances after all. A bit older perhaps, but not unfamiliar. Just like Estrella, many had been with her during the long march up to the surface. Some, they would eventually be reminded during the long descent, had been soldiers in the Naustie Army, freed from their entombment when Felina led an expedition all the way back down to search for survivors. Surging lava flows had trapped thousands following the explosions. They could count their lucky stars that their countrymen had the courage and resilience to burrow through mountains of rubble to save them. That's why Felina was loved so dearly by the citizens of New Australia; veterans and civilians alike. It was another half hour before she and her husband finally made it to their destination.

The visit with the Bandicoots was a friendly one, as would have been expected. A feast was held in the couple's honor that very evening. Stories of Felina's first visit years before were told and re-told. During dinner they paid homage to Murad; honored him for his efforts in defeating Earth. He'd led a band of elite fighters on a raid which resulted in nearly a hundred enemy deaths. Sadly, he was riddled with projectiles and died during the fray. Warriors from that group of heroes were still around to tell the tale.

His wives were too and most of them were Human, though

barely discernible from their fellow tribesmen. They were covered in soot and filth; only their eyes indicated what species they were. Their movements and mannerisms made them seem more rodent-like than human. They'd aged as well. But even though Felina was hard-pressed to recognize some of them, they vividly remembered her. To them she was like an angel, a magical goddess who'd appeared out of the heavens and freed them from bondage. Now they were equal to their male counterparts according to tribal law. Felina had inspired it. Murad had ordered it done. Now it was *tradition*. Felina was proud to hear how several of them owned their own dwellings; living out their old age alone or in pairs and protected by tribal elders who'd never let any harm come to them.

The following day they were given a tour of their hosts' business operations, what they preferred to call "soil reclamation". This was a fancy term for the mixing of dung with dirt dug out of caves. Slart scientists had given them instructions on the proper proportions; now the Bandicoots "harvested" the final product. Standing near these fields for any prolonged period was an ordeal for Solomon and Felina as the fumes from decomposing feces made their eyes burn. Yet they couldn't help notice how tribesmen working the fields seemed wholly unaffected. They raked and tilled the mixture; sprayed water to settle the dust this created, then moved on to other sections. Spent their days speckled with filth and never washed or bathed. Toiled in near-darkness then returned to their village around supper time. Their offspring were just as dirty, Felina observed them scurrying about completely unsupervised and without a care in the world. She could not help but be impressed. They were happy; living a traditional lifestyle undisturbed by the planet's advancement and perfectly willing to keep it that way.

After their brief stay with the Bandicoots Felina and Solomon traveled through several adjoining homelands. Old mining tunnels were the arteries which kept the flow of goods moving from territory to territory; and to get from one to another merely required hitching a ride with electric vehicles motoring past. Drivers always stopped and offered a spot in the back; even if it meant piling in among shipments of vegetables, trade goods, or worse: manure. That said, the couple never complained. This was the way their fellow Nausties lived down in the bowels of the planet and it was something they had deepest respect for. People knew this about them too. Solomon and Felina walked the walk when it came to the agendas they espoused. Everyone, every last person on New Australia served a vital role in the planet's success: that was the message they conveyed in their many speeches. They proved it in the way they treated their constituents; and when the tour was done it would be time to show their generosity. Upon returning there was going to be an event which would include the planet's entire population in a worldwide celebration of Naustie pride.

***

"Welcome," announced a booming voice. "And happy Independence Day, one and all."

A crowd of ten thousand were at that very moment packing into a large festival square paved in gleaming concrete. It lay adjacent to the planet's convention hall and government building. The Tribal Assembly met there every month and when not in session it was often vacant. Not tonight, however. Tonight, once the sun had set and the surface temperature plunged, the expansive five-story structure would be filled to capacity.

"I believe I see them now!" bellowed the announcer.

He was a Human dressed in festive attire; bright clothing with strings of beads around his neck, a wide brimmed hat to shield himself from the sun. His voice could be heard through loudspeakers placed around the enormous town square as he stood on a dais constructed at one corner. Solomon and Felina were seated right behind him underneath a canopy. The crowd had begun filtering in right before dusk, braving the heat in anticipation the parade would soon arrive. Thousands more had lined the seven mile parade route.

"Yes, that's them." he then yelled through his microphone; and he was right. Fifty floats were in the procession, occupied by tribal elders and chieftains of the many tribes, enduring the scorching New Australian heat to toss jeweled trinkets toward the excited throng. Solomon stood and craned his neck to see the first of the floats. His own tribe, the Schpleeftkorkii were one of the first three.

"Parents. Get those little ones up to the front. You'll want 'em to get a good spot for this." he called out, and that was a wise suggestion. Each tribe had decorated their own float for the event, pulled like freight cars past cheering revelers, many of whom already stoned drunk by mid-afternoon when the event kicked off. At the very end of the column marched the one hundred and seventy-eight cadets from the planet's new Merchant Marine Academy, something everyone was hoping to get a look at as well. But that was only the beginning. When the parade passed, masses of people had swung in behind and followed them. Thus by sundown there would be close to thirty thousand people in the capital.

"Let's all be safe and enjoy ourselves today." cautioned the announcer. That was also good advice. They needed to be mindful of what was in store for them over the next six hours or, for some, perhaps longer. Miners and farmers would be celebrating side by side with one another. Smilodons would raise their cups with Templar Knights. Zorgs would embrace Porkos as though brothers and maybe even an Enoshi or two if they got drunk enough. Earthers and Spleefs would laugh and carry on throughout the night.

Of course, they had little to worry about; besides maybe running out of booze, and of that there was plenty. Happiness and global pride would be the order of the day. There'd be no tolerance for violence or mayhem. If so it would be dealt with harshly; and Nausties knew better than to defy the authorities. It was unlikely such a thing would happen anyway. Police were on-hand primarily as a deterrent, instructed to exercise restraint in dealing with inebriants. Short of vandalizing or defacing public property they were to let folks be as wild and care-free as they wished.

And they would, the many thousands who'd traveled from miles around and in some cases spent an entire day getting there. They'd chat with neighbors, renew old friendships, and make some new friends as well. One could expect most any-thing on a night like this. In that mass of beings from six differ-ent species delighted to enjoy a day off work, it was only a ques-tion of how long it could go on. Which it did almost until dawn.

Meanwhile none of them, not a single soul within that crowd of partiers, could have had any idea what was headed their way. It was not an invader. The IPA had enforced a fragile peace ever since Earth's defeat ten years ago. No, it was something else. A spacecraft was fast approaching New Australian orbit.

"Hailing home base, come in home base," was the message flashing onscreen. It was now four o'clock in the morning at Terminal Command and the party was finally dying down, sev-eral thousand yards away over at the convention center. The music had stopped hours ago. Most folks had headed home, if they could still walk that is. Solomon and Felina had slipped off to their private apartment inside the neighboring govern-ment administration building shortly after midnight; looking to spend some alone-time together. They were sound asleep by the time the transmission arrived, startling the team of traffic controllers who'd been enjoying a cask of ale which had been smuggled in. The message repeated thirty seconds later; fol-lowed by a succession of beeps to let the staff know a ship was nearing.

"What the...?" remarked a control room operator, a Suidonji named Moccus. He'd been at the parade earlier and was a bit tipsy; even though it was against regulations to be drinking on duty. But that was understandable. The last thing he'd been ex-pecting was the arrival of another ship. All vessels in the Naus-tie merchant fleet had been accounted for by that point in time. If they weren't out on trade missions, they were parked on the planet's surface, their crews allowed a week's shore leave.

"Who in blazes could that be?" he slurred. He waited several moments while the rest of the team gathered around his work station.

"Do you see this? Who's the lunatic?" Moccus then quipped, starting to chuckle as he swigged his beer. "Someone's playing a prank on us, eh?" It had to be some kind of joke. Question was who in their right mind would find it funny? For that matter how could anyone have hacked into their computers? Slarts had programmed them. What's more, Slarts never made jokes. That's why it had to be real. He suddenly got a cold chill.

"Did they identify themselves yet?" asked one of his colleagues; a human by the name of Nikolay. Moccus already knew the answer and soon everyone else would. Terminal Control computers could do so automatically, based on a ship's transponder codes. All his fellow traffic controllers had to do was look at the screen and see for themselves. The name of the craft was right there in front of them. The inquisitive Earther practically spit up his beer when he saw it displayed across the bottom of the screen. Moccus still couldn't fathom how this could be happening.

"You've got to be kidding me." exclaimed the rotund fellow. Ten years of peace had allowed him, just like many other Suidonji, to pack on the pounds. He swiveled in his chair to respond. "It's already on-screen, brothers. See for yourselves."

The reaction was immediate. The team of seven included four Suidonji, the Human named Nikolay, and two Zorgs. They looked around at each other with bewilderment. No one dared speak. Meanwhile the message repeated onscreen, followed by an alarm. Because the first transmissions had not been responded to, the computer was sounding off to let them know something very large was approaching. Someone had to type in a response or notification would be passed along to Planetary Defense; and if that happened there'd be hell to pay. Moccus quickly thought up a reply to send back in order to buy some time. Transponder codes were impossible to fake but this could still be a "false flag". He had to consider the possibility this might be pirates using the long-lost *Anarchy* to enter New Australian airspace, however unlikely that might be.

"*Verifying identity; please stand by,*" he typed into the computer. It did little to mitigate the situation. The mysterious ship fired back a terse answer.

"*This is the Anarchy, flagship of the Naustie fleet, Ensign Frilbriliram speaking. Everything should be in order. Request immediate permission to land.*"

Moccus wasn't sure just what he could do at that point. Brilly? *The* Brilly? He knew the name well. But therein lie the problem. As far as he was concerned it had been many years since *Anarchy* failed to return from the infamous raid on Star Fantasy. He'd been in his twenties back then; virile and strong, serving on one of the ships in that attack. Now he was overweight and alcoholic. But this couldn't be them, could it? For that matter where could they have been all this time? Moccus soon realized this was a matter best handled by someone with a much higher pay grade.

"*Sorry Anarchy. Unable to grant access yet. Maintain orbit until further instructions,*" he wrote back. If necessary, he figured he could always say they had an issue with the lift mechanism, even though that had been destroyed years ago. It was one of several crazy ideas going through his mind as he tried getting his head around the situation. He waited several seconds for another transmission from the ship. Finally, it came.

"*Roger that, home base,*" the display screen said. That's when Moccus quickly turned to his fellow controllers. There was only one person he wanted to be talking to right about now. And that *person* was either making love to his wife or sawing logs at this ungodly hour.

"One of you, anyone, doesn't matter, for God's sake get First Citizen Mwonga down here and make it quick. I don't care what time it is or what he's doing to Felina. Don't give a damn, okay? We've got a real problem on our hands. I don't know about you but I'd rather it not be me who has to shoulder the blame later on if this turns into a real shit storm. Anyone disagree?"

No one did.

Naturally Solomon was right where they would have assumed he was at 04:00, an hour before dawn. He was in bed with Felina. They'd slipped away from the party after having several drinks; staggered upstairs to their flat, had "a quickie", then passed out. When his communicator sounded off next to the bed, indicating it was an emergency, he was barely coherent.

"This had better be good ..." he mumbled when he engaged the device, even though he knew it had to be serious. Terminal Command never called him directly, not anymore. He'd long since delegated operational leadership to other capable hands. Now he was a politician; far too busy to mind the store. Meanwhile Felina was fast asleep curled up next to him, snoring softly. He decided not to wake her, not until he got to the bottom of this. Instead he got up and took his communicator with him to the bathroom. What he heard next was the frantic voice of Nikolay Suleimanov on the other end, telling him the news.

"Are you sure?" he said in response. "Could it be an attempt at landing an invasion force?" he then asked. But in the back of his mind he realized that was all but impossible. If there'd been a fleet of ships heading toward New Australia, they'd have detected this already and they'd be having a far different conversation right now. A single ship? Landing on a planet and looking to pick a fight? *Nonsense*, he thought. "I'd better get down there," he finally said. "Notify Planetary Defense. No telling what this is."

Seconds later Solomon dashed out of his apartment, leaving Felina alone to continue sleeping. He rushed across the plaza, stepping over empty cups, party beads, and other debris strewn across the cold concrete. In his haste he'd left in just his underwear; pausing only to put on a pair of sandals and his breather unit. The frigid night air woke him up once he got outside. By the time he reached the terminal control tower he was fully alert with a splitting headache from all the alcohol he'd drank. What greeted him when he arrived were seven frightened faces. No one dared comment on the fact he was half-naked. Out of breath, squinting from the pain in his forehead, he addressed them.

"Well then, let's have it. Have they been verified? Are the transponder codes confirming their identity?" he demanded. Of course he already knew the answer to that question; same as they did. He'd been in charge of Traffic Control when it was located inside the terminal loading bay. He knew what the computers did and what they were capable of. If they confirmed it was the *Anarchy*, then it truly was. Only problem was he didn't want to risk believing it. The original Naustie flagship had been assumed destroyed many years ago. At his and Felina's wedding they'd honored the crew as well as their commander by posthumously awarding them the Order of Heroic Merit. No one doubted they were dead back then. Solomon could not imagine how they'd have been alive all this time. Nevertheless, despite his hangover, he tried composing himself.

"Alright then," sighed Solomon. "So, they're in orbit are they, yes?"

Heads nodded. Only Moccus ventured an answer. First Citizen Mwonga had a look on his face like he'd rip someone's head off.

"Aye, sir. Should be coming 'round any minute now," replied the well-fed Suidonji. "We can hail them for you if you like."

Solomon agreed. But he wasn't interested in communicating with them on their ship's computer. He wanted to call them on their voice transmitter once the vessel got within range. Preferred to hear for himself whether it was really them. Could it be? Only one way to find out. There was one voice he'd recognize immediately, even after seventeen years. He sat down at one of the workstations and grabbed a nearby headset. Moccus typed in the command for the *Anarchy* to open a hailing frequency so they could speak with each other live. Solomon then took a deep breath and spoke, slowly and deliberately, his heart pounding in his chest.

"Hailing *Anarchy*, hailing *Anarchy*. This is New Australia Terminal Command. Come in *Anarchy*, over." After that he waited for the transmission to garner a response. When it finally came in, he almost shit himself.

"*Anarchy* acknowledging. Good morning home base, over," answered a voice; scratchy due to atmospheric static yet vaguely familiar. *Oh my God,* Solomon thought. *Could it really be him?* He spoke again, blood rushing to his cheeks when he realized who it must be.

"Good morning to you as well. Uh, this is Solomon Mwonga. May I know who I'm speaking with? Please identify yourself, over," he said. It took about thirty seconds for the return transmission to reach Terminal Command. What he heard next practically made him jump right out of his seat. It was like a ghost from the past.

"What do you mean, identify myself? What kind of nonsense is this? We haven't been gone that long, have we? This is Admiral Slout, Chief Mwonga, don't you recognize me? Over."

CHAPTER FOUR

RETURN OF THE ANARCHY

Word got out fast. Solomon had Moccus and the rest of the staff notify Planetary Defense; they in turn notified the planetary police department. The police department reached out to the different tribal leaderships about what was happening and from there news spread like wildfire. Soon a very groggy Felina Toyger was delivering a freshly pressed suit of clothes to her husband at the Terminal Command building where he'd set up headquarters. From there they hastily made preparations for their unexpected visitors from outer space. Despite the early hour they had little difficulty getting things ready.

It was rather easy to arrange a respectable reception for the crew of *Anarchy*, not to mention their legendary commander. For one thing, half the revelers from the day before were still in the general area. Following the previous night's festivities many had opted for 'sleeping it off' inside the giant convention center rather than attempting a journey home in the dark. Given their depleted condition, many probably couldn't have found their way back. The few that tried were certainly missing out on what was to come.

Within an hour, just as the sun started breaking over the horizon, thousands had gathered near the festival square, awaiting the ship to appear in the sky. Nursing hangovers they stood far enough from the center so they wouldn't get incinerated by the spacecraft's stabilizers or pelted by blowing sand; yet close enough so they could see. Everyone wanted to catch a glimpse of the returning crewmen and especially Admiral Slout. For those born after the raid on Star Fantasy, he was someone they'd grown up hearing about but never imagined meeting. Stories about the famous ship all concluded in the same way: that he and his crewmembers had "sacrificed themselves for the sake of the rebellion," even if that was a bit of a stretch. The rebellion had succeeded years before the mission to capture females on Star Fantasy. It was just a little something folks tended to *gloss over* when it came to teaching their offspring Naustie history.

As part of the preparations the small stage and canopy where Solomon and Felina had been sitting the day before were removed to a safe distance. There the planet's First Citizen and his wife would be seated once again, ready to greet the returning heroes. The announcer from yesterday's parade was also located. He was passed out drunk much like at least a hundred other government officials. He was then delivered to his microphone stand for a follow-up performance. Didn't take a lot to get him to sober up once they told him what was coming their way. A cup or two of strong coffee, a chance to relieve himself, and he was good to go. Having ordered the sound system to be brought out from the convention center and set up to soothe the crowd with heroic music as they waited, Solomon and Felina figured they'd thought of just about everything. Estrella eventually joined them as they waited, watching the sky.

The excitement amongst the crowd was electric. As the story made it around that the planet's most famous ship had somehow survived all these years, many were already starting to question how such a feat could be accomplished. *Our original pirate marauder from a fleet which once terrorized the galaxy ... suddenly appearing in orbit and preparing to land? How is that possible?* they asked. *Where could they have been?* No one had answers, nevertheless it made for lively debate. What better way to cap off an already spectacular Independence Day celebration than to welcome back their long-assumed dead countrymen from the glory days of New Australia? Solomon stood shivering in the early morning light, directing local law enforcement officials to hastily move barricades into place.

"They might still be drunk," he warned them. "Don't let anyone get too close, do you understand?"

They certainly did. Given the size of the celebration the night before things could easily get out of hand once the ship entered Naustie airspace. By 06:00 the crowd had swelled to over ten thousand and was growing by the minute. In the morning gloom a flash could be seen in the distance, indicating *Anarchy* was penetrating the planet's atmosphere. Within minutes they'd be able to view the vessel. This would surely bring them to hysteria. Meanwhile Solomon and his wife sat together on the dais discussing the conversation he'd had with his old friend Slout earlier that morning. Estrella listened in.

"So how did he sound?" asked Felina. "Did he sound okay when you talked to him? Are the crew doing alright?" In her mind she pictured the poor souls having suffered through some terrible ordeal getting home. Perhaps they'd been lost all this time struggling to find their way back.

"He sounded exactly the same, it was just the way I remembered him, dear. And I have to say it was almost eerie the way he talked, as if he'd only been gone a short while. Seemed like he had no idea what's happened to us since the raid."

"Oh? How so? What did he say to make you think that?" she asked. Solomon grew perplexed.

"Well for example I told him how things have changed quite a lot since they've been gone. You know, trying to prepare him for all that's occurred since the war. I would have thought he'd known about it, seeing as wherever he and the crew have been hiding out all this time they would have to have heard at least something by now. But I never got the chance to elaborate. He was too busy explaining his actions; like he'd just escaped from the IPF months earlier, but that's impossible. The raid on Star Fantasy was many years ago. He was talking like it just happened."

"Why? What did he say?" Felina asked. "It's only logical that he'd start off by telling how he got away from them. You were his superior. Maybe he felt compelled to give you his report, don't you think?" Solomon shook his head.

"It's just the way he worded it. That's what sounded so weird. For instance I told him how excited everyone was going to be finding out they'd survived all this time and he responded by asking me if all the ships made it back. That made sense so I told him he had nothing to worry about; everyone got home safe, more or less. But then he started asking about some of the Enoshi who were injured during the raid, asked if they were doing alright, said he was worried some of them might not survive the voyage."

"That doesn't sound strange to me. He was concerned for their well-being, that's all. Seems like a question one might ask; especially the commander in chief of a military operation."

"Sure. I would as well. But then he said something else that threw me off."

"What?"

"Well, I was asking him about his escape from the IPF squadron. That's something we've always wanted to know. And sure, I could have saved that question for after they landed, but his response didn't make sense. He said, 'a couple months back we really thought we'd had it and figured we'd better hide out for a while.' See what I mean?"

"Hide from what?" asked Felina. "We've been at peace for ten years."

"Exactly. That's what got me was the way he said they *thought they'd had it*. Like someone was chasing them recently. Then he said 'I hope you'll forgive our absence, we decided to stop off on a planet we found on the other side of the wormhole.' I asked him to repeat that part and he did. Said they stayed for thirty days then headed home."

"Days?" chuckled their daughter Estrella, finally interrupting. "More like years. So, what have they been up to since then? Did you ask him that? Traveling around the galaxy raiding ships? If they were we would have heard about it by now wouldn't we, Father?"

"Yes, yes of course we would," nodded Solomon. "But it's the part about the wormhole that troubles me. He was talking like they'd actually traveled through one and came back out. No one's ever done such a thing and lived. Certainly not a space-ship. If wormholes even do exist, which I doubt, I've never heard of anybody entering one and returning to tell the tale. They're a myth, something Human scientists came up with when they were first attempting space travel."

"And yet he believed what he was saying. That's what concerns you," his wife observed.

"Exactly, my dear. Unfortunately we couldn't continue our conversation. He had to prepare his ship for the descent and we had to send his navigation officer coordinates for the landing."

"Well then you'll have to find out the rest once they get here," summarized Felina. Estrella sighed in frustration, the way teenagers do. There were so many things she wanted to ask. "Anyway, it's good that he's home," her mother continued.

"He's an old friend. I've known him as long as I've known Keech. And yes, you're right. It's good that they're finally coming home. I have to say though; it's going to be strange seeing him again. God knows what he's been through since I saw him last. I wonder what he'll look like."

Felina then patted his noticeably expanded waistline; sensing he was feeling self-conscious about his appearance. Solomon had packed on nearly twenty pounds since she'd first met him and that was only natural for a Human over age forty. Nevertheless, she could tell it might be bothering him.

"Don't worry, Husband. We've all gotten a little older," she assured him. "It *has* been seventeen years."

Following a sonic boom sounding off from above, all eyes were on the clouds, searching in vain for the fabled pirate ship. Only a handful knew precisely from what direction the space-craft would be coming. Solomon was one of them.

"They should be visible soon," he commented, pointing toward the eastern horizon. Their daughter meanwhile still had more questions.

"So, what does he look like Father?" she asked. "Slout, I mean. He's a Porko, right? Big and fat?" Solomon wondered if perhaps she was trying to address his earlier concerns that he'd soon be encountering a colleague who might have done a better job maintaining his figure. Not so. She honestly wanted to know how to recognize her dad's famous friend. That would be no problem.

"Big," Solomon replied committedly. "Not fat though, at least not the way I remember him. Working the mines all those years... you can't imagine how horrible it was, Scout. The work, it wasn't all that different from the way things are done today, but it was the food that was the problem. The lack of food, I should say. Even Suidonji like Slout, we all slimmed way down. Those who couldn't work, starved." Estrella dutifully filled in the rest.

"The prison guards rationed food, gave you outrageous production goals, and refused to feed you if you didn't achieve them. Evil Zorgs. They deserved what they got." she boldly declared. Felina felt compelled to interject.

"Yes, they were evil, but that's not to say all Zorgolongians are that way. We should be careful how we put things, Daughter. There were Earthers in league with them back in those days. Enoshi, Suidonji, Schpleeftii, sent from our original planets to run the prison and all had a hand in the abuse. It was an evil perpetrated on those who had no say in their circumstances and the shame shall be forever borne by the governments who enabled it to happen. No one was without at least a share in the guilt."

"I know, Mother," Estrella responded confidently. "The history of our planet is one of struggle against oppression. This world is now completely ours, but only because brave warriors like Slout Epididymus and Archibald Hicks had the courage to rise up and defeat their masters. Also Architeuthis. We can't forget about him. He was the one who brought the tribes together and led them to form an alliance in order to win their freedom. Even then they underestimated us; for that we made them pay. Now they treat us as equals, with respect. We gained our independence once they realized they could never defeat us."

That was the official version of things, of course. As for reality? That was a little more complicated. Felina was happy with the answer nonetheless. The next generation of Nausties didn't need to know *all* the details regarding Rijel 12's past as a global penal colony for the galaxy's many criminals. They did not need to know what prisoners had actually done to be sent there. The youth of New Australia could and should be spared the troubling truth regarding their fathers being former convicts. For that matter, what of their mothers? What stories should they be told of how their dear mothers had once been pirate captives? No, a sanitized version of Naustie history was preferable. That's what the younger generation had grown up hearing; even if they'd pieced together the rest on their own. What wasn't revealed to them could easily be found out with a bit of poking around.

"There they are." exclaimed Solomon suddenly. He'd been half-listening to his wife's conversation with Estrella while anticipating the *Anarchy's* appearance. A dot in the sky was growing ever larger over the eastern horizon and he knew it to be them. By then Moccus and the other staff from Terminal Command had joined them, leaving no one on duty. Solomon decided against pointing out this obvious security breach, given the magnitude of the occasion. Frankly there was nothing else for them to do back at their workstations even if they'd been there. Admiral Slout was in command and he was an experienced ship captain. In minutes they'd be landing anyway.

"How exciting." observed Felina. She wasn't the only one barely able to contain herself.

"This is amazing, Father. They're finally coming home, I can't believe it's really happening." yelled Estrella over the growing roar of the crowd. *They'd seen it too.*

Mesmerized by the approaching craft, people cheered and jumped up and down. The announcer took over at that point. He'd been downing coffee from a thermos that had been handed up to him on the dais and was trying to get himself together. The thrill of the moment was plenty to get him over the hump. He took out his breather tube and called out over the public address system.

"Alright, folks. That must be them coming toward us right now. Let's all get ready 'n give 'em a hearty New Australia welcome, shall we?" He then paused a moment, wincing at the throbbing behind his temples while the crowd whooped it up.

"Now, for safety-sake, those of you with children be sure and hold on to them tightly until the ship has landed and the all-clear signal is given. If you've ever been out on the surface while a space craft is landing you'll surely understand when I tell you this: it can get pretty dicey when those stabilizer jets kick in. It won't be very much longer before they're centered over the festival square, so…"

By that time the noise created by the crowd mixed with the roar of the *Anarchy* overhead was drowning him out. Also, he was running out of breath. He replaced his breather tube before getting lightheaded. That was a good way of losing consciousness.

As the *Anarchy* set down, practically nothing else could be heard. People covered their faces or held on to their offspring, squinting their eyes until the swirling dust subsided. Within a few minutes they could hear the whirring of the ship's stabilizers winding down, indicating they were no longer in danger. All that remained was for the cloud to settle so they could see clearly. Fifty yards away Solomon was already walking toward the craft, bedecked in the suit Felina had brought him earlier that morning. It was the same one he'd worn during treaty negotiations with Suidonj and Zorgolong: charcoal black with red piping and epaulets, colors from the flag of New Australia. On the breast was the national symbol: crossed spear and pickaxe superimposed over a clinched fist with claws.

Solomon didn't wait for the dust cloud to finish settling. He hopped up and marched right out there. Felina hastily caught up with him as Estrella followed. He walked out to a spot not far from where he knew the landing bay door would open, descending like a gigantic drawbridge to form a ramp. He could hear the hissing sound of the doorway depressurizing so he knew the order had been given to disembark. Wouldn't be much longer before the motors would activate and it would begin opening. Once it did he took a long hit from his breather tube then let out a deep sigh. This was the moment everyone had been waiting for.

Only there was a problem. The thought occurred to him immediately upon exhaling. *Breather units.* How did they know the crew still had them after this long? They certainly knew their home planet; would probably have them in stock, but who's to say the devices would still be functional? Solomon thought long and hard about rushing to grab some, only he didn't have a clue where there'd be. Then he remembered his brilliant daughter and her resourcefulness. She was standing right there with him. Over the roar of the ship, he spoke to her.

"Breather units." he cried. Estrella looked up at him inquisitively. She couldn't hear him clearly but she could read his lips once he removed his tube and repeated himself. "Breather units."

"What about 'em?" she replied, realizing immediately once she got the words out just what he was implying. "Oh. You're right. *God.* They might need those, huh?" Looking about for a second or two, Estrella appeared to be determining where she should go find some. After the chaos from the day before she wasn't too sure anymore. Felina sensed what was going on and put a halt to it. It was far too late at that point and besides, Slout was no fool. Years later wouldn't he remember how thin the air was on New Australia? Of course he would.

"No, young lady. Stay where you are. Solomon, seriously. They're *from* here." she yelled over the din. "I doubt they've forgotten." Her nervous husband nodded in response, looking toward his daughter who was about to run off and look for a carton or two of the new breathing devices from Suidonj. Felina was right of course. If Estrella tried something like that she'd be lost in the crowd for over an hour and miss the entire event.

"Forget it, Scout. Sorry, my dear," he called out. At that point the freighter's rear door was already descending. In seconds they'd be gazing upon faces not seen in a very, very long time. And then, after a moment or two, they were all standing there, eyes adjusting to the morning sunlight: the entire crew. It was like in a dream.

"Chief Mwonga." yelled the old skipper. Then he laughed, causing Estrella to giggle at his ebullience. This wasn't something he was known for; he typically didn't express outward emotions, though the youngster wouldn't have known such a thing. But there was something else. He looked just the way Solomon remembered him. Perhaps it was just that Slout was wearing the same outfit he would have had on prior to boarding the *Anarchy* years earlier. That the crewmembers standing around him were dressed no differently than the way they'd been prior to the Star Fantasy raid was equally intriguing. Even weirder was how they, like their commander, appeared young and fit like they hadn't aged a day. This thought occurred to Solomon as well.

"Admiral." he yelled back with a welcoming smile. "Ensign Brilly. We've been expecting you." He stepped forward, trying not to dwell on the fact that the admiral was still in spectacular physical condition. It was just what he'd feared.

"Yes. It's been a while, hasn't it?" laughed Slout. Of course Solomon was only being humorous in stating they'd been expecting them all this time. Slout seemed to take it literally. He descended the ramp with a spring in his step, youthful and energetic as though he hadn't missed more than a day at the gym since the last time they'd seen each other. "Like I said earlier, my apologies for the slight detour but it was necessary. The IPF were closing in on us so I made the decision to take us off the grid for a while. Wanted to make sure they couldn't follow us.

Glad to hear the other ships made it back in one piece. Saw several of them as we descended, saw a lot of other things as well. My how things have changed, you weren't exaggerating."

He then held out a hoof to greet his old boss, glancing briefly at the man's balding head but opting not to mention it.

"Right." smiled First Citizen Mwonga. "We'll have to show you around later on. But first I believe there are some people here who are rather anxious to meet you." At that point Felina stepped forward, prompting Slout to rear back with a toothy smile. The big beast went over and embraced her excitedly, lifting her off the ground and causing her to yowl. When he set her back down he then looked over to see Estrella standing next to her, beaming with delight.

"Ah, yes. Delightful. And who might these beautiful creatures be?" he asked, getting a lusty look on his face, raising up to put his hooves on his hips like back in the old days. "You saved these for me from the raid, did you? Nice selection, thanks Chief, very nice indeed." He then snickered, causing both females to eye the fellow warily. Solomon intervened before things got icky.

"Admiral, uh, this is my wife Felina. And our daughter, Estrella. You wouldn't have met them yet. Felina came from Star Fantasy and Estrella, well, she came along shortly after that."

Now it was Slout's turn to be confused. Solomon was Human and so was the girl. His "wife" as he referred to her was an Enoshi. He stepped back, hooves still on his hips, grinning embarrassedly. "Wife?" he snorted. "And daughter, you said?"

Solomon nodded, briefly shifting his focus toward Felina to cock an eyebrow as if to say, *"See what I mean?"* Felina returned the gesture with a *"Wow, you weren't kidding"* look on her face.

"Well, then. A lot *is* different than before we left," Slout remarked. He hastily changed the subject. "And what about my first officer, Keech? You said they all made it back okay. The *Chengshi* among them, right? So where is that old reptile?" It was an ironic choice of words.

By then Kscheeeech had emerged from the crowd and was

walking toward them. The sight of his comrade from years past was destined to be yet another shock for the befuddled skipper. That Solomon was clearly fifteen to twenty pounds heavier than before the raid was one thing; and yes, Slout had noticed that too. Kscheeeech's appearance was a much different story. As the rest of his crew fanned out from the base of the craft to greet friends and acknowledge the cheering crowd, Slout followed Solomon's gaze to find an aging version of his former shipmate approaching him. He looked back at Solomon with an expression of profound desperation. *What the hell is going on?* he seemed to be asking. Then he nervously looked back at Kscheeeech.

"Keech?" he called out. The elder Zorgolongian waved jovially as he neared. Stooped slightly, scales peeling from his body, eyes milky white compared to when they'd parted ways after the capture of the *Chengshi*, Kscheeeech smiled and shuffled along as though attempting to run. Slout now grew agitated. Zorgolongians were well-known for their agility and speed. Sprinters by nature, from the dire necessity when it came to hunting in prehistoric times, Kscheeeech should have been able to do just that. But that was only because the poor admiral still had no idea just how long he and his crew had been gone. He was about to find out.

After making small talk, the big Suidonji finally inquired as to his old friend's circumstances. "So uh, at the risk of sounding impertinent, what happened to you? Have some trouble getting home perhaps? I mean, uh, I have to say you look rather worn down." That's when Kscheeeech, not yet realizing what was actually going on, shrugged his narrow shoulders and ventured an answer.

"Trouble getting home?" he repeated. "From what, Star Fantasy? Why no, Admiral. I quite enjoyed the journey, to tell you the truth. Made a new friend or two in the process. I guess I didn't age as gracefully as you did, that's all. You see, this is what happens to Zorgs when we get old. You've probably never seen an aging Zorgolongian before, have you? Skin dries out. Scales start to flake off. And by the way, since you brought it up, how in the hell do you still look so fit after seventeen years?"

Slout wasn't sure how to answer something like that. He stood up straight, muscles rippling, raising a thick eyebrow with his gigantic head cocked to one side.

"Seventeen?" he snorted.

No one spoke ....

CHAPTER FIVE

GREEN PLANET

"Y ou wanted to see me, Admiral?" asked the studious looking Earthman. Science Officer Minggatu had just arrived on the command bridge to find all eyes upon him the moment he crossed the threshold. It had been two days since the *Anarchy* had survived the wormhole and his commander was awaiting his report. While the converted freighter orbited the mysterious planet, he and his team had been completing tests in order to determine whether they could attempt a landing and search for provisions. The results were positive: "Green Planet", as crewmembers had taken to calling it, was teaming with life, and as far as anyone could tell there was no perceivable danger.

"Ah. Minggatu. I believe you bear good tidings for us today, am I correct?" replied the fleet commander. He was as always seated in his custom fitted captain's chair, swiveling 'round to face the Human. Minggatu was happy to accommodate him.

"So far, so good, Admiral. I can at least say that much. Oxygen atmosphere, breathable, no indications of toxicity. Gravity slightly less than what we're accustomed to. The probe came back full of data and we've been sifting through it since this morning. I'd consider it a safe environment overall. We won't know for sure until we land of course, not without further tests, but it's worth giving it a shot. Surface is solid. Fresh water in the interior. We located a logical landing site too; near a massive lake in the center."

What Minggatu was referring to was that Green Planet possessed only one major land mass: a single continent which occupied half the globe. The other side consisted of an enormous ocean; in the middle of which was a storm the size of South America which had likely been active for centuries. Evidence indicated that hurricanes regularly plagued coastal areas making it inadvisable to attempt a landing near the sea. It wouldn't be necessary, Minggatu's science team decided. The interior was bursting with plant life and only one identifiable desert located in the southern hemisphere. The rest of the continent, according to pictures taken from thousands of feet above, showed endless plains covered in grass possibly supporting herds of grazing animals and complemented by lush forests. After all they'd been through this was sensational news indeed. Slout liked what he was hearing.

"Great job, Lieutenant, outstanding. And by the way, nice work getting us through the wormhole. Seems like we came through it okay, wouldn't you agree? No damage to the hull I've been told."

This didn't exactly line up with the facts.

Minggatu knew the admiral was already aware of the ship's questionable condition. Engineering section had done their tests while *Anarchy* circled the planet; hence the reason his team had been given so much time to do research. The findings regarding *Anarchy's* exterior were "inconclusive". That was the official word, anyway. However, he'd heard through sources of his own that the ship's engineers feared deterioration in the hull's integrity. Contraction and expansion caused by the 'walls' of the wormhole may have weakened the metal skin of the craft. On the bright side he now knew better how to stabilize the portal once they tried traversing it a second time. This they must do if they were ever to make it home.

"None that I know of, sir," he said ... lying of course. And besides: why have that argument? His job was to find out if the planet was safe to explore and that's what he'd accomplished. Once they landed he knew his colleagues over in Engineering would perform a whole battery of tests. *Let those poor bastards confront the big swine with their findings*, he figured. *Maybe they can take the admiral around and show him.* Meanwhile he had a much bigger concern and it was one he'd be wise not to bring up in mixed company. If only he could have kept his mouth shut.

"We'll have plenty enough to worry about when we try going back," said the short-statured fellow, instantly regretting his choice of words. The backlash was immediate.

"Oh? How so?" snorted Slout. His eyes grew intense, even though his face still held the same snarky grin he was so well known for. It was something the admiral did in order to intimidate subordinates and it was highly effective in snuffing out insubordination.

"Uh, well, it's kind of complicated, sir," continued Minggatu, digging himself an even deeper hole. "Boring science stuff. Has to do with a disruption in the space-time continuum."

"Disruption? Sounds painful." quipped Slout with a patronizing smirk. This prompted several crewmen to chuckle, Brilly among them. Minggatu suspected his audience wouldn't benefit from a detailed explanation even if he tried providing one. He tried playing it off.

"Oh, it's nothing we can't manage I'm sure. Perhaps we can talk about it later?"

He could only hope his far-too-busy superior would see the opportunity to cut things short and focus on the more immediate issue of setting down on the planet's surface. To achieve such a feat would require collaboration between Engineering and the command bridge. Minggatu's team of scientists would have to provide precise coordinates for them to find the location he'd spoken of. After all, they were talking about a ship the size of a 70,000 square foot office building. The surface would have to bear the weight of this. They'd have to get it right the first time and if they did not it could spell disaster. Even when successful that would be only the beginning of Minggatu's challenges. Those would begin shortly after touching down.

"Very well then," snorted the admiral. Minggatu was dismissed and told to return to his duties.

In reality the landing went off without a hitch. Just like with the *Warthog* years earlier, following that ship's attempt to hide out near an abandoned plantation out on Frabrak 3, the crew of *Anarchy* were able to exit their spacecraft to find a pristine, unspoiled world, lush with vegetation. Slightly humid but otherwise quite comfortable, there was nothing really to complain about. Not that anyone would after five months in space. To the Human, Suidonji, Zorg, and Schpleefti pirates of the Naustie flagship it was as if they'd found paradise. They celebrated by increasing ale rations for twenty-four delightful hours before getting to work.

The first task was to set up a suitable encampment. Few wanted to be stuck sleeping on the ship at night if they could possibly avoid doing so and since there didn't appear to be any immediate threat of attack from beings native to the area, the admiral allowed this. Work crews were formed then ordered to build a stockade. Inside of this crewmen fashioned huts using whatever material they could acquire from the nearby forest. Within days a proper fortress had sprang up in the middle of the large meadow where *Anarchy* had set down. Using the ship to secure one end and having ordered a gate with watchtowers constructed at the other, Slout and his senior officers decided it was finally safe to send out teams of explorers.

Now was their chance to go find food. There was a massive lake less than a mile from the landing site, they were told. A squad was sent out to acquire fish samples and if any could be found, bring them back to the ship for testing. They returned a few days later empty-handed. The lake was filled with plant life but no fish or aquatic animals in the depths below. No reptiles or amphibians either. Disappointed, they looked to the nearby forest.

Teams of forty to fifty then fanned out in multiple directions in order to gather fruits, nuts, or leafy plants which might appear edible. All were delivered to Minggatu's lab onboard *Anarchy* where he ran tests to determine what was poisonous and what could be consumed. This turned out to be quite successful by way of comparison and it didn't take long before the teams were being instructed as to which plant varieties they could harvest. Crewmen then ventured forth to bring back containers filled to the brim with edible produce.

Meanwhile groups of hunters were formed for the purpose of tracking down available game. That's when things started getting weird. Bands of Nausties explored almost fifty square miles of terrain over the next two weeks searching high and low for animals which might be butchered for meat. Ship rations were typically bland-tasting cereal bars with whey protein and dehydrated vegetables or fruits pressed into prepackaged squares. Not much to look forward to at the end of one's work shift. When the ale began to run out there wasn't even that to rely upon for sustenance. Now they were on an alien planet with billions of acres of grasslands able to support massed herds. There was water in abundance. Berries growing in the forests. Budding wildflowers dotting the meadow surrounding their ship. There simply had to be an abundance of land mammals ready for the taking. All they had to do was figure out where such creatures were grazing. A game trail. Tracks. Droppings. Burrows. Bedding areas. Something.

Only there was nothing. No signs of animal life whatsoever. Wherever they looked and no matter how far they traveled they could find no evidence any had ever existed. Insects aplenty, oh, there were lots of those and quite happy to alight upon their skin as they searched in vain day after day. Minggatu himself was amazed whenever groups of hunters would report back to *Anarchy* with the same story. It simply didn't add up. Conditions were ideal for a countryside populated with any number of quadrupeds. What's more, the insects didn't bite. That was yet another clue as to what they'd truly found here on Green Planet: a world ruled solely by plants.

Admiral Slout was livid.

"You mean to tell me we came all this way, risked our necks, only to find out there's not even a furry little bunny we can roast on a spit? No roaming herds of beasts we can slaughter and feast upon? No tiny lizards or mice scurrying about? No primates jumping from tree to tree? No wild birds we can shoot down from the sky? How could that be? Dammit Minggatu, what kind of upside-down world is this anyway? Tell me, please. You're my science officer."

He was right of course. There were no birds either; that also made no sense. A vast ecosystem, brimming with vegetation, devoid of all winged creatures besides curiously large bugs? How? The angry fleet admiral wasn't done with his tirade.

"Fifty species of insects? Probably a million more if we were to scare up an entomologist among our staff and put him to work on it, but since none of us eat bugs who gives a shit? They're crawling all over me every morning when I wake up, I can tell you that much. I just don't get it, do you? And no fish either? How can that be? There has to be fish. Not even in the rivers? Not a one? Maybe they're wise to us and hiding deep below the surface; any theories?"

Minggatu had none. There simply wasn't an explanation. Or then again perhaps that's just the way things were. Perhaps there once had been great creatures walking the planet. It was certainly possible. If so, they must have died out millions of years before and their fossils buried beneath the forest floor. As for the lack of aquatic life he had no answer for that either. The two should be unrelated, unless there'd been some form of global cataclysm during the planet's evolution. The Devonian Extinction back on Earth 360 million years ago came to mind. During this period vascular plants growing on the surface had a powerful impact on sea life. Tree roots penetrated the ground, breaking up rocks, creating soil, but also releasing nutrients and minerals. These washed into rivers and subsequently the oceans. Such nutrients became food for microscopic algae, enabling them to flourish. And then? Algae were broken down by bacteria, which used up the sea's oxygen. Creatures began to die out; all thanks to the success of land plants. Maybe that was the answer.

But Slout was far too exasperated for him to explain something so intricate. Simply put, they must accept their circumstances. No telling what they'd find in the stormy ocean on the other side even though that was out of the question. The good news was they had plenty of food to re-stock their ship. They had an endless wilderness to meander through gathering food without fear of being stalked by meat-eating predators. As long as they could find their way back out, crewmen could harvest all the fruits and leafy vegetables they could carry.

"No sir, Admiral," answered Minggatu, determined to point out the positives. "It is what it is, I guess. However, I'm sure you'd agree, it truly is a magical paradise when you stop and think about it. To have found such a place, I mean, what were the chances? You realize, don't you, statistically we'd have been more likely to find a gaseous orb with toxic air and no definable surface. As for the abundance of food, it's not exactly what we'd hoped for but it will solve our immediate needs. What's more, a vegetarian diet is healthier in the long run. Helps one stay fit."

Slout snarled, temporarily lacking a clever comeback. *Of course* it was healthier for his crew to be dining on vegetables and fruits rather than wild game meat which might bear unknown diseases. How could he argue? And to be fair, he should fully appreciate his CSO's logic. There was a lot to be thankful for: only weeks before they'd been running for their lives. Now they could live each day without care or concern. Green Planet had all one needed for a pleasurable coexistence with nature and a place to live out one's life in peace and tranquility.

That's when the admiral thought of something else he could gripe about.

"Yeah, well it's easy for you to say that, isn't it?" he grumbled. "You're not sneezing your head off every day like some of the others." Slout was right again. Green Planet *was* a magical paradise to the majority of the crew. It was only those who suffered from allergies who saw things differently.

There was a large variety of flowers including several million splayed across the giant meadow where *Anarchy* was parked. This particular type caused no issues. Yet in the forests it was different. There the predominant species was a rather tall plant with lavender-colored petals. In the center of each was a grouping of white or gray stamens surrounding a bright yellow pistil. To the visitors from New Australia nothing seemed so remarkable about them other than their size.

That and their numbers, of course. In any clearing and between clumps of towering trees there'd be hundreds; sometimes thousands, with insects the size of fruit bats alighting upon them busily consuming their nectar and fertilizing them with pollen from the anthers of other nearby flowers. There were other strains of course, too many to count. An overzealous botanist with nothing better to do could make a career out of gathering, categorizing, and classifying specimens from Green Planet. Adding in the many local tree varieties and a particularly organized plant specialist could stay busy for decades. However, the lavender giants seemed to thrive in far greater numbers than any of their neighbors and there was no doubting who wore the pants in that relationship when it came to bug versus plant. Any questions regarding this were quickly laid to rest once bands of foragers came across predators of a far different kind.

"Killer flowers", as some nicknamed them, could be found growing on the perimeter of large beds, strategically located so as to get a piece of the action. They had large leaf blades or *laminas* which were many times larger than a Venus Fly Trap. They stood five, sometimes eight feet tall, ensnaring prey as fascinated crewmen observed them doing so from afar. Their efforts had little effect on their prosperous cousins. The lavender giants were far too many even to venture an estimate. Meanwhile, those among the legions of insects who managed to avoid being snatched and smothered to death seemed to be doing a more than adequate job of spreading their genes to future generations. The constant activity of flying bugs hopping from one flower to the other produced billowing clouds of *pollen*.

This became the second major drawback to life on Green Planet. Pollen emitted from the lavender giants quickly became a problem for crewmembers who were susceptible to allergens. It collected everywhere: on their clothing, on their hides, and in their fur. Gatherers returning to the ship brought it in with them. Those affected the most would often have to be confined to quarters, making their time on Green Planet especially disappointing.

"Yes Admiral," answered Minggatu. "It is unfortunate." Allergy attacks would continue to be a bother and couldn't be avoided. Not that the salty old ship captain didn't appreciate all of his CSO's efforts; he'd simply gotten his hopes up that they'd find something more filling than fruits and leafy vegetables. Suidonji were omnivores just like humans, but they especially loved meat.

After thirty days it became clear no one had followed them; Slout called a meeting of his senior staff including Brilly his navigation officer and Minggatu his chief science officer. Now that it had been a month he was growing impatient and a bit nervous too. They'd been gone for some time now and there was no telling what might have happened to their brethren back on New Australia. His goal had been to lead the IPF battle squadron on a wild goose chase and he'd succeeded. It was clear they'd shaken off their pursuit. Either the enemy had chosen not to follow them through the space anomaly or they'd simply not seen it in time and might have been racing after them only to find they'd disappeared. Either way it was time to head back.

Assuming they could, that is.

"We have what we need, even if it's not exactly what we'd hoped for," Slout began, referencing the crew's excellent work in restocking the ship's cargo bay. Slout had ordered them to pack the hold with as much as they could fit. They took samples of plants, plus soil samples and seedlings in hopes these could be utilized. "That's why I think it's time for us to go," he then said, prompting a melancholy sigh from Ensign Brilly. Brilly was among those who found Green Planet to be a veritable wonder-land.

"Not what some of you were hoping to hear, I take it?" added the admiral with a snort. This inspired chuckles from the group, despite the formal nature of the meeting. What would be decided today was going to affect the fate of the entire crew and possibly mean a safe return to their home planet. It might also spell doom, and for two very good reasons. Maybe they'd come through it okay; the wormhole that is. Then again maybe they'd be crushed like a walnut. No one knew for sure just how much more the hull of *Anarchy* could take. But the second reason was just as deadly. What if the IPF knew where they'd gone? What if they were waiting for them on the other side?

"Now I know it's been discussed and you know how things get back to me one way or another. I've heard rumors that perhaps those bastards are back there right now watching for us to re-emerge and make an easy target for them, am I right? That's why I think we should talk about this; perhaps allay our fears. We've got Minggatu here to set things straight. I'm sure he's got some opinions on the matter, don't you Lieutenant?" Momentarily surprised at being put on the spot the science officer hastily responded.

"Well, if they are, they'd have been sitting there waiting for a very, very long time," he replied. He'd known all along about the theoretical implications of traveling between galaxies using holes in the fabric of space. Only problem was in explaining this in layman's terms. "I don't think you gentlemen realize what might have happened to us," he then added. "We may have been gone much longer than what everyone believes." As usual, Slout and the other officers struggled to understand his meaning. Debate ensued.

"Why do you say that?" argued Lieutenant Muhendis from Engineering. "It's only been, well, let's see, first we left Star Fantasy and traveled to Earth's solar system. Then what? About three months racing toward Kapteyn B, right? Another two months or so trying to elude the IPF? Plus a month here?" Slout tried calculating this in his head as well.

"What does that total, five, six months?" he interjected. "Sounds about right. Mr. Brilly, what say you? Could they stay in space for that amount of time without having to make port? Got to run out of food some time, don't you think?"

"Just under six," said Ensign Brilly. He'd run those numbers in his mind hundreds of times. Adding in for their three week voyage to Star Fantasy and it totaled *six months* since they'd departed the former penal colony. It'd be another three weeks or more before they'd make it home. "A battleship squadron can be provisioned for extra-long voyages though. I've always assumed they were equipped to follow us wherever we might go; to the ends of the galaxy if need be. Who's to say they might still be patrolling the area where we were last seen?"

This was precisely the type of negative feedback which aggravated their commander. That said, he'd invited open discussion and this was what he was getting.

"Fair question. But you aren't seeing it that way, are you, Minggatu?" he asked, directing his attention back to the CSO. The little fellow was supposed to know about this sort of thing. Astronomy was once his profession. He'd even taught the subject at the collegiate level. Obviously he disagreed with Brilly's timeline, so what was the correct answer? "Does this have to do with that *space-time continuum* you were speaking of just before we landed?"

"Yes, Admiral," replied the science officer, leaning forward in his chair, trying to ignore the looks he was getting from the other staff members. "You see, with wormholes we are shifting from one side of the universe to another. When doing so time itself becomes fluid. That is, we cannot be sure how it is affecting us as we move through. Myself, I experienced bizarre sensations, I don't know about the rest of you but as I sat at my computer I noticed time actually slowing; not to mention other things. Dreamlike is the way I'd describe myself. But that's not all that I noticed. It seemed as though we were only inside of the anomaly for a few minutes."

"I agree," interrupted Slout. "Same thing happened to me. So?"

"Well Sir, when I went back to my system after things returned to normal I calculated the actual time we'd been inside the portal. Turns out it was a lot longer than a few minutes."

"What, like an hour then?" clarified the ship's commander, raising an eyebrow.

"No sir. More like sixteen. According to the ship's computers we'd been traveling sixteen hours before command stepped in and halted the ship. Myself I was a bit woozy afterward and felt like I'd drifted off to sleep. The rest of you might have noticed this; as well as being terribly hungry."

"Me too," commented Brilly. Others sitting around the table confirmed experiencing similar sensations. Slout, for his own part, distinctly remembered having to override the helm and operate the ship's controls because Brilly was passed out. And yes, he remembered being ravenously hungry as if he hadn't eaten in days.

"Explain," ordered Slout. He wasn't too sure he even wanted such a thing but he sensed that Minggatu would do a bang-up job of confusing the hell out of everyone, to the point they'd stop worrying about the issue. That or it would make things worse.

"Yes, perhaps I should try and do that," responded the science officer. It was time to unload as much science as they could absorb, then see what questions they still had. Clearing his throat, he began.

"Space-time is but an expression of the quantum continuum. It's not a solid, but consists of space, time, *and* vacuum. It may contract. It can be twisted, stretched, or even torn apart. In our case we have gone through such a vacuum and we are about to do so a second time. When we do we will once again be exploiting a *tear*, if you will, within layers of space time. You see, negative versus positive energy levels within this vacuum and the pressures above or beneath become extreme, thus any weak points that have been forced open allow passage between these layers."

"Layers of what? Layers of time?" asked Brilly, trying to keep up.

"Something like that," replied Minggatu. "When a vacuum forms between layers it is permeated by negative energy and that's what Casimir proved nearly a thousand years ago. The layer which is lining one cavity may also be differentially affected by gravity, thereby affecting the vacuum between them. What we did was force open this cavity from the outside as well as hold it open as we shot across it, right?"

Heads nodded.

"Well, wormholes presumably tunnel through a negatively charged vacuum between the layers of space time which would strip away positive energy in order to equalize energy gradients, such that we and the *Anarchy* would have a negative charge when we emerged a month ago. Now that we've all agreed there might have been missing time when reaching this side of the wormhole, it's pretty clear there will be additional effects traversing it a second time when we try returning to the other side of the galaxy."

"So, let me clarify," said Brilly, not waiting for the admiral to summarize. By now Slout's facial expression was indicating he'd heard enough. He understood a lot of what Minggatu was saying and astronomy was a big part of being a ship captain, always had been. It's just that science tended to bore him. He knew what he needed to know and the rest he delegated to those who had an appetite for it. For example, the status of the *Anarchy's* exterior and whether it was safe to re-enter the wormhole: if Engineering gave the okay, then that was plenty enough for him. His young navigation officer had reason to probe further.

"You're saying we've gone through time. By traveling from one side of the universe to the other using a space anomaly we've what, gone *back* in time? Or have we gone forward, which is it?" He sounded vaguely impatient but since it was likely that others mirrored his concerns Slout remained silent. He could already sense Minggatu had absolutely no idea what the answer might be. His Chief Science Officer was an astronomer and astronomers were like that. They could talk for hours and hours but still not explain a thing.

"Am I older or younger than before?" Brilly then queried, making the CSO realize he needed to simplify things.

"It doesn't work like that," Minggatu responded with a timid smile. Nevertheless, Brilly still wanted to try and grasp what the Chief Science Officer was driving at. If reemerging from the wormhole meant they'd arrive many months later and or even better, many months *earlier* and then that was useful information. No, he could not fully understand the rest of what the former astronomy professor was saying regarding "quantum continuum" but he could certainly see himself taking full advantage of the situation if they'd be popping out the other side a month or two *before* they'd entered.

"My theory is that since time slowed for us, we should consider it likely that upon returning to our original point of entry we'll see time has advanced noticeably."

"Well of course it has." retorted Lieutenant Muhendis, stating the obvious. He was a human just like Minggatu and came from the Middle East. Unfortunately he was missing the point entirely. "Thirty days, more or less, right? Plus sixteen hours? Is that what we're talking about here?"

"No, Lieutenant," answered Minggatu, realizing his colleagues weren't getting it. "My guess is it would be much, much longer than that ...."

CHAPTER SIX

LOST TIME

It would end up taking Anarchy just over four weeks to travel to New Australia after coming back through the portal. During the journey they took extra care in avoiding detection by other space craft, still believing they were being hunted by the IPF. Arriving, they found things had changed a great deal. That's because they had no clue just how much time had passed.

There were subtle differences, the way Terminal Command responded to their electronic transmissions, when they finally got around to doing so that is. In the past they'd come to expect military precision and a businesslike approach to traffic control. Before they'd left, response times were instantaneous. The place functioned like a well-oiled machine. Yet when they'd hailed terminal command this time around it almost seemed like no one was taking their job seriously. They noticed other procedural violations as well.

The Naustie fleet, most of it anyway, was parked out on the planet surface, completely vulnerable. Sensors onboard *Anarchy* detected their transponder readings and there was no particular pattern to their arrangement. That wasn't the issue. If attacked they'd be sitting ducks. Why weren't they in orbit or out on missions? What special occasion warranted beaching nine converted pirate ships all at once, and if so *how were they servicing them?* Sandstorms, searing heat, thin oxygen, not likely they'd be able to accomplish such a task with the kind of climate New Australia was known for. Were the ships moth-balled? Damaged during the Star Fantasy raid? *What the hell was going on?*

Slout's conversation with Solomon Mwonga did little in shedding light on the situation. And as they rounded the planet they picked up on yet another shocking alteration. As dawn broke they saw buildings, lots of them. It caused quite a stir when Ensign Brilly brought this to everyone's attention. That wasn't all. Structures they knew of were not just out of place but missing entirely. Dozens of new ones now dotted the land-scape.

Plus there were farms. When Brilly first pointed them out Admiral Slout sneered in disbelief. Took a while to convince him. *"Nothing grows there, you idiot."* he'd retorted, but Brilly knew it to be true. Ship sensors identified hundreds of acres of farmland in various stages of development. He found roads, and along these he found row upon row of rectangular structures which could only be multi-family housing given what he'd dis-covered already. Nausties had apparently colonized the surface in a matter of months.

The obvious question was how they could have done so in such a short amount of time. It sparked lively debate amongst the ship's officers as they awaited instructions from their old boss Chief Mwonga. He and Admiral Slout chatted for several minutes as *Anarchy* passed over what must be the new Naustie capital but nothing was gleaned from this exchange besides co-ordinates and timetables, all of which were delayed as if they weren't prepared for a ship to arrive.

Little could they have known what was in store for them when they did land. Drawing closer they began to see just how right Frilbriliram was. Descending to what would have ap-peared to be a concrete slab the size of a track stadium, the truth was revealed. What they could not have known is the number of years that had transpired during which all of this was con-structed; not to mention that their homeland was and had been at peace for over a decade.

***

"Yes, seventeen," quipped the aging Zorgolongian. Shoulders slumped, his eyes squinting in the sunlight as he stood at the base of the *Anarchy*, glaring curiously upward toward his old friend, he wondered as to how Slout would not have known this. "I can still count, Admiral, I'm not *that* old you know?" Then he hissed the way beings of his kind often did. To other species it was difficult to tell whether it be anger, joy, surprise, or despair whenever a Zorg started hissing. In this case it was mirthful humor.

"Why? Do I look that bad?" he then asked, glancing over at Felina, inviting her opinion. She, like her husband, was still trying to wrap her head around the situation. Good manners required that she address Kscheeech's query and save their honored guest Admiral Slout further embarrassment.

"Not to me," she replied kindly. "You look as young as ever, Keech."

Solomon laughed, prompting Slout to eye him warily. He wasn't quite sure what was going on and it made him uncomfortable. Minggatu's cryptic words, spoken right before they'd re-entered the wormhole, were echoing inside his brain. The ship's science officer had foretold this, even if he'd not been terribly specific. Deflated, Slout shrugged his shoulders and shook his head, searching for something to say.

"Uh," he stammered, looking around at the faces of Solomon as well as the young female human he'd introduced as his daughter. Slout looked into the milky eyes of his old pal Kscheeech, then toward the gorgeous Enoshi who he suspected was reading his mind. *Must be an Empath*, he figured. "I'm afraid I'm at a disadvantage right now. You'll have to forgive me."

Solomon reacted quickly. Whatever was afoot they'd have to deal with it *after* the ceremony. Statesmanlike, he intervened.

"It's alright, Admiral," he said, reaching over to grab Slout's massive arm. "We'll talk later. For now, let's go greet our countrymen who've turned out to see you this morning. This is your day, my friend. You're a hero. They've come here to welcome you back."

With that he gestured toward the cheering throng, turning toward them to flash his best politician's smile. This elicited a deafening response. He and Felina then led the poor fellow around like a visiting dignitary. It was more than that of course. This was history in the making. A truly momentous occasion on par with the greatest events in the planet's storied past. The *Anarchy* and her captain, along with all her crew, had returned home safely after being assumed dead for many years. Only problem was, the ship's heroic leader now looked like he wanted to throw up.

"See what I mean, Admiral? They haven't forgotten you, not one bit." yelled Solomon over the boisterous crowd, many of whom were reaching out to touch the bewildered ship captain as he passed. He looked exactly like the day he'd left seventeen years ago and to most in attendance this only enhanced the experience. Of course, the faces looking back at him, calling out to him, chanting his name, he could barely recognize. He wanted to stop and cry out indignantly, *"Wait. Stop your cheering. I don't understand, how could this have happened?"* But he did not. Solomon was his host, leading him by the arm, Felina gently guiding him by the other. This required that he maintain his poise. It also required that their honored guest try and forget what he'd just learned about the amount of time that had passed since he and his ship had set off for Star Fantasy. He never got the chance to dwell on it; the ceremony was just getting started.

"Once again, let us welcome back our returning heroes." bellowed the announcer. He'd been goading the crowd into screaming ever-louder and when Admiral Slout was led up to the dais, escorted by First Citizen Mwonga and his wife, the people roared until their eyes nearly popped out of their heads.

"It's been a long, long time, but worth the wait." the announcer then called out. By that point baffled crewmen whom he'd recognized and introduced had noticed the same thing as their commander. As he stood with Solomon and Felina, Slout returned their confused looks with a shrug of his shoulders or a "don't ask me" expression on his face. Ensign Brilly panicked, looking about at the buildings, overwhelmed by the sight of friends he'd just seen months earlier in the prime of their lives. He was not alone. Several of his shipmates stood frozen in dismay. Next came the big climax, complete with music and a recorded drumroll.

"And now. Brothers and sisters. I give you commander in chief of the Naustie fleet, champion of the great rebellion, captain of the legendary anarchy, scourge of the galaxy ... admiral Slout Epididymus."

Slout dutifully raised his right arm, as if to acknowledge the many thousands in attendance. Solomon could tell he was barely hanging on, seriously in need of an explanation or even better, a stiff drink. He may not have known precisely why his favorite ship captain had not visibly aged, not to mention why his crew looked the same as when they'd left many years ago. This would certainly have to be dealt with. Thankfully it seemed the ceremony was about over.

"Admiral?" asked Solomon, worried for his old friend. "Think you could manage a glass of Scotch right about now?" Slout maintained his pose while leaning slightly toward the former Terminal Chief, continuing to wave toward the ecstatic crowd. His answer was the first thing that had made sense all day.

"I could murder one," he replied ....

That afternoon, once the crowds had melted way, once Slout had reacquainted himself with a hundred old friends and expressed gratitude to a thousand or more well-wishers, Solomon invited the exhausted fleet commander back to the private apartment he shared with Felina. Here they could finally have a chance to talk. Solomon had questions. Slout had questions. Chances were they wanted to know the same thing: how did all this happen? The two sat down at the dining room table together, grateful to be out of the heat.

"Well, where should we start?" chuckled the admiral. "Do you want to go first or shall I?"

He'd just downed his second glass of whiskey and was already feeling better. All they had onboard the Anarchy were barrels of ale, not the best of quality, certainly not by Suidonji standards. Good liquor was a luxury he'd sorely missed for the past six months. Seeing he was a bit more relaxed Solomon gestured for his guest to proceed.

"Right. I should probably go before you, shouldn't I? I'm guessing your version of things will take a while," said Slout with a smirk. He then went on to detail what he had experienced since the raid on Star Fantasy. Never one to overload a superior with information, the admiral finished in only a few minutes. Solomon sat in silence while he spoke, recalling Slout's preference for brevity. He wasn't much for specifics and that's what the former African dictator always used to like about the fellow: always left it up to the boss to ask clarifying questions. Given the circumstances Solomon had plenty, especially when it came to the "missing time" experienced by the crew of the *Anarchy*.

"I see," he said eventually. "So back to this *missing time* you mentioned a moment ago. That, you believe, is what Minggatu was talking about. A disruption in the space-time continuum. Yes, I read about this once. I recall that a wormhole operates by boring a hole through time and space in order to connect two distant points within the universe. It makes more sense now that you told me what it was like. I understand it better now."

"Really?" scoffed the admiral. "Well I'm glad one of us understands 'cause I sure as hell don't." Solomon appreciated his bluntness ... yet another thing he'd missed about his old friend.

"Well, I'm not saying I grasp the concept fully ... and I absolutely couldn't explain it to you the way an astronomer could..." Solomon began to comment modestly. His guest was quick to interrupt.

"Thank the gods for that." joked Slout, slurring his speech

now that the drinks were finally hitting him. "I've had just about enough of listening to all that scientific mumbo-jumbo by now. I don't get it and I don't want to. It happened and there's nothing I can do about it. Whatever that damned wormhole did to our ship, whatever made us go through time, it doesn't matter anyway, does it? We're home, aren't we?"

That seemed like a fair assessment. Sensing it was his turn, Solomon began the daunting task of describing for Slout all he'd missed out on since the Star Fantasy raid. It ended up taking nearly half an hour. The return of the ships, ending with the arrival of the *Warthog* months later, made for a good starting point. From there he told about the bold transformation he'd proposed to the Tribal Confederation. He told of the resistance he'd encountered in changing the modus operandi of the planet from an ever-expanding pirate enterprise to that of *nation-building*. This drew an odd look or two from the brawny pirate. Only there was more, *much* more for the big fellow to learn.

The building of an agricultural dome for the purpose of farming on the surface as well as plans for building five of these massive structures in order to feed their people: this sounded particularly insane to Slout, given that any enemy worth its salt would target these immediately in an effort to destroy the planet's food supply. Who in their right mind would have agreed to such a thing? Obviously a majority of the tribal delegates.

Then there was the construction of an enormous service garage, capable of being sealed off while ships could be serviced and refitted for further missions, all peaceful of course. Slout couldn't begin to imagine how his old boss might have convinced the former convicts of New Australia to accept such an idea. Such a facility should exist only below ground. What were they thinking?

Also, there was the return to mining the interior of the planet in hopes of exporting New Australia's rich natural resources; secretively using the black market to try and establish trade between New Australia and Suidonj. That, they'd never

dared attempting in the old days. In fact, it was Solomon himself who'd defied the Tribal Confederation when it had ordered
that very thing years ago. It was originally Solomon's idea to
turn the *Anarchy* into a pirate marauder. He even championed
the recruiting of raiders to accompany future missions. That's
how Slout had been recruited in the first place.

Finally came the establishment of a system of laws for the
inheritance of property, as well as promoting legal marriage as
a means of fostering lines of succession among tribes. With it
came the advancement of rights for New Australia's female citizenry, leading to the spawning of a new generation of Nausties.
This at least explained how people appeared during the welcome ceremony earlier that day. How they were dressed, for
instance. Slout remembered his countrymen dressed in rags at
one time, barely covering themselves. Big difference with children around.

He listened patiently while Solomon spoke, occasionally
raising an eyebrow or shaking his head in amazement. Otherwise he didn't make a sound and never interrupted other than
to snort when Solomon offered to refill his glass. This he politely refused, prompting his host to cap the bottle and return it
to the liquor cabinet.

"Of course it all came crashing down, I'm afraid," admitted
Solomon, returning to his seat at the dining table. "Quite literally, too." The now middle-aged Human went on to describe
how, after all they'd done and after all they'd tried to accomplish, war was visited upon them in the form of a deadly invasion force from Earth. This, Slout concluded, they should have
expected to happen all along.

"You can't imagine what it was like," Solomon went on to
say. "And I'll be the first to tell you we were *this close* to going
out for good. We only got rid of them by blowing up the
planet. One of our Slarts figured out how to do it. I myself set
the charges. I figured if it was going to be the end of us then I'd
rather be the one pulling the trigger." Slout was particularly
interested in this part of New Australia's history. He'd been ab-

sent throughout; now he was learning just how awful things had been for his countrymen.

"And then it was over," continued First Citizen Mwonga, looking directly at his guest. "In a flash the war was over." He went on to tell of how the explosion cleared out the main shaft, killing thousands from the invading army, effectively spelling doom for the operation. Earth forces evacuated as many of their troops as possible and then, within days, abandoned their mission. New Australia had won her independence.

"Many of our people were killed. The fireball was so devastating that people died on both sides. I probably would have perished right along with them if it hadn't been for my wife and daughter. They led a team down to rescue me. At the time I was passed out from a lack of oxygen. My breather unit had run out of water. I had tried making a run for the surface for some reason. I'll never know why. I guess it made sense at the time. Anyway, I didn't get far before I fainted. That's where Felina and Scout found me. That's what I call my daughter Estrella, by the way, *Scout*."

"Adorable," commented Slout. Yet he did so coolly. Solomon could tell he was thinking about something else. Apparently the tale he was telling of dramatic rescue in the tunnels below the planet surface wasn't terribly interesting to the admiral. Still, he pressed on. There was a lot to cover.

"But we never could have pictured what would be the result, you know, from that volcanic eruption we set off. Colloidal carbon, you see. Water vapor from exploding glaciers. Dust particles. All of that was jettisoned into the atmosphere. And then, amazingly enough, it rained. No kidding. It rained here for the first time in history. That's when we realized we could start farming the surface. You wouldn't have believed it, even if you'd seen it with your own eyes. Thousands of us, rushing over to the terminal bay to see for ourselves. They'd destroyed it. The Earthers, I mean. Blew it to pieces. Many of our people were already outside celebrating when we got there. It was, well, we didn't know what to think at first, to be honest. When we real-

ized it truly was water falling from the sky we danced and celebrated like little children. As for the rest, well, it didn't take
long to move our entire agricultural industry topside."

Slout was finally ready to speak. The rest he could put
together on his own. They were already mining the interior.
Suddenly they were farming the surface, somehow figured out
how to do so in New Australia's brutal climate. They made
peace with other planets no doubt. That shouldn't have been
difficult. No one was going to try attacking them again, not
with their infrastructure in tatters. It would require enormous
capital investment before any money could be made and who'd
take on such a burden? Why not leave it to the survivors? And
how did they manage to do such a thing, those poor souls who'd
managed to drive off the invaders from Earth? How did they get
the funding? Must have borrowed money from Suidonji investment bankers. Knowing his species the way Slout did, they'd
have jumped at the chance to invest in a revitalized New Australia, especially a peaceful one and of course for a share of the
profits. In reality, Suidonj *and* Zorgolong put up the dough, leading to military alliances with both. Slout wasn't thinking about
that however. There was an even bigger issue here.

"So, you turned us back into miners did you? Farmers as well,
I see ... made farmers and laborers out of all those bloodthirsty
killers we'd created. Good for you, Chief. That's something to
be proud of. Once upon a time they were frightened, starving
convicts weren't they? Then we turned them into warriors,
into pirates 'n cutthroats. Not anymore. Now they can finally
settle down, can't they? Raise families? I guess that's every warrior's and every sailor's dream, isn't it, once he gets older?"

Solomon detected a hint of sarcasm but decided to go along
with Slout's line of questioning for the time being. The admiral
would never be insubordinate. Could have, naturally. Solomon
had no real power anymore. No single individual did on New
Australia these days. Nevertheless it wasn't Slout's style. Not
the way the old terminal chief remembered his friend, anyway.

"Yes, I suppose so, I suppose that's what they dream of," responded Solomon, being careful not to reveal his suspicions.

"Well then," Slout continued. "You've surely done what's best for them. The best for everyone concerned. And as for me, I have to confess. Piracy, you know? It's a zero sum game, isn't it?"

"A what?" clarified Solomon; knowing what Slout meant but wanting him to expand on the comment. He'd used terms just like that many years earlier when trying to convince tribal leaders to embrace his concepts. There'd been several who'd pushed back and told him their warriors would never agree, that it would lead to insurrection. Some warned that if they tried selling the idea to the more violent among their constituents it could end up causing their own deaths. *"They'll kill me if I try going back with rubbish like that."* was a common excuse he'd hear.

"Zero sum, it basically means one side always has to lose if the other is to gain. That's basically what piracy is. Problem is, one way or another the losing side will eventually seek recompense. When they do there'll be hell to pay. Hell, we knew what we were doing was bound to get us killed one day. My whole crew did, and if not, they were fools. I'm surprised we even made it back alive after what happened with the IPF back at Star Fantasy. If they'd been there only a few hours earlier they'd have destroyed my entire fleet. You realize that, don't you?"

Solomon wondered whether Slout was merely trying to rationalize his new existence. Nevertheless he had plenty more to say.

"It was all I could do to try and play chicken with those bastards long enough that they'd take the bait and follow me. Even then I knew it to be a death sentence. I've never told anyone this. Frankly I haven't thought about it much lately. It used to be on my mind all the time. It was only when we landed on Green Planet that I dared believing we might make it out of the mess we were in. You know, come to think of it, I honestly never thought we'd arrive home alive until this morning when we made orbit. Just between you and me, I wondered what we'd find when we got here. There were a lot of angry folks after us ... turns out they found their way here to try and destroy us after all. Did a bang-up job of it, didn't they? How many did they kill, by the way? Fifty, eighty thousand?"

Once again, a taste of Slout's bluntness. Solomon adored that about him, even if others might find it abrasive. To be sure, if Felina were there she'd pounce on his cynical words and admonish him, fleet admiral or not. For ten years she and her husband had worked tirelessly to create a more digestible version of Naustie history so that citizens would not dwell on the horror they'd experienced. They focused their efforts on building a more perfect society for future generations, tidying up the facts in order to make things cleaner, more palatable. It was getting easier for the aging former convicts of New Australia to accommodate her and Solomon's "spin" on their planet's wicked past. As Slout had so keenly observed, they'd evolved from criminals into brave warriors. They'd defeated their captors and won their freedom, then in desperation resorted to piracy, attacking and plundering lightly armed merchant vessels. Captured crewmembers were given the choice of joining them or being jettisoned into the blackness of space. Few chose the second option. It was no wonder that someone would eventually retaliate. The only surprise was in Earth's failure to achieve victory, not to mention how Solomon's desperate act, which very nearly destroyed the planet itself, ended up causing permanent alteration to New Australian weather patterns. That being said, it was more desirable to apply terms such as *destiny* and *heroism* to the history of their world. Slout simply chose to call it the way he saw it.

His host chuckled darkly. "We can only estimate the total. There are parts of the interior which have never been excavated. No telling how many bodies would be found." His guest was quick to offer a summary of what he'd gleaned from the conversation; along with a warning.

"Doesn't matter, does it?" remarked the admiral. "We won. To the victor goes the spoils, as they say. Only problem is, how in the hell will my crewmen react to this? To them they left this place only six months ago, on a mission to raid a space station full of females. Now they've come home to a place they hardly recognize. What're we gonna do about that?"

Solomon paused, choosing his words carefully before responding to his guest. Had Slout just raised a valid point? Absolutely. And though the admiral was apparently sold on the concept of attempting to civilize former murderers, thieves, and criminals, transforming them into exemplary citizens of the galaxy, what of the several hundred crewmembers from the planet's most notorious pirate ship? How would beings such as these be able to re-acclimate? For that matter, could they? In their minds they were still raiders and New Australia was still at war with the Interplanetary Authority. This would have to be dealt with immediately; otherwise there was bound to be trouble. Slout could be trusted; only question was could three hundred space pirates be re-assimilated into modern Naustie society?

CHAPTER SEVEN
FIRST SIGNS OF TROUBLE

It wasn't long before trouble began. And it started, not surprisingly, once the returning crew of the Anarchy encountered females for the first time in months. Few could blame them. That is, initially.

There were females of every species, practically everywhere they looked. Some were older and less attractive than one would normally desire but it was their sheer number that was so overwhelming, not to mention a veritable cornucopia of teenage off-spring who were decidedly even more appealing to all those lonely sailors who'd spent a near-eternity in space. Meanwhile, as for the younger generation of Nausties, they were celebrities. Most anyone, including their parents, could only admire their bravery and fortitude in keeping the Interplanetary Fleet preoccupied all those years ago following the raid on Star Fantasy. None dared to question the role they'd served in ensuring New Australia's survival. Therefore it was understandable to people like their former Terminal Chief that they'd be allowed to run wild for a while, which they did, with reckless abandon.

To be fair they'd been gone since the attack and never gotten to see the result, never gotten to share in the spoils. Before they'd departed they'd never have experienced such a thing as female Humans, Suidonji, Enoshi, and Zorgs walking about, going to work, going shopping, and meandering freely through the streets of the capital. When they'd left there was no capital. Plus all females were captives back then. They'd been taken as plunder; distributed among the tribes. Now they were full-fledged citizens of the independent world of New Australia; a fact which was of little interest to crewmembers craving companionship. Star-struck citizens, inclined to treat *Anarchy's* veterans with reverence and even awe, rapidly found themselves having second thoughts.

Bars and saloons were packed to the rafters with the newly arrived guests from outer space, carousing and drinking through the night. Bartenders often "comp'd" their drinks and when they did not, fellow patrons usually paid the tab. The former pirates had no money per se; could only trade for what they required using exotic foods they'd brought back from Green Planet. What they desired was liquor most of all and of that there was an endless supply, even if it seemed there'd never be enough to slake their thirst. Unfortunately, that wasn't all they sought for pleasurable entertainment.

Solomon was constantly being called upon to get involved; for the rapidly overstretched Naustie police force he was often their last resort for guidance when it came to repeat offenders. *Disturbing the Peace* was the common charge. Sometimes it was far worse: Battery, Assault, Indecent Exposure, Corruption of a Minor, Destruction of Property, Unlawful Entry, the list went on and on. Within a week the jails were filling up with *Anarchy's* crewmen. Slout was of little help, even if he always seemed 'willing'. When called upon to advise how to deal with his unruly subordinates, incarceration was about all he could suggest.

"*Throw 'em in the brig; let 'em sleep it off for a day or two.*" he'd snarl, as that was the usual punishment. Beatings with electrified whips hadn't been employed for over a century. The only common infraction was being drunk while on duty, resulting in confinement to quarters, and if available, the ship's brig. The admiral figured they'd eventually "get it out of their system," as he liked to put it. That never seemed to materialize.

During the thirty days following *Anarchy's* return, the number of incidents only increased. Solomon and his old friend Slout were hard pressed to find a way to deter such behavior. Being *drunk in public* and getting in fights with husbands or fathers of the females they'd attempted having relations with? About the only solution the admiral could offer was a night or two in jail. "It'll cool 'em down a bit, you'll see," as Slout would say, "if not, make it a week next time." Sadly that only worked until the jails were filled to capacity, which occurred within weeks. In desperation the *Anarchy* herself began to be utilized as a prison. This Solomon instituted, with Slout's blessing of course, as a means of isolating serious offenders until they could think of something better.

It did little to quell the growing tumult over how to deal with the planet's returning 'heroes', though. Victims and relatives of victims were growing impatient. Solomon feared how this might degenerate into further *unpleasantness,* especially when the Tribal Assembly met the following month. For now they'd isolated the threat by imprisoning the miscreants by confining them to quarters onboard their own ship. But there was another issue, and that's why Solomon sought out a private meeting with his admiral to discuss a more long-term strategy. It had now been only a month since the *Anarchy* had landed. As bad as things had gotten they could easily get much worse, especially when those now incarcerated were released. That's because Naustie legal code regarding misdemeanor charges stemming from public intoxication, vandalism, minor assault, and the like, were purposely lenient. It was a little something left over from their pirate past, but what it meant was those currently locked up on the *Anarchy* could only be jailed for up to *twenty days*. Major infractions, such as murder, were dealt with by the different tribes, but in less than a month they'd be going through this all over again once the nearly three hundred former pirates would once again be out on the streets raising hell. That, among other things, concerned Solomon most.

"You see, my friend, there is potential for an even bigger

problem if we don't come up with a plan," Solomon said to Slout as they sat together at his dining room table. Felina had been present when the conversation began. Then, sensing Slout was uncomfortable with a female listening in, she quietly departed. Estrella came home at one point during the meeting, even sat in on the discussion for a few minutes. Their guest, though cordial, didn't seem to appreciate her presence so she too left, claiming to have some errands to run. This left the two embattled leaders alone in the Mwonga family apartment. Once they could finally talk privately, Solomon revealed what he was most afraid of.

"It's the old guard, you know, the ones who never fully accepted what we were trying to accomplish here. They're still out there. Not so many as there were right after the invasion, I have to admit. Many have passed on. Before the war there were thousands, many times that of today. Nevertheless they're still a thorn in my side. They miss the good old days, is what they'll tell you. We all do, I suppose, but their type especially ... they won't let it go. They're obsessed with our past." Slout didn't see where there was an issue.

"So?" he pithily observed, not being insubordinate, just Slout being Slout. Blunt, no-nonsense, get-to-the-point, tell-it-like-it-is, Solomon didn't notice anything unusual about his friend's curt response. It was only when he elaborated that the middle-aged African realized what the admiral meant.

"That's what you want, isn't it Chief? For them to remember fondly? Be proud of what they've accomplished? Respect the names of the fallen and those who sacrificed for the cause? Sounds to me like good old fashioned patriotism. They love their country, they *should* love their country. What's the issue then?" Solomon could see where this might require some explaining.

"It's more complicated than that, admiral," he sighed. By then he'd offered Slout a drink, but his guest declined. This by itself was not terribly unusual, given the seriousness of their meeting. "There's a lot about our history. Well, I'll just come

right out and say it. There's a lot we'd rather try and forget."
The former fleet commander now got a look on his face like he
might be taking offense to such a comment. Solomon instantly
regretted his choice of words.

"Forget?" snorted Slout, clearly with a lot more to say but
possessing enough common sense not to do so. Didn't need to.
His piercing black eyes spoke volumes. Solomon tried walking
it back.

"Oh, I don't mean forgetting our heroes, no. We'll never
forget what you veterans did for our country. You risked your
lives, no question. It's just that, and I'm sure you can appreciate when I say this, but there are certain, uh, *details* if you will.
Thing's we'd like to leave out when it comes to discussing our
history. Pieces of the puzzle which may be disturbing to the
next generation. That's because we now wish to be a peace-lov-
ing planet."

The burly ship captain cocked an eyebrow. His response was
wholly unexpected.

"We?" retorted Slout, causing Solomon's eyes to widen.
"Who's *we*? And just who do you think you speak for when you
say that word? All of us? Is that what you believe ... *Mr. First
Citizen*?"

He then formed a half-smile before continuing.

"I heard of this, you know?" They say you're more of a politician these days. Politicians say things like that. They say *we* and
us when they really mean *I* or *me*. I guess that's why you think
you can make such a statement."

Solomon had never seen this side of Slout's personality. The
big fellow was sober as a judge, so what in God's name had come
over him? True, the former dictator had to admit that his barrel-chested, brawny houseguest was asking a fair question. And,
to be fair, perhaps it was difficult to accept, the way Naustie
society had evolved. That said, Solomon wasn't the same man
anymore; didn't want to be. He was, as Slout indicated, a politician. Thus a politician's answer was what he gave.

"I assure you, admiral," Solomon countered, clearing his

throat, "the vast majority of Nausties feel the same as I do. They love our modern society. Ask them and they'll tell you. They get up and go to work each day in the mines and on the farms. Some are mechanics. Some farmers. Some homemakers. We even have a college now, did you know? A Merchant Marine Academy where we can send our best and brightest to learn how to be ship captains and first officers someday. And as for those from our own generation? They have no interest in being pirates. They're fed up with war. They want to raise families. Grow old and do so in peace, with no threat of seeing their wives and children butchered at the hands of an invader. They tell me these things. I travel throughout, visit all the old homelands, not to mention the housing districts on the surface. Have to, just to know the pulse of our countrymen. I travel far and wide, ensuring that the message is conveyed and adhered to. We, both Felina and I, remind them of how far we've come, remind them what we're striving for, remind them of what it takes for New Australia to be a citizen planet. We're a democracy now, and that's how it should..."

Slout started shaking his head dismissively, causing his host to trail off. Apparently, he possessed an opinion on the matter.

"*Propaganda*," he quipped, now shocking his host with his candor. It was as though he were mocking his former boss. This was highly unusual for the normally respectful ship captain.

"Propaganda," he repeated. "You know it. I know it. Noblest of intentions, I'll grant you that, but Chief you have to admit, it reeks of a whitewash. I get it of course. You had the vision years ago. Knew what needed to be done. Told me the day I arrived, remember? First you sold the tribal chieftains on it, most of them as you said, then you turned all those thieves, drug dealers, and murderers into farmers, laborers, and merchant seamen. And no, you don't have to sell me on it. I told you before, I agree. Problem is my crew. They're bound to see through something like that. They're still young, most of them. They just wanna go out and have a good time ... been cooped up on that ship for half a year. It won't do any good tellin' 'em it's not acceptable or that it's *illegal.* You want them to become *villagers?* That'll take some time, old man."

Old man? thought Solomon. He'd never been called that before. Didn't particularly care for it, either. Only there was more. Slout wasn't done with his tirade.

"Then you go and speak of democracy. Is that what we are? *Pffft.* Democracy is an illusion, my friend, always has been. Leaders still must make decisions affecting public policy or national security, and their stewards must enforce the rules. They'll tell you the beauty of democracy is that there are systems in place, checks and balances, which prevent a tyrant from advancing a potentially disastrous agenda. But it doesn't matter, don't you see? Elected leaders simply inspire public sentiment which pressures lower level officials into throwing their support behind them. In that regard it doesn't work any better than with a dictatorship. Either way a leader is at the mercy of advisors who may or may not provide him with accurate information. Operations planned sometimes ignore common sense, based on bad intelligence or incomplete data. Sure, it may take more time to commit an enormous blunder, but the result is the same. And when it fails, it's the people who pay the price."

Something had definitely changed regarding Slout's personality. Perhaps he'd grown cynical now that the world he'd known so well was a thing of the past. That might serve in explaining his skepticism. Once firmly in charge of the Naustie pirate fleet he was now fleet commander of nothing. The ships he'd once directed in battle had been converted back to freighters. Vessels he'd once known, captained by homicidal maniacs he'd led during the Star Fantasy raid, were now loaded with mineral ore, industrial diamonds, and perovskite crystals for use in powering factories and cities throughout the galaxy. What made it hard for Solomon though was that his friend was absolutely right. It *was* a whitewash. He'd simply spun that message so many times, in so many ways, for so many years, he'd grown to believe his own bullshit.

But that wasn't the point he was trying to make. There was

a danger needing to be addressed. If Slout's crewmen were to get mixed up with right wing radicals it could mean a potential threat to the stability of the confederation. There were those who still, even after ten years of peace and the challenges they'd endured rebuilding, demanded bloody revenge. *"Earth."* they said, *"Earth should be made to pay for all the destruction they caused."* It had always been a tenuous peace with Solomon's original home planet. And it was one that he wished to maintain.

He'd be the first to say it, perhaps to his wife Felina and no one else, but in his heart of hearts he'd love to agree with them. What Earthers had done to his people was unforgivable. Yes, they should be avenged: eighty thousand killed by the invaders, most of them noncombatants. However, it wasn't that simple. Nothing was as simple as it was seventeen years earlier, when *Anarchy* and the rest of the Naustie fleet set out to plunder a remote space station which had been converted into a floating brothel.

The problem with settling the score was that Earth's aggression had provided a golden opportunity for Solomon to seek peace with the rest of the IPA's member planets ... an opportunity he was wise to exploit. All his countrymen had to do was *behave*. Raid one ship, just one, and all bets were off. Today the other planets trusted them, more or less. New Australia had a thriving economy and the planet's youth were flourishing. What these radicals were still clamoring for ... in the pubs and in the saloons ... in caverns far beneath the surface ... was ludicrous. There could be no going back.

Violently suppressing such thinking was also quite out of the question. Perhaps it was part of the illusion which must be maintained in a democracy and to which Slout had smugly referred. There must be freedom to believe, freedom to express opinions, and live one's life however one saw fit. It merely required a system of laws, along with a police force and judicial system adequately empowered to enforce those laws. If those hard-heads insisted upon criticizing the direction things were going they must be allowed to say whatever was on their minds.

And frankly they could bellyache all they wanted. Tribal leaderships heartily supported Solomon and his agenda. Chieftains and their families were rich beyond belief. Their constituents were by and large happy. Up until now it had been quite easy to convince the majority of citizens not to listen to such vitriol. And yet, three hundred returning pirates from a bygone era could endanger this. Even with all the turmoil they'd caused since re-entering society, such incorrigibles could very easily rekindle hope among right wing radicals for a return to "the old ways". What if these radicals started recruiting sailors from the *Anarchy* to their cause? Then what? Who might be next, the planet's youth?

Solomon considered all of this, then spoke. "Yes, I see your point, admiral," he said.

Solomon was well into his forties by now and the years had made him, among other things, *tolerant*. Less inclined to argue. More inclined to seek common ground or simply agree to disagree. A lot of it had to do with the way Solomon viewed his purpose as an enlightened leader. Power, true power, must be derived via a mandate from the masses. Encouraging proper ways of seeing things through campaigning and stump speeches notwithstanding, it was the will of the people which surpassed all else. Believing he was right, confidently touting his ideals of peaceful coexistence, certainly aided him in steering public opinion. And yes, his reputation and past heroism were a huge factor in this. Having Felina reinforce his message with tribal chieftains was even more crucial to that success. Still, he preferred to have people believe it was they themselves making the decision to pursue the proper path.

"But try and see things from my perspective. They're out there, my friend. Older now and lacking physical prowess, they speak of war and conquest with fire in their eyes. You should hear some of the crazy things they say. Our youth find them to be eccentric, and in many ways, ridiculous. Teenagers refuse to listen to them; laugh at them behind their backs. Yet here come your crewmen, back from space and right out of our own history books, a history which we've tried to protect them from. Please understand. This could change the way our young people see things."

Slout had never been a parent. Never been married. Rarely been around teenagers. Thus he had trouble relating to his host's concerns.

"Even now? After the way those idiots conducted themselves?" questioned the admiral, referring to how his crew were out making jackasses of themselves night after night. If anything, this should have proven to the youth of New Australia why their fathers had become the way they were, why they'd suppressed tendencies toward violence and encouraged their offspring to do the same. Returning pirates running rampant through the streets and getting into fights with locals couldn't possibly inspire young males to do the same, could it? Then again, it was all in how one looked at it. Aging Nausties who'd been bragging about their exploits all these years: who's to say such shameful incidents might seduce Naustie youths into believing there was good reason to pursue a life of piracy?

"Especially now," Solomon retorted. "Young people, it's always been their tendency to latch onto a revolutionary idea. As they develop a sense of independence they start rebelling against their parents. Not all of them, mind you, but you know what I mean. You were young once, I was too, and I remember what I was like as a teenager. I left home, joined a band of hooligans, and in time became their leader. Perhaps you remember my story. I'm sure you heard what happened to me years later when authorities caught up to me. But my dear mother, she tried and tried to make me stay. Tried telling me I'd end up dead before I was twenty. And did I listen?"

"Obviously not," chuckled Slout.

"Exactly. And it wasn't that I didn't love my family. I adored my mother and my brothers and sisters, too. Looking back, our village was like a paradise compared to what I experienced once I left. But I wasn't going to listen. Wasn't a rebellious child and yet that's just what I did once those ideas got into my head."

"*Baaah.*" scoffed Slout, once again surprising Solomon with his nonchalance. "I wouldn't be so concerned about all those young people out there, seeing pirates committing mayhem all over town. Really Chief, I wouldn't let it worry you. They're kids ... teenagers who don't have a clue what they want. If they get out of line, scare the shit out of them. That's what my parents did and look how I turned out, I'm a goddamned admiral."

Solomon quickly grasped the big fellow's humor. He laughed and even slapped the dining room table to let his guest know how much he appreciated the irony. Slout was a ship captain and a very good one, but he was also a ruthless pirate ... before that a smuggler. Not exactly a bona fide fleet admiral within the ranks of the Interplanetary Fleet. Solomon was starting to like this new version of his old friend. However, it was Slout's next comment that brought him back to reality.

"No, I wouldn't give it another thought," the admiral continued, absent-mindedly reaching up with a hoof to scratch his armpit. "It's my crewmembers locked up in their cabins out there on the *Anarchy*, that's who you'd best be worried about. You're worried about broken down former prison inmates stirring them to action? Join a political movement? Try convincing tribal elders that we should plunder the galaxy once again? Nonsense. They certainly don't need some shriveled old Porko, some silver haired Earther, some withered old Zorg they used to raid ships with ... don't need some old fool like that to tell them what they should be longing for. They already know what they want. They're pirates."

CHAPTER EIGHT

A VILE ACT

Clearly the solution was to go have a talk with the prisoners. That's what seemed to be the most logical approach. Speak to them and tell them what was expected and what was not allowed anymore. Chew the fat too, let them vent their frustrations. A good leader has to do such things from time to time. A great one inspires his followers to choose for themselves between right and wrong.

Considering Slout's initial reaction to what he was experiencing a month earlier when they'd first landed, Solomon could only assume *Anarchy's* crewmen must have been equally baffled and not to mention *distressed*. They deserved an explanation, it was only fair. Solomon could only wonder as to why he hadn't tried this already. Perhaps it was because with the hearty welcome those returning sailors had received it simply never crossed his mind there'd be any fallout. Obviously, he'd been mistaken. And it wouldn't do any good bringing Slout along for the visit. The admiral had changed and given his attitude regarding New Australia's transformation from pirate paradise to 'citizen planet of the galaxy', he'd only be a hindrance. Best tactic was to deliver the message which needed to be conveyed and do so alone.

To accomplish this, Solomon arranged to have the entire group of malcontents assembled in the enormous cargo bay of the *Anarchy* where they were being held. He anticipated no security threat since these crewmen had known him for years as Terminal Chief. They'd view him as an authority figure and be hesitant to question what he was saying due to his former rank, not to mention he was nominally still head of the Schpleeft-korkii tribe.

"Good afternoon, gentlemen." Solomon announced as he stood front and center. Guards had moved a metal crate to the middle of the now-empty ship's hold for him to use as a platform. First Citizen Mwonga was used to giving speeches by now. Only difference was he didn't have his beautiful wife Felina tagging along, yet another potential distraction, he'd decided. The returning pirates had likely heard what she once was, and even if they had not, the appearance of an attractive female wouldn't help his cause. They needed to hear from a male authority figure, one they both recognized and respected.

"I'd like to begin by apologizing to each and every one of you. This is not what we would have preferred, I am embarrassed to say."

Aside from a few grumbles, nothing. Blank faces greeted his gaze. Otherwise the crowd remained silent. It was an inauspicious start.

"Of course by now you've all been told the rules. There's no need for me to detail them for you at this point. And I don't wish to belabor why it is we've had to sequester the lot of you inside your own ship especially after what you've been through. New Australia is aware of the sacrifices you've made and you've heard this, no doubt, from your own countrymen. We are so deeply grateful for the risks you took as well as the many hardships endured in making your way home. Despite all you've experienced let me make this abundantly clear, as one of your leaders, and while I'm at it, as a fellow Naustie: what you did for our planet will never be forgotten."

Silence still. Solomon was undeterred.

"It's why I came to speak with you today. This needed to be communicated in person and from the highest echelon. Things have changed and it is not your fault you've returned home only to find New Australia far different than the way you left it. You've undoubtedly been informed how many years have passed since your departure. I realize this was something you were unprepared for when you arrived four weeks ago. Seeing old friends who've aged many years, unfamiliar buildings and the like, must have caused stress and confusion. For that I am also sorry. I cannot begin to imagine the shock and dismay you may have suffered seeing such things. My heart goes out to you."

Nothing, not even a head nod to let him know he was getting through to them. Solomon tried not to reveal how this was unnerving him.

"However, you must try and adjust to your surroundings. That's why I've come here to meet with you in person, to let you hear this from someone you recognize, someone you trust. A little older, yes. A little rounder in the middle, I suppose. Nevertheless, I'm the same man who ordered the raid on Star Fantasy. To you it was only half a year ago. To us it was much longer, but let's move past that shall we? I prefer emphasizing just how grateful I am for what you did. But that's not all. It is my desire that you find your place within our new modern society. A society which values its heroes and offers a quality of life unsurpassed in the galaxy."

Solomon paused for a moment to look out at the sea of grimy faces. Most had not showered since being ordered back to their cabins and hadn't been inclined to do so the whole time they'd been in space. Their odor, combined with the stale air inside the ship's hold, was stifling.

"We are a citizen planet now. Member of the Interplanetary Authority," he continued, trying to ignore the smell. "It came at a great cost, but that is what we've achieved in your absence, I'm proud to say. Please, become a part of this new society, a society which your sacrifice and bravery helped create. That, gentlemen, is what I wanted you to hear today. Welcome home, all of you, welcome home."

Solomon then paused, extending his arms in a gesture as if to express the warm tidings he'd just expressed. He'd given speeches like this so many times. Unfortunately, the response was far from what he would have anticipated.

"Rubbish." shouted one of the prisoners, giving Solomon a jolt of reality. He'd forgotten what his fellow Nausties used to be like. Memories came rushing back of that fateful day when a thousand warriors gathered to hear Architeuthis deliver a similar speech inside the recently conquered terminal bay. Arguments broke out between rival gang leaders arrayed at the base of an earthen ramp used in the attack on the warden's stronghold. Civil war was the result.

"Yeah, that's what I'm sayin'." bellowed another, just as a swell of laughter began to rise among his fellow prisoners. "Save that crap for all those *peasants* out there working in the fields. And by the way, if you're so happy to see us then how about doin' us all a favor 'n bring us some liquor, will you? We been cooped up in this shithole for two days and there ain't a drop o' booze to be found nowhere."

They'd seen past his attempts at diplomacy, apparently. Now the gloves were off. Solomon braced himself for further backlash.

"Amen to that." hollered yet another. The voice sounded Human. "You tell us how thankful you are, then how about a keg or two of beer? Or better yet, let us go. We ain't done nothin'."

"Besides keep the IPA off your asses?" joked a fourth, sparking a spirited debate. It fast became a free for all.

"Maybe what he really means is what we did don't need doin' no more. We're relics." cried a voice from the back, inspiring yet another round of derisive snickers. Solomon's eyes darted about in hopes of identifying who was talking but could not. This only fed the tumult.

"Since when did that matter, brother?" quipped a prisoner near the front. This time it was a Zorg. He averted his eyes when he said this, not willing to look Solomon in the face. Either that or he simply didn't care. "We raided all over the galaxy and took whatever we wanted, whenever we wanted, and no one told us we wasn't supposed to until we got back, to the very place it all started. Now, we get here 'n find shriveled faces looking back at us, including the same old geezer who sent us off raiding when we was supposed to be doin' somethin' else. That sound like anyone we know, brothers?"

He then looked directly into Solomon's eyes. Obviously New Australia's de facto leader was the 'old geezer' being referred to. Wisely he did not respond. He was a statesman, not a stand-up comic, had no background in responding to hecklers.

"Or have you forgotten? Eh, *Chief Mwonga*?" asked the pirate. The Zorg was quite astute. Solomon had been the one to initiate pirate raids as a means of securing food for the planet. Following a brief civil war the newly established Tribal Confederation had assigned him the task of seeking trade relations with Suidonj, but he'd disobeyed. To do so would risk losing their one and only ship and the same converted freighter they were now located inside of. Meanwhile the other pirates, some two hundred fifty of them, redirected their attention toward their once-powerful Terminal Chief from days past. He'd recruited them, a lot of them anyway. For Solomon that was nearly two decades ago. For them it was only yesterday, and yes, he understood their confusion, even if he had no interest in debating the issue. That he'd changed his focus and later convinced tribal delegates to do the same was immaterial. It was the proper thing to do. Not that it was worth explaining to these ruffians. They weren't going to let him off so easily. The Zorg then turned his attention to their more recent mission.

"Then came Star Fantasy. You were there, up in your office atop the loading bay, weren't you? You saw us off, hoped we'd bring back thousands of fresh females. Which we did, or at least our colleagues did on other ships, I should say. By the way, I hear you made out quite well in that regard. Got yourself a nice tasty Empath when it was all said and done, didn't you?"

This inspired a roar of grumbling from among the crowd of brutes. Those who'd heard the story of Solomon securing for himself one of the legendary creatures from planet Enosh, passed on the news to those still uninformed. At the time Felina was captured and taken onboard the *Chengshi*, no communication was allowed between ships, a security measure ordered by Admiral Slout so to disguise ship identities. Thus they'd never known of Solomon's spectacular good fortune until now.

"Yeah, *Chief*. Seems like you did quite well for yourself." reiterated a different pirate, this time an Enoshi. That Solomon would have taken one of his kind as a bride didn't sit too well with him. Judging by the tone of his voice, frankly all Enoshi males sounded like they were growling when they spoke, it didn't appear as though the snarling beast meant it as a compliment. The big cat had more to say.

"Or shall we call you, *'First Citizen'*?" the warrior added. Must have been a marine onboard the *Anarchy*, retained by Slout as a security officer, Solomon figured. There was no way to tell. Crewmen from back in the old days wore no uniforms. What's more, Enoshi never wore clothing. This caused a rumble among the mass of bodies huddled around Solomon's feet. He took a quick inventory of his surroundings: two hundred plus pirates, at best fifty policemen, the majority of whom were Enoshi as well. Problem was they too were getting on in years. Same as he, they were overweight and past their prime. Thoughts of a riot now ran through his mind. If that happened he'd never make it out of that cargo hold in one piece. Question was, would they attack him? Would they kill him just for sport?

Maybe. Given the way they were looking at him right now and sizing him up like a porterhouse steak, it wasn't out of the realm of possibility. Sensing things were coming undone, Solomon signaled for guards to return the inmates to their quarters. There was no point in continuing; the meeting was over. For his own part, the former Terminal Chief headed for the safety of the command bridge. Only when the ship was secure did he make a hasty exit.

Following the disastrous encounter with the imprisoned pirates, Solomon returned to his apartment. Felina was home already after spending the morning doing volunteer work at the community outreach center. Months earlier she'd created a literacy program. It was a great opportunity to connect with at-risk youths, which was something she was rather passionate about. Whereas their adopted daughter was home-schooled and well-educated, many growing up around the capital didn't have such opportunities. Their parents rarely knew how to read and write and Felina had made it her mission to remedy this. She greeted her husband as he walked in, sensing immediately his frustration.

He'd no sooner pulled off his breather unit than Felina was offering him a glass of Scotch to soothe his nerves. They'd been married so many years; by this point she no longer needed to ask. Solomon sipped it slowly, letting the alcohol do its job. Felina then sat down with him in the living room, waiting for the man to speak. He wanted to open up about what was bothering him, she could tell. The key was to be patient. Since her husband was not asking about her day at the community center, this could only mean he had things on his mind. Felina purred softly while he collected his thoughts. He eventually set down his whiskey and spoke. What he had to say surprised her, especially considering all they'd been through since the legendary ship's arrival.

"We have to let them go; that's all there is to it," said Solomon finally, looking down at his aching feet. He'd walked all the way out to the *Anarchy* in sandals, then back again through the mid afternoon heat. Now he was exhausted, physically as well as emotionally. "It's wrong to keep those crewmembers locked up, not accomplishing a thing, besides, it's only going to make things worse."

This was the last thing Felina expected. After thirty days of almost constant reports coming in of assaults, vandalism, and mischief going on in the streets at night it would almost seem they'd be better served in sending the pirates back where they came from. Only that was the problem. This *was* where they came from. They couldn't very well exile them to Green Planet. Next time they returned, Estrella would be a grandmother.

"I understand," replied Felina, even if she wasn't so sure that she did. Saying that was more a way of coaxing Solomon into explaining his logic. It always worked.

"You see, we have to show them how they can assimilate into our society. If we keep them in cages they'll never be able to rejoin their tribal communities. They'll always resent us for it and who knows the consequences we may suffer later? I saw it in their eyes, Felina. It shocked me. Frightened me. And yet I have to say, I could only feel sorry for them."

Felina chose not to press him for details. If he'd felt it necessary her husband would have done so, might still. Being an Empath she knew not to make him describe what he'd just experienced. That would only distress him. Besides, it was unimportant. Solomon was suggesting a potential solution to dealing with the returning crew of the planet's long-lost pirate ship. That's what needed to be focused on. An Empath's skill was in diplomacy after all. That, and other things of course.

"Bottom line is it's not their fault, the circumstances they're in. That is the key. And I know from experience how people respond whenever the unthinkable happens. Let me assure you. Those victimized by violence want to believe it was under someone's control; even when it was not. They'll start saying that someone should bear responsibility for the disaster. Then guess who they'll point their fingers at? Their nation's leaders."

Felina knew her husband was drawing comparisons to events leading up to his imprisonment on Rijel 12 many years ago. As a young man he'd led an armed coup to take over the government of a small African nation. The ensuing conflict saw death squads employed by the warring factions in order to gain an edge. Hundreds of thousands died; most of them civilians. Judges at the world court needed someone to blame. Solomon and his men had seized their government's headquarters, initiating the conflict, thus he made for the perfect fall guy. Now he was in a similar position.

The former terminal chief could see how it might unfold. Right wing radicals within the different tribal councils would decry the 'despicable treatment of our returning heroes'. Citizens who'd been affected by the sailors' behavior would urge the government to keep them locked up, but such pleas would largely be ignored. The Confederation would be meeting later that month and heated arguments were bound to occur within the assembly hall. Feeling pressure, they'd likely decide to suspend sentences and put *you-know-who* in charge of creating a program for the 'proper assimilation' of the crewmen. Then he'd have no choice, and if someone, or several people, got hurt due to acts of violence, Solomon would inevitably face criticism for worsening an already difficult situation by having detained them in the first place. That's because every day those miscreants remained in lockup, they'd grow increasingly belligerent. He had to bite the bullet. Better to be proactive and deal with it now before the Tribal Confederation ordered him to. Only challenge was in how he'd ever be able to face them again, those former pirates who'd sent him scurrying for cover.

Felina was deep in thought, a trait of hers he'd come to appreciate. Solomon waited patiently for her to finish meditating on the matter. Finally, she looked up and met his gaze. "I agree. We'll begin first thing tomorrow," she said, as a determined expression formed on her whiskered face. "In fact, I'll do it myself. You just leave this one up to me."

For the first time that day, Solomon cracked a smile. He was glad that she agreed. And she was right. The best person for a job like this was a female. Slout would only make things worse. That Felina was an Empath and could adapt instantaneously to the feelings and needs of others was crucial to their success. He'd seen her in action so many times in the past. He knew she wouldn't let him down.

"Tomorrow. Yes, tomorrow, we'll begin trying to win them over," he repeated. He then leaned back in his chair and sighed. Felina got up and fixed him another drink.

***

The first task was to meet the initial demand he'd been informed of by the prisoners themselves. Liquor. Lots of it. In fact, Solomon's initial strategy was to get them all they could consume and then some. Let them drink themselves into oblivion. Get stoned drunk. When accomplished he next ordered showers constructed so they could wash the filth off their bodies using fresh water. This, he conceived of as a means for improving their morale. It had an immediate effect.

He concealed his involvement, naturally. That was also part of his strategy. Guards were given bonuses as a reward for the imposition of having to supervise such a process, and from there they left it up to the prisoners to assume it was all a gift from the community. Later he sent in Felina with a delegation of citizens to attempt a fresh start. The sailors' reaction to seeing her was one of astonishment. When she spoke, they settled right down like unruly children in a classroom when the teacher walks in. Her beauty and kindness shown through. Her patience and compassion turned them around ever so slowly until one by one they opened up. Foul language and lewd comments quickly ceased, especially when they saw how little effect these had on the lovely Enoshi. When they'd all said their piece and both sides had aired their grievances, and all crewmembers and citizens had expressed their discord, it was finished. Solomon was not present but had already signed the order. Felina was charged with delivering the wonderful news: *they were free to go.*

The next few months saw a steady improvement in the way crewmen from the *Anarchy* conducted themselves. The meeting of the Tribal Confederation came and went. Delegates discussed policy, passed a few measures. By that point the troubles had for the most part died down. Of course, there were still a few hard cases. Some of the crew simply could not adjust. The majority settled into new lives within their tribal homelands. They found their place; joined work crews or took jobs on merchant ships. Slout, for his part, was put in charge of the planet's navy and given an office within the same building as the Mwonga family's apartment. Solomon saw to that personally.

It was a great way to keep tabs on the admiral. New Australia's navy existed only on paper of course. At least it gave him something to do during the day.

It was those hard cases that continued to be a challenge though. Solomon anticipated this; despite progress made with large numbers of the crew, there were a minority who showed little sign of accepting their new environs. Stories made it back to Solomon of fights occurring, assaults on females, drunken debauchery going on well after curfew. It didn't always prove to be the same individuals involved; to be fair there were those among the population who were goading them on ... provoking them in some cases, encouraging them in others. As for teenage girls, of whom there were quite a few, it was apparent that more than a handful were drawn to these repeat offenders. They were attracted to them like rock musicians. This only perpetuated the cycle of arrest, incarceration, followed by returning them to society with a warning of more dire consequences if they didn't shape up. Nevertheless, Solomon could only assume the worst was behind him. He and Felina returned to their regular practice of touring the planet's interior and checking up on what progress was being made with those who'd tried making a go of things. Their first stop: the tribal homeland of the Lacertilias, all of whom were Zorgolongian.

The reception was lukewarm at best, even if that wasn't terribly unusual. For one thing the Lacertilias had welcomed back several returning crewmembers from the *Anarchy*, and though this had been accomplished with no incident, the tribe was also home to several so-called "ultra-conservatives" among its elders. These individuals were part of the old guard who would love nothing more than a return to plundering the galaxy and getting even with Earth. He and Felina did the usual glad-handing and took the customary tour of their tribal homeland. Felina made the rounds and checked in on how females were being treated, something she was known for. Otherwise their visit was uneventful. When finished, the chieftain and his entourage escorted them back to the border between theirs and their neighbor's homeland, that of the Cave Lions. This was also a known bastion for right wing radicals, even if Felina and the Cave Lions had a past.

The Cave Lion Tribe were Enoshi, like herself. They had relocated following the war with Earth. Their original environs were located atop an enormous magma chamber. During the war this area had been selected as an ideal place to lay a trap for the invaders. Wired with nuclear detonators, it was destroyed by an epic blast which resulted in the eradication of the enemy's forces and effectively ended the conflict. The tribe had nevertheless held on to their traditional existence, believing that the planet itself had decided they should survive when the volcanoes erupted. Actually, it was Felina who had originally suggested such a notion during a rousing speech she'd given ten years earlier. It had been necessary to tell them this in order to get them to leave; however, stories passed down had been conveniently *altered*. Nowadays, Cave Lions believed they themselves had decided to vacate their lands and been richly rewarded due to their faith. This, Felina and her husband had discovered during a previous visit. Their main village was less than a mile from the border.

The good news was that they wouldn't have to walk very far to get there. Over the past few weeks, Admiral Slout had expanded his duties as "Admiral of the Navy". Finding little to do after revamping the planet's naval defense protocol, he'd taken over the task of inventorying hundreds of mining vehicles, something that was long overdue. Years of losing track of dump haulers, excavators, drillers, and the like, had led to production delays resulting in disputes between tribes whose economies relied on the mining industry. Arguments ensued over who possessed what within the vast motor pool inherited from the mine's previous owners. Thanks to Slout, things were now organized and running at optimum efficiency, with his office employing several crewmembers from the *Anarchy* including Ensign Brilly, a natural at keeping his boss updated and informed. Due to this Slout had been able to arrange for a small transport to be delivered to the very spot where Felina and Solomon would cross into Cave Lion territory. It made things so much easier finding a parked vehicle with the keys left in it, waiting for them just a hundred yards or so beyond the border crossing. In only minutes they'd be arriving in the Cave Lions' capital.

Unfortunately, they'd never make it to their destination.

Within an instant of turning the switch to activate the battery and propel the vehicle forward, tragedy struck. A bomb had been attached to the undercarriage. Suddenly an explosion tore through the chassis, lifting the entire vehicle off the ground. It sent debris hurtling through the tunnel in both directions, injuring several members from the Lacertilian delegation who were standing some distance from where the transporter had been parked. Meanwhile the horrendous noise could be heard as far away as the Cave Lions' main village. Smoke and dust caused by the explosion filled the chamber and made it impossible to approach the wreckage for nearly a minute. When the cloud settled the dazed Zorgolongians raced to the scene looking for survivors. That's when they discovered the sad truth.

First Citizen Solomon Mwonga, Chieftain of the Schpleeftkorkii, legendary hero of the Great Rebellion, along with his beautiful wife Felina, beloved champion of the people, were no more.

CHAPTER NINE
OUTPOURING OF GRIEF

In the days following the assassination there was shock and dismay, followed by an outpouring of grief. Nothing like this had ever happened on New Australia. Solomon and Felina had been the most famous couple on the planet; though in older times Chieftains would often be challenged and sometimes killed by rivals whenever a change of leadership was desired, the Mwongas were like royalty. It was unimaginable that anyone would murder them.

That's why it was so devastating. Who could have been behind such a vile act? Better question, who in their right mind would want them dead? Public reaction was overwhelming. People were concerned, not the least of which all those tribal leaders who feared a coup d'état was in the works. If the assassin wanted Solomon and Felina out of the way in order to pave their way to power, who might be next? Most were deeply saddened by the loss of the planet's First Citizens. Even those who'd opposed or defied them felt the same.

It was little comfort to their daughter Estrella. She, like many, was heartbroken. For days she didn't leave the family's apartment. Kscheeech stopped by to check in on her. Megalocyathus too. By and large she remained silent throughout their visits. It always appeared she'd been crying prior to their arrival, likely continuing to do so after they departed. Her grief along with confusion over a possible motive was shared by everyone else on New Australia. *Why? Why would someone do this?* Whatever the reasons they wanted her parents dead, an even bigger question remained. Was it one person or several? Was it part of a plot? If so, what was the goal?

At the funeral Estrella put on a brave face. This was expected, even if everyone knew how inseparable she and her mother had been. As for Solomon, her love and admiration for her father was widely spoken of, as well as her tendency to mimic his manner and replicate his finer qualities. No one doubted she'd one day follow in his footsteps as the planet's preeminent statesman, even if no one expected that day to come so soon. Perhaps that's what made it so difficult to bear.

The ceremony was deeply emotional, attended by over fifty thousand Nausties. The bodies of the deceased had been mangled, dismembered, and horribly burned due to the explosion, making it difficult to identify them. Estrella was not forced to go through the traumatizing experience; instead Kscheeech performed the grim task of confirming they were indeed First Citizens Mwonga and Felina. It was a complicated process, yet by the day of the funeral they'd been painstakingly prepared for their final public appearance. Limbs reattached. Felina's fur scrubbed and cleaned. Solomon dressed in his best suit. When done their bodies were placed side by side on the pyre for cremation. It had to be done just so the citizens of New Australia could say their goodbyes.

Following Enoshi custom, those who fought with or served with Felina and Solomon were required to chant their names. This tradition went back centuries; in the case of New Australia it had been replicated perhaps a thousand times following the return of the ships from Star Fantasy. The location chosen for the cremation was right next to the great pit which had been dug seventeen years ago. Once again, the *repeating of the names* was not coordinated, and it wasn't intended to be. Warriors who'd served with Solomon or those who'd worked with Felina or campaigned with her for equal rights softly chanted, causing a cacophony of sound. There were precious few on the planet who'd never had dealings with, fought for, battled with, or served alongside the planet's most easily recognized couple. That's why there were so many voices speaking at once. It was truly the saddest day anyone could remember.

As the funeral pyre was set alight it was easy to see that it was them, even from a great distance, prompting tens of thousands to wail pitifully. It was like they were losing a grandfather or grandmother, the loss they felt was so overwhelming. Many swooned and collapsed. Estrella was not among them. The poor girl had already cried a river of tears the past few days while the event was being prepared and her parents' corpses were made presentable. Upon seeing the way people were acting around her, it emboldened her to maintain her composure. She'd wept enough already, enough for a lifetime or two. It was time to begin calculating her next move.

For it may have been true that Melody Estrella Esperanza Milagros Mwonga was adopted, and genetically unrelated to the brilliant statesmen now being mourned by her countrymen. Her real mother had died in childbirth. Her biological father, a warrior nicknamed *Feathers*, had been killed in the war. Her skin was olive hued; her hair shiny black, same as her eyes, whereas her adoptive father Solomon was African. Skin chocolate brown, tall and muscular in his youth, Solomon Mwonga was far different in appearance than the slightly pudgy, notably plain-looking teenager. However, they had one thing in common and it was becoming increasingly well-known with each passing year. Estrella Mwonga possessed every aspect of the great man's intelligence.

Her eyes darted about the crowd, studying facial expressions. In her heart of hearts, she knew this was a time for strength. Her people needed her now. They needed to see her holding up well, maintaining her dignity despite debilitating anguish. She was past that, Estrella kept reminding herself. Just like she believed her father Solomon would have been doing at a moment like this, she was preparing for what needed to be done, rather than dwelling on what was already out of her control.

Megalocyathus was there, along with many others from the Ministry of Science and Agriculture. They spoke Solomon and Felina's names with reverence, or at least a Slart's version of it. And there was Kscheeech standing nearby, his head craned back slightly and his eyes squinted shut as though in a trance. The tragedy had affected the old Zorg as much or more than anyone. Clearly the deaths of his "two best friends" as he'd regularly described them in happier times, had hit him hard. He'd been the one to introduce the couple, he'd often boasted, a fact which her mother confirmed even if the details of how she'd been 'found' by the now-elderly lizard had typically been glossed over when Estrella was little.

But then her eyes made it to yet another individual, Admiral Slout. He wasn't far away, in that he'd been assigned a spot among the chieftains and their wives now tearfully chanting her parents' names. She fixed her gaze upon him for several seconds, perhaps for too long, watching him mouthing the name *Solomon* over and over again, much like the many thousands who'd fought in the Great Rebellion and remembered the great man's role in preserving the planet. She wondered what he might be thinking.

It was then that the hefty ship captain looked back at her, giving her a cold chill as she realized he must be sensing someone was staring at him. Only she didn't look away, not immediately. It was in that moment that their eyes met. A shiver ran up her spine.

The next day Kscheeech again stopped by to pay a visit. This time it was business. He had been appointed executor of the Mwonga's estate, as directed by the couple's will. In the interest of tact, he'd decided to delay discussing the young girl's future. It probably could have waited a few days longer and wouldn't do any harm if he did; only Kscheeech no longer felt it wise. He was concerned for how Estrella was coping with her new life.

She had no family now, and though many Nausties from the older generation had never married and never sired offspring, hers was a special case. She'd been left parent-less at a relatively young age. How in the world was she going to get by? There was little chance she'd be forced to go take a job working in the spinach fields. That was out of the question and Kscheeech, among others, would never allow it. The tribal leaders of the Schpleeftkii would see to her welfare and what's more Kscheeech was officially her guardian, as per the section of Solomon's last will and testament pertaining to FINAL IN-STRUCTIONS:

"Regarding the care of my cherished daughter Estrella, in the event of my untimely death, and assuming the absence or incapacity of my beloved wife Felina, I hereby bequeath to my loyal and trusted friend Kscheeech of Zorgolong, Captain of the Chengshi, complete and total discretion, as well as full responsibility in seeing to her daily welfare." It had been written right after the war with Earth, back before Kscheeech had retired.

Technically Estrella was already an adult. She was sixteen, plenty old enough to take on the burden of finding a way to support herself. Yet her situation was different than other teens on New Australia. The apartment she was living in, for instance. There was no lease; none had ever been drafted. There was no deed to it either. It was in effect property of "The Government of New Australia" but that was a misnomer. New Australia was a confederation of individual tribes with sovereign rights to their territories. There was a police department, there was a planetary defense force, and of course there was a Terminal Command Center, which was manned around the clock. The salaries for these functionaries were accomplished via an assessment paid by member tribes. Solomon's and Felina's situation was complicated by the fact they served the planet in far different ways, prompting the confederation to compensate them by providing a comfortable living. Solomon and Felina never asked for this, of course, and it never occurred to them to ask for much of anything. The Assembly simply decided it was the right thing to do. Problem was, that 'special arrangement' was with her now-deceased parents, not Estrella.

"How are you holding up?" asked the aging Zorg when he entered the apartment. The place looked rather 'lived in' at the moment. Clothes were strewn about. Dirty plates were stacked up on counter tops. In her mother's absence it didn't look like the girl wanted to be bothered with maintaining a clean house. Given what had happened, Kscheeech was inclined to ignore the clutter. He'd never grieved for the loss of a loved one and couldn't begin to imagine how devitalizing it must be.

"Fine, I guess," she replied. She was lying of course. Estrella had been in a daze the past few days. After the killings she'd drawn within herself, avoided most of her friends, and thwarted their efforts to try and console her. Her many pals she'd grown up with in the capital had reached out to her any number of times and begged her to go out and get snot-slinging drunk. It was a tempting offer, but Estrella was uninterested. She had bigger fish to fry.

"You need anything? Can I bring you something?" he then asked, probing for answers as he found an open spot on the couch. Surrounding him were dirty laundry and the smell of decaying food from the kitchen lingering in the air. The girl clearly needed a maid sent in to get the place in order. Then again, was that really necessary? Maybe she just needed a friend.

"No," she said, otherwise revealing nothing. Kscheeech decided it was better not to press. Despite not having gone through it himself, Kscheeech knew that the grieving process can vary from individual to individual. There will be those who seek comfort in the company of close friends. There will be those who seek comfort in their own personal solace. Then again there will be those who seemingly do not grieve at all. They internalize feelings of loss and separation, focusing the intensity of their emotions on the only available outlet: *justice*. For an intelligent young lady like Estrella, this was what consumed her. Kscheeech was soon to discover this.

"I'm glad you're here," she then said, redirecting the conversation from what she assumed he'd try focusing in on: namely, her future livelihood. That was the last thing on her mind. Her parents had been murdered. She wanted nothing more than to find the killer and put him on trial.

"I've put a lot of thought into this and here's what I've concluded. The bomb went off just inside the border with Cave Lion territory. That means the assassin had access to the vehicle my parents died in long before the explosion. Have you considered that at all, someone from the motor pool perhaps? And while we're at it, what of the Lacretilias? They too could be involved. They would have known the transport was waiting for my parents when they escorted them to the border crossing. Plus, I heard they were virtually unharmed in the blast. They somehow knew to stand far enough away before the car went up in flames. That's a clue if I ever saw one. They very well could have known there was an explosive device inside that vehicle and knew to stay on their side of the border."

Kscheeech knew what she was doing and was quick to caution her. There were rules to be observed here. Estrella couldn't just go off half-cocked and conduct her own investigation, even if it was rather obvious she'd already begun one.

"Oh yes, my dear. All of those things will be considered, I'm sure, once an inquiry is conducted. But you have to allow for the process to be completed. The crime occurred on tribal lands. Each tribe has jurisdiction within its territory per our constitution. When a crime occurs, the individual tribe is responsible for pursuing its own inquiry, in this case The Cave Lions. Unless or until they seek assistance from the Assembly, we have only to await their findings before any further investigation can be conducted."

That was correct. The tribes of New Australia held sway over territories ceded or granted to them by the Assembly. This governmental body functioned as a panel of nobles made up of the chieftains of the planet's many tribes. It had worked for decades, this system of government. It wasn't perfect. Quick decisions in times of crisis were often problematic. Solomon had regularly butted heads with stubborn delegates getting them to enforce his policies. Yet it had worked in keeping the peace since the end of hostilities following the devastating civil war which at one time threatened to destroy their civilization. Estrella knew plenty about her planet's unique system of government having received a little reminder only hours earlier.

"Thanks, Keech, but I already got reminded of that this morning from Megalocyathus. Seems the two of you really know the law," she smirked. Kscheeech could tell she was being sarcastic. She probably knew far more than he did, given how she'd grown up hearing about it night and day. "And for the record I don't give a shit, okay? Those morons down there, seriously? They won't find out what happened. Won't identify who actually did it. You know they won't. Plus, we'll have to wait several weeks until the next Assembly to hear what their so-called investigation determined which will be nothing. Fuck those idiots. By then the killers will have covered their tracks or fled the planet. We're talking about my parents here. Besides, who's to say it wasn't part of something much, much bigger?"

Kscheeech knew what she was implying. That is, he thought he did.

"Ah, I see. You believe those responsible may be wishing to destabilize the government, do you? I doubt that's the case. Think about it, Estrella. How would it benefit our tribal leaders to murder Solomon and Felina? And while we're at it, why would they pursue such a path and risk all they possess? Your parents were above tribal politics and wanted only to advance our society. No one failed to recognize this, no matter what they might say at Assembly meetings and no matter what they might spout off about back in their tribal homelands. Your parents sought only to lift us up from barbarism. Everyone knew this to be true."

"You mean everyone except for my parents' killers, of course," she flatly stated. For the umpteenth time Kscheeech was to receive an education on just how bright Estrella was, not to mention *direct*.

"But you raise a valid point, Uncle," she then said, referring to him as her uncle, though that was not the case. It was just a nickname she'd been taught when her parents were raising her. "I suppose I can eliminate the Lacertilias. They're too careful. Even if they wanted to, I mean it's pretty clear what they'd *like* to happen. They'd love nothing more than for New Australia to return to plundering the galaxy. Plus, they've got all those dirtbags who returned from space with the *Anarchy*. That said, I don't consider them a prime suspect. And the Cave Lions? They're a bunch o' dumb asses. They'd never try and pull off something like this. Not the way it was done, anyway. No, it was more sophisticated. It'd have to be someone with the wherewithal to arrange things and put things in place days, even hours in advance. He would need to make sure the vehicle was parked and wired with explosives and moved into position long before my parents arrived with the Lacertilian delegation."

Kscheeech knew who she referring to. She didn't have to say his name. His first instinct was to try and prevent his 'niece' from making a fool of herself tangling with the powerful admiral. Over the past few months Slout had expanded his influence, to the amazement of practically no one. Moreover, Kscheeech was certain he was completely innocent. Admiral Slout had no motive. To believe otherwise was absurd. Yet he did not argue with her. Convincing a teenager that what she believed was implausible? That would be futile.

"Well, I see you've given this some thought," he replied sweetly. "You better get some rest. Perhaps you'll feel like your old self in a day or two." He left not long after that, sensing she'd never heed his advice. Not the daughter of Solomon and Felina. In that he was correct.

Estrella understood fully what Kscheeech was saying. She'd already considered how foolish it would be for the Lacertilias to involve themselves in a plot to murder the Mwongas. Solomon's economic policies had made them stinking rich. They controlled a section of the mine which ensured them unlimited wealth for generations to come. Their chieftain and his nobles were direct beneficiaries of this and would do nothing to jeopardize the steady flow of royalties. As for their constituents, the members of the tribe, it was much the same. Peace with the rest of the galaxy meant they had all they could desire. The tribe provided everything: food, water, housing, and they had only to work the mines and fill transports with mineral ore. Granted, one could argue that a commoner lacked any opportunity to improve his lot in life by distinguishing himself in combat, but that was a foregone conclusion for the typical Lacertilian miner. Seventeen years ago perhaps, when he was young and virile. Not so much anymore.

The same held true with the Cave Lions. They were Enoshi. However, they'd cast off their war-like ways in favor of maintaining a primitive society far below the surface, devoid of outside influence. Their strange religion clashed with modern Naustie culture and they'd avoid doing anything which might interfere with their preference for isolation. Killing Solomon and Felina would achieve nothing but an endangerment to their way of life. She could scratch them off her list of potential suspects.

That left only one logical choice.

There was one gnawing question, however. Why did the killer or killers go to so much trouble in planting a bomb? That was something which made no sense at all. The Mwongas traveled everywhere throughout the planet and never required nor even requested any form of protection. If anyone had wanted them dead, it would have been quite easy to pull it off without putting much effort into it. Solomon and Felina could have been ambushed any number of times when traveling from homeland to homeland. If they'd wanted her parents out of the way, the plotters merely needed to find them walking down a dark mining tunnel, which they frequently did. Opportunities abounded. Their bodies properly disposed of, no one would ever find them. So why complicate matters by constructing an explosive device which detonated when they started the vehicle? Others could have been killed right along with their primary targets and thus provoke conflict between neighboring tribes. Why risk that?

The more Estrella thought about it, the more her suspicions fell upon the crewmen of the *Anarchy*. Ability to pull it off? *Check*. The ship had engineers, scientists, mechanics, any one of whom could construct a bomb. But what about a motive? That was the key. Not just *who* might want them out of the way, but who *needed* them out of the way, in order to advance a political agenda. That's where her upbringing as the only child to an Empath came into play. She considered everything she knew, carefully and thoroughly, and came to one conclusion: crewmen from the *Anarchy* had to be involved. But it didn't answer the nagging question as to why the assassins felt inclined to rig a vehicle with high explosives. When looking at it that way, it almost sounded like they wanted to commit an act of *terror*, not just kill the First Citizens of New Australia, the primary obstacle in affecting regime change, but to frighten and terrorize the populace.

Could it really be so diabolical? And if so, how was it arranged? How did they achieve total secrecy in rigging the device ... without anyone seeing them doing so? This had happened within a hundred yards or so of the border. If their plan was to topple the government, how many people would have to be in their pocket in order to stage a coup, assuming that was the goal? She had only to recall what her late father had told her about his days as a rebel leader back on Earth.

"*Taking over the government wasn't the difficult part,*" he'd intimated. "*That was accomplished in an afternoon. We merely took out the president then the army melted away. That's how you do it, see? Cut off the head of the snake and the body ceases to function. Our coup d'état was relatively easy, looking back. It only turned sour once our neighbors across the border thought they saw an opportunity to settle old scores. But no, it only took a handful of us to storm the palace and drive off the guards that day. Once we had their leaders in custody many even joined us. For eighteen months I was absolute ruler of the country. Me, this old fool, can you believe that? And I was only in my twenties."*

Her father's self-deprecating humor aside, this was precisely the wisdom she needed. A blueprint for an eventual hostile takeover. Create confusion and instability. Quickly install a new regime and proclaim it to be legitimate. That could only mean there was another shoe to drop. In other words, it might be only the beginning of the violence. Who would they go after next? Estrella herself? She had no influence in the Assembly. That said, she was a living legacy to her parents' beliefs. Thinking it that way, maybe she too would become a target. The best answer seemed to be in confronting her fears face to face. If Admiral Slout truly was behind the murders, she'd see it in his eyes when she visited with him.

So that's precisely where she went the very next morning.

***

"Now what? Who is it this time? Dammit, Brilly. How do they expect me to get things done with all these bloody interruptions?" bellowed a voice from the next office. Brilly's eyes widened with anxiety. His boss, Admiral Slout, was clearly perturbed. Meanwhile the young ensign tried putting on a brave face for his guest. The person now standing before him in the outer offices of New Australia's Department of Naval Defense was a bona fide 'V.I.P.' and someone worthy of respect, not to mention extreme courtesy and compassion given what had happened days earlier.

"Uh, well, sir," stammered the *Anarchy's* former navigation officer. He quickly switched from intercom to a wireless headset. Being a Suidonji it was rather hilarious the way it had to be stretched over his bulbous head. "My apologies for bothering you, Admiral, but it's Estrella Mwonga. She says she has important business to discuss. Shall I tell her to come back later?" Slout's subsequent response could be heard not only through the walls of the adjoining office but even the headphones affixed to Brilly's ears. It almost made Estrella step back, she was so startled.

"By the gods, no. You fool, don't you know who that is? Shit. Uh, tell her I'll be right out. I need to tidy up a bit. Stall her for a minute, do you hear me?"

Estrella desperately wanted to chuckle. A deaf man could have heard that. After Brilly acknowledged the admiral's instructions he hastily pulled off his headset that was designed for humans but altered for Suidonji to use. Then he stood. When he did, he towered over her, shirtless, wearing nothing but worn trousers which barely covered him up. It was the same thing he'd been wearing when *Anarchy* landed, no doubt. Estrella recognized him but didn't know his name.

"My apologies, ma'am. I'm Ensign Frilbriliram," he said, extending his hoof. "The admiral, you see, well anyway, it's an honor to finally meet you." Estrella reached out and grasped it, recognizing that the polite fellow was attempting to greet her in the fashion of Earthmen. It was his way of being respectful.

"And please accept my condolences for your recent loss. It was a terrible tragedy that affected us all," he then added. Now she was impressed, not to mention perplexed. He was so disarming. How could such a sweet, good-hearted individual stand working for a monster like Admiral Slout? For that matter, how could he have been a pirate at one time? She came to the department's offices half-expecting thugs and hoodlums. She knew they were all Slout's cronies working there. Given the way he'd been so standoffish toward her in the past, she could only assume they'd be bullies, just like their boss.

"Can I get you something?" he asked. Estrella politely declined but the beast was adamant. It seemed important to him that she be comfortable. "Are you sure? It's very hot outside today. A real scorcher. You look like you could use a bottle of water. Here, you have a seat right there on that couch and I'll get you one. Let 'ole Brilly take care of you, okay?"

When he put it like that, how could she say no? And with the way he got so excited, fetching her a bottle of chilled drinking water from the cooler? It was as though he were bringing out a vintage bottle of wine. It made sense once she put some thought into it. Having purified rain water to drink instead of the recycled swill they had to consume on long voyages must have been heavenly for the young buccaneer.

Once he delivered it to her, Frilbriliram returned to his desk. Estrella sat in silence and sipped her water. The mannerly Suidonji then went about his work, once in a while looking up toward her smiling. Meanwhile in the back office could be heard the rumbling of chairs or furniture being moved around and clutter being removed from surfaces. She almost felt inclined to tell the Ensign that his superior need not go to so much trouble. Then she remembered why she was there.

After a few minutes, Slout emerged from his office, yanking open the door and stepping into the outer office. Brilly surprised her by once again springing to his feet. Estrella almost did the same. Instead she sat and tried to remain calm. She was a guest, after all. It was up to her host to follow social protocol. And besides, if he did not? Well, suffice it to say he'd better show some respect, admiral or not. Estrella may be an orphan, but she still had friends in high places.

"Ah. Young Mwonga. Welcome, and thanks for waiting. I hope you'll forgive us. We don't get too many visitors." That was how he greeted her. She had no idea what to say. Nevertheless, she mustered an answer. Her upbringing once again paid dividends.

"Please don't trouble yourself, Admiral," she stated coolly. "I'm sure this will only take a few minutes of your time." The muscled giant nodded politely and formed a crooked grin. She could see it was mostly an act. Saying nothing else, he gestured for her to enter. This she did, pausing only to thank Frilbriliram for the water.

Once inside, she was immediately hit with the smell of food, half-eaten and decomposing, stuffed inside a nearby waste basket only seconds before. His desk was cleared off hastily, no doubt. Either he was embarrassed she'd see something he didn't want her to see or maybe he just wanted to portray an image of a good administrator, she wasn't entirely sure. Not waiting for an invitation, she promptly took a seat. He closed the door and came 'round to sit across from her, causing a distinctive odor to waft toward her. It was a smell she recognized from visiting 'Porko' tribes who worked in the fields. They rarely bathed. After a day in the sun they were often quite pungent. Now she was smelling it once again.

"So, what can I do for you, my friend?" he said, sighing and snorting as he leaned forward to rest his elbows. "I understand you have some business to discuss?" His crooked grin faded as he studied her eyes. He was trying to read her thoughts. It wouldn't be necessary.

"Yes, Admiral," she said, having prepared and rehearsed that morning what she was going to tell him. She had every intention of opening up with both barrels. Trying to be courtly wasn't likely to impress such a creature as Slout and she knew not to attempt it. The best strategy was to spell it out for him, and in no uncertain terms. Chances were good he already figured he was a suspect. If he did not, he was fooling himself.

"You see, I've begun my own investigation into my parents' death. Perhaps you wouldn't mind me asking you a few questions; would that be alright?"

Slout shrugged his shoulders as if to say, "*Go ahead*". Otherwise he only stared back at her blankly. It was amazing how quickly his demeanor turned ice cold, like he was studying an enemy and predicting their next move. It was terribly intimidating, yet Estrella soldiered on.

"By now everyone knows it was your department that provided the transport vehicle my parents were killed in. A polite gesture on your part, fair enough. I guess I should commend you for that, but you have to realize how suspicious this might appear to those of us still uninformed as to your true intentions. You delivered it; ordered it delivered to them, I should say. It came from the motor pool, which you and your staff have recently taken charge of. The Lacertilias knew it would be there waiting. The Cave Lions may have known as well since it was parked just inside their territory. You would have had to notify them it would be there, I assume, so that no one from their tribe would drive off with it, forcing my parents to have to walk all the way to the Cave Lions' main village. Same with the Lacertilias since it was parked only a hundred yards from the border crossing."

Slout remained silent. He merely raised an eyebrow as if processing what she was saying.

"Now of course the Cave Lions will have to conduct their own inquiry, as that is their right, since the crime occurred on their lands. But perhaps you'd be so kind as to explain your side of things. You see, it was you or your staff which selected the vehicle and determined where and when it should be delivered. You had the opportunity and the time in which to park it in a location of your own choosing. That gave you or your staff all the time they needed, time to have access, time to attach explosives, and wire them to the ignition. When you look at it that way..."

Slout's grin returned. He'd heard enough.

"When I look at it what way?" he quipped. "What are you driving at, my friend? Are you saying I or one of my crewmen or one of my *staff* as you called them, would have had the unmitigated gall to commit such a heinous, cowardly, and treasonous act? Betray their own planet?"

Estrella braced herself for a tongue-lashing. She'd said too much even if it was her intention to provoke him. He was not about to disappoint her.

"Young lady, I believe your sadness regarding the loss of your parents has imbalanced you. That is understandable. You want justice. I respect that. It fills you with a desire to seek vengeance, eh? That's only natural and shows me all I need to know about your character. You're Solomon's daughter, no doubting it. You're just like him too ... the way I knew him before, if you'll forgive me saying so, when he was younger. That Human wasn't afraid of anyone, not anything, no matter how big the threat. If he was, he surely didn't show it. I see a lot of him in you. But like I said, these crewmen who now work for me, absolutely not.

They may be bloody pirates but they're patriots. And they respected your father. Me, I loved him like a brother."

Estrella wasn't sure how to respond. His words smacked of manipulation. Taken at face value, the compliments he was paying her could easily be construed as an attempt at smoothing her over, getting her to drop her guard, distracting her from what she was attempting to do, which was uncover whether Slout and his henchmen had been involved in the murder of her parents. All she could rely on was instinct at this point, and her instincts were telling her Slout was being sincere. Indignation? Yes. Facing accusations of treason would invite such an emotion. Then again, reversing quickly and acknowledging her wanting justice for her parents? If he or his men were the killers that might be a useful tactic in distracting her. *What would father do?* she wondered. The answer she already knew. *He'd press on.*

"Much obliged. However, that doesn't answer my question," she replied coolly. Slout was unmoved.

"And what question was that?" he countered. Estrella pushed on.

"Actually, it was more of a statement," she clarified, raising her voice only slightly. It was quite effective. "As I said, you or your staff members had the opportunity to park that vehicle and choose a location some distance from the border crossing. Thus, your men would have had plenty of time to wire the car with explosives and connect them to the battery. When it comes out that you and your crewmembers are the only likely suspects, these same observations will be made in front of the Assembly once the Cave Lions have completed their investigation. But we don't have to wait until then, do we? That car was parked a hundred yards from the Lacertilian border so that none of their delegation would be killed in the blast. They had no prior knowledge, that's what they'll claim, anyway. Either that or they were too fucking stupid not to stand back far enough and that's why some of 'em got hurt. As for the Cave Lions? Their village was nearly a mile away. They'd have had no idea you were there; never notice your men planting the bomb. And the Lacertilian sentries? Even if they *were* patrolling the border diligently, which I doubt, the vehicle was parked too far away for them to notice what your men were up to. So, let's save everyone a lot of time, shall we? You did it, and soon everyone's going to find out. The only thing we don't have is a motive. That's what they'll want to know at the Tribal Assembly coming up. That's what I want to know too, Admiral. Why? Why did you do it?"

Slout remained silent for a moment. For a second his grin returned, then faded almost as quickly as it formed. It seemed like he was thinking deeply all of a sudden.

If anything, he should have been offended by these accusations. He should be arguing vehemently regarding his innocence. Lash out. Scream at her. Insult her. Question her sanity. Something. Instead he appeared as though he were solving a riddle by piecing together bits and pieces of it. As Estrella awaited his response, he'd occasionally look at her, then look away, still appearing like he was arriving at a conclusion to some philosophical dilemma. She dared not interrupt him. He was either about to confess to the whole thing or suggest who it was among his staff likely to have done it. That or he might just spring across his desk and strangle her.

"Wait," he finally said. "Did you say the transport was parked some distance from the Lacertilian border? Did I hear that correctly?"

Estrella confirmed this with a nod, then specified with, "A hundred yards or so, plenty of distance from the Lacertilan delegation so as not to..."

"So as not to harm them, yes," he interrupted, finishing her sentence. "*Hmmmph.* Well my young friend, we seem to have a discrepancy, I'm afraid." He then reached down to access his computer. Estrella wondered as to what he'd do next. "May I show you something?" he then asked. She could only nod. *What in the world is he up to?* she wondered.

Slout then started typing something into the computer on

his desk, pausing after hitting a few keys to turn the monitor slightly so his guest could view it. Instantly she could tell what it was: pick-up and delivery records for all vehicles throughout the planet on the day of Solomon's and Felina's murder. Comprehensive in its scope, Estrella could only marvel at how organized Slout and his department had become in only a short period of time. He did not know she was coming that day and there'd have been no time to alter what she was looking at, unless it already had been. Judging by Slout's actions it was clear he too was checking to see when and where he'd ordered the transport vehicle to be delivered, and by whom.

"There, you see that, Daughter of Mwonga?" he eventually said, pointing at the screen with his hoof. He enlarged the view slightly so she could see the entry. "It's clear that the original instructions were to deliver that vehicle to the Lacertilian border and leave it with the sentries. *Not* a hundred yards inside Cave Lion territory. Not ten feet, either. It says the car was to be parked right at the border crossing."

"So, they disobeyed you?" asked Estrella, raising up and leaning in to view the screen side by side with Slout. By now she was used to the smell.

"No, they didn't. Look here, my friend," he replied, pointing out that his employee had delivered the car, noted the location where he'd left it, and this location was transmitted to the department's database using monitoring devices embedded in the vehicle's on-board computer. It was right there on screen: where the car was located upon completion of the task. Estrella's next question was obvious. Slout didn't wait for her to ask it.

"And no, these cannot be faked," he remarked. "That's where the transport was left waiting for your mother and father to find once they got to the border crossing. Obviously it had been moved by the time they got there."

"Yes, obviously," Estrella remarked, sighing in frustration. "But when? That's what I want to know, and if we solve that mystery we're one step closer to finding our killer."

"When? Oh, that's easy," Slout observed with a smirk. He then scrolled down to a later entry. The computer program created by his former science officer Minggatu had automatically attempted to update the vehicle's precise location later that day. The new location had not been a great enough distance to register a change in coordinates, yet the fact it had been moved was enough to trigger a new entry. Plus, it showed the exact time this had been done.

"There's your answer," he said in a calm voice. Estrella read the screen then looked him in the eyes. From this point on, Admiral Slout was no longer her primary suspect. He was now going to be her partner in solving the crime.

CHAPTER TEN
SEEING A PATTERN

Predictably, the Cave Lions' attempts at conducting an investigation sputtered overnight. That was understandable, given their lack of sophistication. To expect more was unrealistic.

Then again, they, and for that matter every other tribe on the planet, had simply never dealt with anything like this. Chieftains had certainly been challenged by rivals during the history of the planet and forced to battle them for power. Not only that commoners had fought with and even murdered one another in cold blood from time to time. But these crimes were easy to solve. Confessions would be extracted, either willingly or otherwise, and the result was typically the same. Most tribes treated capital murder in a similar fashion: a brief public trial followed by immediate execution of the perpetrator.

That's why this was so different.

As the days passed and it got ever closer to the monthly meeting of the Tribal Assembly, it was getting clearer and clearer the Cave Lions weren't getting anywhere. That's because they weren't really trying. Didn't need to. All they had to do, per the rules regarding criminal investigations conducted on tribal lands, was concede their failure to resolve the issue and grant access to the crime scene. Since the location was nowhere near their main village and would present little disruption to their daily lives, it almost begged the question, "*Why didn't they do that in the first place?"* Not that it mattered. Estrella hadn't been waiting around for them.

Now, she had help. She had her very own team in fact, and it was flying under the radar so as not to rile the Cave Lions. Having recruited Admiral Slout to her side, she was able to secure the help of Kscheeech in analyzing their findings. Wisely they kept these efforts secret. No one outside their group could know what they were up to.

"So then, is that our killer?" asked Estrella. She was at that moment sitting next to Kscheeech, across the desk from Slout. They were in the admiral's office at the Department of Naval Defense, examining his computer screen which he'd pivoted for all to share in looking at. He'd sent Brilly out on an errand, just to make sure they would not be overheard. He was now showing them what he'd concluded from his research.

"Yes, I'm positive that's who did it. And if I may say so, I'm quite impressed. Actually, *amazed* might be the better term, considering the recent unpleasantness, but it's him, I'm sure. To be honest, he'd have been the last scaly devil I'd have expected being mixed up in something like this." Slout then sat back in his big desk chair and shook his head in disgust. Sneeeep, the Zorg in question, formerly of the *Anarchy's* engineering section, was someone he knew only vaguely. This was just what Estrella was expecting to hear: a stooge set up to be the trigger man. If so, they merely needed to figure out who else was involved.

"So, you're saying it might be a plot, then?" she inquired leadingly. "That's what I've been thinking all along. No way he acted alone. It's gotta be part of a plan to destabilize the government. Wouldn't you agree, Admiral?" Slout wasn't about to get roped into such wild assumptions.

"I'm saying nothing of the sort, Young Mwonga. I'm only noting that he was the one member of my crew unaccounted for during the time after the vehicle was delivered, up until your father and mother arrived with the Lacertilians. That's it. He alone could have planted the bomb and he alone would have had enough time to pull it off. By the time of the explosion he had retrieved another vehicle and was driving it back to the motor pool, yes, but I can't determine his whereabouts prior to that. Maybe he can."

"Then I guess we'll have to ask him, won't we?" interrupted Kscheeech, finally joining the exchange. It was interesting watching Estrella and Slout *mix it up*. The admiral was obviously charmed by the girl and recognized her intelligence as well as her lineage. He'd been unwavering in his loyalty to Solomon back in the day. This he no doubt intended to continue with the man's daughter. That said, if Estrella had been anything less than brilliant he would have dismissed her long ago as little more than a presumptuous teenager. That was not the case. He argued with her when he disagreed, nodded and grunted when he did not. It would appear the fleet commander considered her *an equal.*

"Yes, but we need to be careful," Estrella stated matter-of-factly. "If he's involved with others then we don't want to risk alerting them as well. Also, if he gets spooked, he may try and make a run for it. There are a million places he could hide down there." The admiral scoffed.

"Nonsense, you just leave it to me," remarked Slout. "He's one of my crew. I was his commander. If I tell him to do something, he will obey." Estrella did not agree and was happy to tell him so. What's more she did so without hesitation, demonstrating how she had no fear of the admiral. Like her mother would have done, she challenged him.

"No, no, not like that, big guy. We've already taken enough chances as it is, meeting here. We can't risk word getting out to the rest of the conspirators by having you order him up to your office. One little slip-up and they'll know we're been figuring things out. For now, they think it's just the Cave Lions bumbling about, searching for evidence and with no clue how to even reconstruct bomb components ... assuming they have any idea how one could have been made in the first place. What they don't know is that there's no need to bother. We only have to identify the plotters themselves, *they'll* tell us how they..."

Once again, Kscheeech interjected.

"Oh, there you go again talking like it was some big plot to overthrow the government. I wish you'd quit doing that, I really do. We don't know if that's truly the case and we shouldn't be speculating. It could cause a panic out there among the masses. Besides, we've got an even bigger problem in bringing our suspect into custody. Our friends from the capital police have no idea what we're up to, and on top of that we have no authority to order an arrest. We'll literally have to bring him in ourselves and coax a confession out of him, assuming he's guilty that is, then turn him over to the authorities, which we cannot do yet." Slout however agreed with her.

"Yes, but Young Mwonga makes a good point, old friend," quipped the former pirate captain. "We're treading on thin ice as it is, using my office to meet. But, we had no choice as I had to show you how I drew my conclusions as to the killer. I sent Brilly down to the market saying we were about out of food, which was a bit of a stretch." He then gestured toward a shelf that was stocked with a variety of dried meats, along with some raw vegetables and day-old bread. If pressed, Slout would have had a hard time explaining such a request. "And no, I'm not saying anything about Brilly. He's completely trustworthy ... known him for years. But I'd rather not have to explain any of this to him, if you know what I mean."

"Well then, we only have one option and that's to put a tail on our suspect," offered Estrella, using a colorful term she'd heard in a movie once. Unfortunately, it had dual meanings.

"Put a what? A tail? On a Zorg? Why?" queried Slout with a snort. Kscheeech knew what she meant but let her provide the necessary clarification.

"Not literally. What I mean is let's *track* him for a day or two. We can't access the crime scene and don't need to really. If we follow Sneeeep around to see who he's in cahoots with, that will be sufficient for the time being. Once the Cave Lions report to the Assembly what they've found, which is likely nothing, we'll have identified who he might have been working with. Interrogating him will only draw attention. We can't have that."

"Oh, I see. *Tail* him, follow him in other words. Yes, that's very clever. We should do that," agreed Slout. "But who will do it? Has to be one of us three and I certainly can't be involved. I'm always here. Keech, you're getting up there in age. We can't expect you to do it, not for long. Besides it wouldn't make sense. You're supposed to be retired. And as for you, Young Mwonga, I can't imagine how that might appear, a young female milling about in the motor pool. Talk about suspicious. Unless I were to give you a job of course, that could work."

Kscheeech shook his head in response. Estrella thought it was brilliant.

"Yes, that's a great idea, Admiral," she proclaimed, to the astonishment of her guardian. Kscheeech shot her a look of profound disbelief.

"Now wait a minute. Think about what you're saying, my dear. The daughter of our planet's venerated First Citizens working a menial job? You can't be serious, girl. Out of respect for your parents I simply cannot allow that. I'm sorry but that is not an option. Please, let's not pursue this. I can do it myself; if we're trying to avoid tipping off our suspect that he's being watched, how better to avoid suspicion? I'm well-known, yes, but he's a fellow Zorg, am I right? I can use any number of stories to explain my presence, report back what I've seen, then let you two monitor his whereabouts whenever necessary." Slout realized how completely ludicrous that sounded. Estrella was a far better choice.

"You'd never keep up with him, old friend. No, I think we'll need someone more, uh ... nimble for this task." His words emboldened young Estrella.

"He's right, Uncle. We need someone on the *inside* and someone who can blend in, work alongside the other crewmen. We could pull it off. My parents are dead. I'll obviously have to take a job to support myself ... eventually, if not immediately. It'll make sense to them I'm sure; meanwhile my Dad and Admiral Slout were known to be friends. Who's to say..."

Kscheeech wasn't going to wait for her to finish that sentence. He had to put his foot down.

"It's out of the question, my dear. They're pirates, we all were once, but this lot are fresh off the boat. And they aren't well known for respecting females, as we all know. If we're looking to imbed someone in their midst, a teenage girl has got to be the very worst choice imaginable. If something happened to you, then what? Another scandal. No, this is far too dangerous. I'm your guardian, young lady, and I cannot allow it. I *won't* allow it."

"Then what do you suggest?" asked Estrella, growing agitated. Kscheeech sensed they needed to find a compromise, otherwise the bright youngster might simply strike a deal with Slout later on and pursue it behind his back. And next? She'd quickly discover her mistake once she found herself surrounded by a group of those hooligans and by then it'd be too late. As her guardian he'd be blamed for not protecting her, and what's more they'd be right. He'd never live it down. Fortunately, Slout already had a solution in mind.

"How about you both go?" offered the admiral. This prevented further argument. "Neither of you will be missed. Keech, you're retired. And Estrella, you're not terribly busy, are you?"

"Not really, no. Just my mother's volunteer work to tend to. But no, I don't need to be there on a regular basis. Why, what are you picturing us doing?"

"A tour, basically. That's what I'm thinking. Say I assign some of my crewmen to pick you up and drive you around, both of you, but at different times ... Sneeeep being included among them. Meanwhile you two keep track of where he goes and what he does. Split up occasionally. Distract him if need be and see what you can find out. There's no hurry after all. We have our primary suspect. Just need to wait on the Cave Lions to admit they don't have one. How does that sound?"

"Excellent." Estrella exclaimed. She then looked at Kscheeech and raised her eyebrows, inviting his reaction. The old lizard only shrugged his shoulders. "Then let's do it," she responded, indicating Slout should proceed with setting the whole thing up.

Later Estrella and her uncle concocted a story that they were going out on a mission to *"continue the noble works of First Citizen Mwonga and his wife Felina"*. It was touted as a peace mission and *"an opportunity for healing"*, thus making it quite easy for Admiral Slout to make the arrangements for transportation and avoid raising suspicion. Better yet he was able to use the excuse, when ordering drivers to cart them around, that due to Kscheeech's advanced age this was a requirement. Sneeeep, naturally, was the first driver selected. Their plan could now go off without a hitch.

However, it was not to be. Come the following evening, as Estrella and Kscheeech arrived at the offices of the Department of Naval Defense, word had already reached the admiral that the situation had taken an unexpected turn. A body had been found at the bottom of an elevator shaft. Sure enough, it was that of their prime suspect, Sneeeep.

What's more, it was abundantly clear what had happened. Sneeeep was still a young Zorg in the prime of his life and not likely to have fallen accidentally. And though police theorized it was a suicide, Estrella thought otherwise. Someone had wanted Sneeeep dead. Nevertheless, and despite all her efforts, the investigation into her parents' murder had stalled.

***

In the days following, Estrella found herself at a loss. What could she do now? Their primary suspect was dead, and she was no closer to finding her parents' killers than when she'd first gone to visit Admiral Slout. With no other options and no other leads to pursue she figured it wouldn't hurt to pay him another visit. His position as head of the motor pool had made him invaluable in that he had employees operating throughout the planet. Who's to say they might one day turn up something? she surmised. Thus, she sought out Kscheeech, and with her uncle in tow, stopped by to see the former fleet commander yet again.

Their timing couldn't have been better. For not more than five minutes after they'd sat down with the big fellow, reports came in of yet another murder. A former crewman of the *Anarchy*, this time a Suidonji, had "gone wild", said the message, brutally assaulting one of his former shipmates. Perhaps it was because the murderer was Suidonji, Slout wasn't sure, but the police were actually requesting his assistance. The situation seemed to present a brand new opportunity for the three to join forces. Perhaps it could develop into something useful in terms of solving her parents' murder, Estrella could only hope. Either way, the first step was to go visit the saloon where it happened while the crime scene was still *fresh*. Nothing could have prepared them for what they were about to see.

What they found when they got there would have appeared at the outset as though cattle had been butchered inside the place. Blood spattered the walls. It formed puddles on the floor where it had drained from the victim's body. In the center of the bar room lay the corpse. It was an Enoshi. Splayed out grotesquely on the cold, gray concrete, he'd bled out from multiple stab wounds, all delivered by a single assailant. It looked like he'd been through a wheat thresher ... hard to believe there was only one killer. Patrons had fled during the attack, police had learned, terrified they'd be the next target. The bartender, for his part, had cowered behind the bar. When police had arrived on the scene, they didn't know where to begin. In desperation they'd called up the admiral begging his assistance. This gave Estrella and her cohorts the excuse they needed to take over the case. Once the trio arrived at the scene, Slout told the obviously troubled police officers to take the suspect into custody while they performed a preliminary investigation.

Luckily, all of the witnesses to the crime were still present. Most of them were standing outside the saloon, too shocked to go home, badly in need of another drink to calm their nerves. Estrella took over the task of interviewing them; leaving Slout and Kscheeech to speak with the bartender. Their stories were consistent, that was evident from the start. The killer "*seemed possessed by demons*," as one person put it. To a man, they told of the Suidonji crewman arguing with the deceased before leaving in a huff, only to return brandishing a knife. No one had any idea where he could have gotten it, which presented the three detectives with a quandary.

Was it premeditated?   Every witness confirmed the same frightening story. The barrel-chested beast was noticeably shorter but "freakishly strong like most Suidonji". He had been "drinking all afternoon" with his shipmate. They'd gotten along fine, or so it would have seemed, until there was a "disagreement of sorts". It started off innocently enough with the Suidonji grousing about his frustrations in attempting to find work and the Enoshi chiding him mercilessly for "trying to fit in". The big cat then accused his friend of "betraying their warrior tradition." Sometime after that the Suidonji had stormed out. When he came back all hell broke loose.

Eyes red with rage, the killer flung himself at the monstrous Enoshi. Slicing his neck, severing his windpipe, the pig-like crewman seemed to know precisely what he was doing in disabling his much bigger opponent. Witnesses detailed how the surprised Enoshi was compelled to grab his own throat in a vain attempt to try and hold his trachea closed. Inebriated to begin with, the giant was said to have struggled to fend off repeated knife thrusts, reeling from the shock of the attack, as well as the speed with which his assassin moved. It was clear the victim was just as overcome by confusion as he was the damage being caused.

"He wasn't just quick either," one witness reported, claiming that the killer seemed to know just where to strike. "Kidneys, lungs, then a hamstring, he was like a surgeon. A surgeon of death."

The Enoshi was reduced to gurgling and choking on his own blood, curling up to shield his torso from further injury, instinctively protecting vital organs even though it was soon more of an afterthought than a survival tactic. He was dying and knew it. With others too terrified to assist him for fear they'd be the next victim, the giant could only fight to breathe as reality set in. Then, just as suddenly as it had begun, the attack stopped. Sensing his drinking buddy was mortally wounded, the assassin merely dropped the knife and sat down in a chair across the room, hanging his head, gasping for air. That's exactly the way police found him when they'd arrived.

After securing the crime scene and allowing crews from the city's morgue to come in and remove the body, Kscheeech, Slout, and Estrella sat in the empty bar and discussed their findings. It turned out Slout knew something about the deceased, something Kscheeech had overlooked and Estrella could not have known. The dead sailor was once the brother of an Enoshi chieftain. That's when they all realized why the police had been so hesitant to get involved.

Years ago, mere months by Slout's standards, the victim had joined the crew onboard the *Anarchy* as a marine. He was assigned with providing security as well as serving as part of a unit of shock troops used in raiding ships. He'd been reliable. Slout had given him responsibilities including the management of his security staff. While on Green Planet he'd even commanded several hunting parties sent into the wilderness looking for game. His decline into alcoholism and depression had been a shock to those who'd known him. As for the Suidonji who was now in custody for murdering him, Slout had little knowledge of the beast. "Worked below decks," was all he could remember. Slout could not recall his function.

"But we're about to have a problem on our hands. I can tell you that much," the admiral then pointed out. The bartender had left by that point. The saloon had been closed. Meanwhile the bar was stocked with a plethora of liquor. Kscheeech figured they could all use a stiff drink, pretty much anything they fancied. However, Slout declined. He next told them why.

"No, we won't be drinking for a while, my friends," he informed them darkly. "That he was a noble is only part of the issue." Kscheeech already knew what he was referring to. The murder had been committed in a bar owned by the victim's tribe, the Smilodons. What's more, the killer was from another very successful Suidonji tribe which was once its rival. Compensation would be expected.

Enoshi were notorious for their traditions, many of which went back centuries. One of these pertained to the death of a nobleman killed in combat. To die in battle was, to an Enoshi, the epitome of glory. And it didn't matter if the fight occurred on a battlefield or in a seedy dive bar out on some distant planet. There'd been an argument. The argument had led to a confrontation. The confrontation had led to the death of one of their own. To the Smilodons it would be black and white. Not vengeance, no. They'd demand an 'honor debt' be paid for their loss.

In olden times it might come in the form of a lavish gift, payment for the funeral arrangements at the very least, or an offering of females to the surviving male heir. For example, Empaths were often used for this purpose and given as a sign of respect so to ensure no further hostilities or blood feuds between clans. But therein lay the problem. Slout knew his people well. Suidonji were known for many things, generosity was not among them.

"So, you think there'll be controversy? Seriously? After all these years? You really believe the Smilodons will demand an *honor debt*?" Estrella asked. Slout was convinced they would. Kscheeech agreed.

"Most likely, in fact I'd say definitely," replied the old Zorg. "Sorry to say but given the circumstances we're faced with I'd have to assume there will be demands made."

It hadn't been seen in years, not since the Naustie Civil War, but he still remembered. So did Slout. Luckily the admiral had some level of influence and so did his Zorgolongian colleague. Plus, they had Solomon Mwonga's very own daughter to aid them. Their next stop would *not* be at the jailhouse to interrogate the crewman now in custody. That would have to wait. They first needed to pay a visit to the Smilodons and do a little damage control.

"That's why we won't be drinking today, my friends. We'll need a clear head on our shoulders," stated the admiral. "I suggest we go there right now and meet with their current Chieftain, before he finds out on his own. Besides, it's starting to stink in here."

That too was correct. Schpleefti cleaning crews would arrive later that evening, once the sun went down. There was nothing left for them to determine there anyway. The deed was done. Time to focus on the matter at hand.

Their meeting with the Smilodon tribal council went about as badly as they could have expected. None of them being Enoshi, the three were hit with questions and demands they couldn't possibly address. Slout was owed respect, being that he'd led them to military victories in years past, and to that end the Smilodons were gracious hosts. Estrella being female was only a minor setback in that she was still Solomon and Felina's daughter and, to an Enoshi, that meant she was worthy of their hospitality. Kscheeech was due the same, if not more so. He'd once directed one of the ships used during the raid on Star Fantasy to rush wounded Enoshi home to New Australia. Many of these had earned the coveted *Order of Merit* and that would never be forgotten. That said, it was a tense exchange.

"You know our traditions, Admiral," said the Chieftain, an Enoshi named Chartreux. His father had been the tribe's leader when *Anarchy* had set off for Star Fantasy. That meant the victim was in actuality his uncle, however bizarre it must have been seeing a creature roughly his own age arriving months earlier after seventeen years in space and knowing how they were related. "My uncle was a great warrior. We were saddened to see how he sought to destroy himself with drink, but that doesn't change who he was. It also doesn't change how he died. He died as a warrior and he must be treated as such."

"Yes, I know your laws," responded Slout, eyeing the big cat calmly. "I will deliver your demands to the Entelodonts in person. If you'll grant me this, I believe I can keep tensions to a minimum. We certainly don't want any ugliness between your two tribes at next Assembly. Please, let me try and handle it from here."

"Be sure that you do, Admiral. That's all we ask," remarked the Chieftain. After that the three of them dined with the Smilodons as honored guests. It wasn't until later that night when they finally made it to the city jail to interview the killer. It was 20:00 by the time they arrived.

"Seaman Blafmer, ma'am. Blafmer is my given name," the prisoner said when introducing himself at the station. "I go by Blaff," he then added, and he was surprisingly polite despite being stained with dried blood on his hooves as well as his face and torso. Chained from head to toe, he sat in the station's interview room while Estrella, Slout, and Kscheeech leveled questions at him. His explanations for his actions made no sense, mostly because he had none.

He had no recollection of what had happened that day. Not one snippet of it could he recall. Estrella didn't believe him, even though he was adamant that he remembered nothing until being hauled away to the police station. He acknowledged that he'd been in the bar, that was about all. Beyond that he said his mind was a blank.

It did no good reading off to him details from the police report compiled from eyewitness accounts. These read like a script from a really bad 'slasher' movie; this only distressed the poor fellow, causing bewilderment. Nevertheless, he couldn't muster even a speck of memory from that gory afternoon in the bar with his victim, a beast he considered one of his "best friends", he claimed. He simply refused to believe he was capable of such a heinous act. He didn't remember going back to the bar and had no idea where he'd gotten the knife. He couldn't seem to fathom how he could have defeated the big cat in physical combat; which was precisely what anyone else would have observed, knowing the two species. Something didn't add up. Suidonji, even larger ones, were typically no match for a full grown Enoshi.

This left the three investigators baffled. What had come over the poor fellow? Had his mind blocked out the awful experience? Kscheeech believed that might be the case: called it a "Dissociative fugue." Slout dismissed such a notion, saying Blaff had simply gone "space happy". But Estrella didn't cotton to either of those theories. Something very strange was going on. First her parents assassination and Sneeeep's mysterious death, then this.

***

For the next several days Slout worked on reaching a settlement between the Entelodonts and the Smilodons. At first the Entelodonts rejected the idea that their tribe "owed" anything to the Smilodons, other than the life of their tribesman. This the Smilodons had no interest in. Blafmer could rot in prison for all they cared. What they required was indemnification, the amount or form of which was up to the Entelodonts' own choosing. None was forthcoming. The Entelodonts simply claimed this was not one of their traditions and not enforceable, which was technically correct. Slout for his own part thought they were being cheap and told them so. Still they would not budge.

"If the police wish to release him to us, then we shall deliver him to the Smilodons in order for them to mete out their own form of justice. That's all we can offer," replied their chieftain, knowing this to be unrealistic. At the next Tribal Assembly there would most assuredly be heated arguments between the two tribes. But what else could he do?

That's when they received the awful news. During the night Blafmer managed to cut his own throat while languishing in his cell, using a metal food utensil which he'd sharpened into a makeshift blade. Slout was called in the next morning. Estrella rushed over as well. By the time they both arrived he was dead. Nothing could be done for him.

With only a few days left before Tribal Assembly, Estrella could now look forward to the Cave Lions announcing their findings. There was no mystery as to what would happen next. They'd admit their failure to identify a suspect and 'allow' the

Assembly to conduct its own inquiry. At that point Estrella would make her move, requesting that the delegates appoint her *inquisitor* and what's more allow her to choose her own team for the investigation. No one would object. But then something even more astonishing occurred, an event which would send shock waves throughout the capital. In the aftermath, citizens would no longer believe they were safe.

Yet another former sailor from the *Anarchy*, this time a Zorg, had gone berserk. Brandishing a knife, he'd rushed through the town market, an outdoor area about the size of two football fields filled with vendor booths. Stabbing several people, screaming obscenities, he'd sprinted through the crowd as folks did their morning shopping, causing people to flee for their lives. Police were already on scene, patrolling like they usually did whenever the marketplace was open to the public. Chasing the crazed crewman, fanning out to outflank him, officers attempted to head him off and make the collar. They pursued him to the very edge of the nearby canyon containing the Terminal Loading Bay. Then, and to their immense frustration, the killer actually hopped the railing and began scaling the protective barrier. Ordering him not to proceed any further, police tried in vain to dissuade him from jumping. This he ignored, instead plunging to his death, 200 feet below. It was over within minutes. Slout and Estrella heard about it later that morning as they convened for their daily meeting at his office.

"Well, I suppose you've all heard by now, haven't you?" asked Kscheeech as he arrived. Estrella and Slout were seated, waiting for him to show up.

"Terrible, yes. We found out a few minutes ago. They're retrieving the body from the loading bay as we speak," responded the admiral. "We heard he made quite a divot. Any word as to which tribe he was from?"

"No," replied Kscheeech. "I know about as much as you two at this juncture. Shall we head down to inspect the corpse? If we don't, there'll be nothing left of the crime scene by the time they scrape up the body." Slout didn't see where that was necessary.

"To see what? A smashed lizard? Why bother? What good will it do? We know what killed him: high speed impact with a concrete surface. What else do we need to know? The fact is, we've had a handful of murders, not to mention one or two suicides."

Estrella noted how he seemed to be speculating that Sneeeep might have thrown himself down that elevator shaft on purpose. *Maybe he was not murdered after all.* She chose not to bring it up for the time being. Besides, they needed to look at the bigger picture. She spoke up next.

"Guys, I believe we need to face facts. I think something happened with the crew back when they were in space, maybe on Green Planet, I don't know. Something happened to their minds. Seriously, it's starting to add up. And no, I have no idea what it is, but something's, well, something's *affected them*. I think we'd better stop denying it. Your crewmen, Admiral ... they're going crazy one by one." Her uncle rushed to the admiral's defense.

"Nonsense," responded Kscheeech. "Just a few isolated incidents, that's all. A mere handful. There were three hundred crewmen onboard that ship, young lady. Slout was among them. We've simply had a few bad eggs. That's all, just a few bad eggs."

Estrella wasn't buying it. The crew had been home for months, thus it could not be that they'd gone "space happy", like Slout had proposed recently. Post-Traumatic Stress Disorder? Sure. That was conceivable. But there was another glaring consistency to the madness happening around them. They had all, every one of them, suddenly and without warning, *snapped*. Slout and Kscheeech disagreed and thought she was reading too much into it, but the young Human was quite sure now. She could definitely see *a pattern*.

CHAPTER ELEVEN

PATH OF A KILLER

The killer awoke shortly after dawn, beginning his day much like any other, only this time with coffee and a hearty breakfast. That was something he'd missed over the years, ever since he'd left his original home planet. He hadn't seen a town market since way back in his youth. Now there was one located mere blocks from his office, and it was the biggest he'd ever seen.

It was to be his last meal, so he took the time to fix up something especially delicious: powdered eggs, imported from Earth, made into an omelet with freeze-dried cheese, then served with locally grown spinach and potatoes. This was quite fancy for the normally low-key fellow. It was more calories than he needed of course, a lot more than he'd normally eat in one sitting and more than enough to tide him over. Not that it mattered. By supper time, if all went according to plan, he'd be dead.

There was a sense of urgency on this beautiful New Australian morning. He had to arrive at his destination at precisely the right moment. Too early and there'd no doubt be conversations with those he knew. Too late and he'd be barred from entry. The key was to get there and be ready to make his move just as things were getting underway.

Not just that. The components within the explosive device he'd been building the past few evenings had to work properly and without fail, he'd only get one chance. It must respond to the triggering system, first of all. Also, he had to arm it at exactly the right instant as to generate the explosive force he desired. He wouldn't be around for long once it detonated. Parts of him would. But that was the idea. His goal was a conflagration that would engulf a thousand square foot area and eliminate as many people as possible, him being among them. That's why he'd worked so diligently in getting things prepared and working properly.

Everything he'd ever known about chemistry, physics, and mechanics had been employed. He'd thrown all he had into the project. The device itself was ingenious as it was makeshift. Moreover, the materials used in making it were devilishly simple. That they could have been purchased separately or all at once and it wouldn't have raised an eyebrow was the cleverest part. He'd used everyday products, in just the right portions. These would be mixed only moments before in order to initiate a volatile reaction, and then, with just a jolt of electricity it would trigger combustion. The net result? An event which would change the face of New Australia for generations to come.

After breakfast he meticulously cleaned his kitchen. He even swept and mopped the floors of the tiny apartment which had been assigned to him by the housing ministry due to his military rank. It was ironic that he'd choose to leave behind a clean house; but somehow it mattered to him how they'd find the place later, once the deed had been done. When it was over they could vilify him all they wanted, so be it. In his heart he knew, they'd label him a hero someday.

Following this whirlwind of activity, he spent the balance of the morning testing equipment. Triggering device: *check*. Timing mechanism: *check*. Fuel lines: *functional*. Fuel reservoirs: *filled to capacity*. And that's where the true genius within the bomb's design could be found: the fuel cells. Of these there were two, containing ammonium nitrate and chlorine, and it would be the mixture of these substances which would create nitrogen trichloride. There was a trick to it of course. They'd have to be combined just prior to activating the detonator; which he must do after a minimum period of time, thirty seconds at the least. It was vital so to ensure maximum effect. In his mind he went over the routine he had to follow once he entered the building, along with a few items he especially needed to remember, otherwise it could mean utter failure and with it a very long prison sentence.

Any delays or interruptions once I reach the west hallway will have to be avoided. Don't talk to anyone, don't acknowledge anyone, nothing more than a wave. I have to keep moving. The lobby may still be crowded when I arrive, that is a possibility. If that be the case, I'll have to slip through and get into position regardless. I can't let anything or anyone get in the way once I get inside that hallway. That's where I'll wait until everyone is seated.

And there was more to consider. That he'd be wearing a backpack weighted down with two liter bottles full of liquid would mean his movements might appear constricted. This could very well invite questions from friends and colleagues as to what he was carrying. The only option then would be to lie and say he'd been to the market and was bringing home groceries. Whether believable or not it must suffice. Timing was crucial. Courtesy was not. It was unimportant if he snubbed an old friend or two. In a few minutes they too would be blown to smithereens.

"First squeeze the priming pump," he continued, now muttering aloud. "This will open the chamber between the two vessels and allow them to merge. Then I begin my countdown. Thirty seconds, *minimum*, before detonating. I've got to remember that. Don't lose count, either. We surely can't have that. Everything must be perfect." He gestured as he spoke, as if sternly emphasizing the importance of each step to some imaginary student.

For instance, the priming pump. This he'd practiced with the evening before using liquids of varying densities just to be sure the device would work. Using a squeeze bulb from a cannibalized blood pressure testing kit, he knew he could draw chlorine from one bottle into the other containing ammonium nitrate and mix them by continuing to pump air via a long tube connected to a valve located inside his backpack. This valve, which kept the two chemicals separated during transport, could be flipped open simply by reaching over his shoulder and grabbing a looped wire he'd fashioned specifically for this purpose. If he missed even one step in this process, or took too long during the final stage, all he'd get would be embarrassment as the two chemicals foamed and spewed, inspiring laughter and ridicule from the audience. But his intended victims wouldn't be laughing for long, not once they pieced together what he was attempting to do. He'd be arrested on the spot.

That's why the detonator was so crucial to his success. He'd gambled on an LPD, or "long period delay", which would give him several seconds upon activation to try and choose just the right spot in order to kill as many people as possible. Because he couldn't be too terribly sure where people might be standing or mingling at the time he made his big move, the killer figured he should leave some wiggle room for last second adjustments. But that was about all he was willing to be flexible on and this was especially true as pertained to the detonator. The switch for it was located on the shoulder strap of his backpack and was easy to find. He could pull it like the ripcord on a parachute. He even attached a large plastic toggle to it so he'd have no problem grasping and pulling it.

When he was sure of everything, he tested and re-tested, and ran through his routine for the hundredth time. He reviewed the route he was going to take through the city then he packed up his homemade bomb and carefully slipped the straps over his shoulders. This truly was the final step in his preparation, for he'd known once he hooked up the connecting tubes and valve separating them ... attached the electrical connections for the detonator ... there would be no explaining away its purpose to anyone curious enough to look inside, especially the police. That said, the killer expected no trouble from them. He left the apartment shortly thereafter, not bothering to lock the door.

Through the streets of the capital he shuffled along, keeping close to buildings and dipping his head so as not to garner the attention of anyone who might recognize him out on the street. This too, he'd anticipated. He'd even practiced walking to his objective a few night's prior, timing himself from his apartment building to the front door. Exacting as ever he'd then walked home in the dark, filled his backpack with potatoes and tried it again just to measure the difference. In so doing he'd memorized the pace he needed to maintain so that he'd arrive "on time", which in this case meant fifteen minutes before the meeting of the planet's tribal chieftains was called to order.

Because that was his goal. He wanted to blow up the entire Assembly Hall during the monthly meeting of the Tribal Confederation, thus destabilizing the government. All he had to do was get there on time and get into position where he could rush the center of the arena. The center platform was where delegates or petitioners would stand when addressing those in attendance; only this time, if all went well, it would be a messenger of a different sort. Barring any interruptions, he'd be just that messenger, ready and waiting, just as the meeting got underway.

That's when things started going terribly wrong.

"Well, good morning Lieutenant." shouted a voice from across the street. The killer tried looking down, pretending not to notice. He recognized immediately who it was. Knew the voice well. Ensign Frilbriliram. Practically the nicest creature he'd ever occasioned to meet and to be fair, capable of brilliance on occasion. He was also known for being long-winded and this was exactly what the man had wanted to avoid.

"Lieutenant. Wait up, I've been meaning to talk to you." Brilly then called out. The killer kept walking, forcing Brilly to have to chase after him. With the midday heat rising from the long strip of bright concrete, this required quite an amount of exertion. Half a block later Brilly caught up, forcing the killer to have to act like he was genuinely surprised.

"Oh. It's you, sorry. I didn't realize you were talking to me, my friend." That was all he could muster for an excuse when the out-of-breath Suidonji overtook him on the sidewalk. Brilly was visibly flabbergasted. They'd spent over six months in space together. Met with each other frequently. On Green Planet they saw each other almost daily. Why in the world did he have to chase the guy down just to speak with him? The good-natured fellow shrugged it off. Clearly his colleague from the *Anarchy* was hurrying to get somewhere and he'd disrupted the poor man's timetable, even it did seem kind of rude that he'd outright ignored him.

Nevertheless, it was business he wished to discuss. The killer was employed by the Department of Naval Defense, same as Ensign Frilbriliram, and there were things Brilly needed to talk to him about. This, his old shipmate could sense and rushed to put a stopper in it. He continued walking, not pausing to find out what the overheated ensign wanted to discuss. It wouldn't matter much longer anyway.

"But you'll have to forgive me, Ensign. I'm running late ... have to get to the market before it closes." That was a pre-planned excuse he'd dreamed up just in case he ran into an acquaintance. To his frustration it only spawned a more expanded inquiry.

"Market?" Brilly inquired, huffing and puffing in the stifling heat. It was a 120° F in the shade. No telling how hot it was out on that cement sidewalk. "That's already closed, Lieutenant. Why, did you forget? Did you sleep in today?" he then joked, struggling to catch his breath. Suidonji had no sweat glands and weren't capable of producing sweat. If they only were, Brilly would have been soaked in it. "Because if that's where you're heading I'm afraid you're going to be disappointed." He then chuckled and snorted the way 'Porkos' often did when kidding around.

"The market stalls, yes," responded the killer, ready with a follow-on excuse. This he'd also prepared for, just in case. "They have to close by midday because of the heat and won't be open again until dusk. That's not where I'm going however."

Brilly knew the man well. He was likely conducting some sort of experiment back in his apartment. This he'd been known to do, even while serving on the *Anarchy*. "*Hobby-related, mostly*." That's what he used to say. Still, the young office manager and special assistant to Admiral Slout had important matters to discuss, despite the apparent standoffishness of his colleague.

"Uh-oh, so what are you up to now? You got something new in the works?" Brilly asked, trying to make conversation. It wasn't working. The killer kept walking, even seemed to increase his pace. This wasn't like his former shipmate at all. He was normally quite cordial.

"Nothing you'd be interested, my friend," answered the man. He said it dismissively, despite the fact he too sounded out of breath. What he said next sounded like he was becoming *annoyed*. "Perhaps this could wait until later? Maybe we could meet later at the office?" He was trying to end further inquiries, Brilly could tell, and this appeared suspicious. He almost wanted to address the matter but decided not to.

"Well, I guess that would be alright," answered Brilly, letting him off the hook. "So, you'll be at the office later, you're saying? 'Cause if that's the case I could sure use your help today. Will you be long? I mean, what time are you thinking? I was gonna run a few errands myself, while the Admiral's visiting the Assembly with Estrella. He's her guest today, maybe you heard. So, uh, what are we talkin', couple hours?" This sounded like a golden opportunity. The killer's next tactic was to come to a dead stop and cut things short.

"That would be fine," he said, turning to face the beast. "I'll see you then. So long, old friend." Then he scurried away, noticeably encumbered by the weight of a knapsack slung over his back. Brilly waved him goodbye then watched as he rushed off. For a second he considered asking what was inside the man's pack. Yet he did not. His former shipmate had made it clear he'd see him later and wasn't interested in talking. *Why anger him?* thought Brilly. *I'll ask him when he drops by this afternoon.* He remained standing there for a few more seconds before realizing he was roasting in the midday sun. He turned and headed for a shady spot where he could cool off a bit before resuming his errands.

Having made his escape, the killer next had to negotiate his way through a wave of oncoming foot traffic, most of which was heading back to the housing projects from the town market. This slowed him further, forcing him to pick up his pace. This could very well turn into a problem. The Assembly always began promptly. Delegates were required to be in their seats the moment the chairman called the meeting to order. He needed to get there long before that and it was going to be at least another ten minute walk. He passed the time by pantomiming how he'd activate, then detonate the bomb. Meanwhile he muttered to himself the details of his now well-practiced routine.

"Reach back and pull the strap connected to the valve opening. Grab the squeeze bulb. Start priming it; fast at first, then slowly. And for God's sake, count. Thirty seconds, not a second longer. If I wait too long the bottles will start foaming and I'll have an awful mess on my hands."

Next, he went over the final phase of his plan.

"Wait until the chairman calls 'order'. Give it a moment then rush into the arena. Grab the ripcord and pull down forcefully. Sprint if necessary but get to the middle as quickly as possible."

He even fantasized about announcing something to those in the audience who were about to die. Maybe he'd yell *"Anarchy."* Maybe he'd cry out some famous quote from history like *"Sic Semper Tyrannis."* But that just wouldn't be his style. He was far more pragmatic. All would be killed and it would serve no purpose in taunting them. Why bother alerting them to their doom?

Arriving at the front entrance to the enormous convention center which housed the Assembly Hall, the killer once again tried to avoid eye contact with anyone who might recognize him. He was not a delegate and not part of any entourage traveling to the meeting from across the planet. This could spark curiosity. However, he had a built-in excuse. The Department of Naval Defense occupied an office within the same complex. If questioned he could always attribute his presence to the fact he was merely on his way to work. That he would have a backpack wouldn't necessarily raise any suspicion. He was a recognized crewmember from the *Anarchy* and by now most everyone knew he was a decent, law-abiding citizen. He was one of those who'd never taken part in any rebellious behavior after arriving ... showed no interest in such debauchery. When Slout had been given back his original position as Admiral of the Navy, the killer had been one of his first recruits. He could thus explain away his presence without further argument.

Nevertheless, he had no intention of risking that sort of encounter. He moved quickly through the crowded lobby into the West Hallway where he awaited his opportunity to strike. He chose a spot along the wall, anticipating that delegates would soon be heading to their seats. When that happened the hallway quickly emptied, leaving him alone to his thoughts. That's when he felt a large hoof on his shoulder, and the distinctive odor of a Suidonji wafting past his nostrils. It was Brilly.

"Ah. You made it back. Well, I'll be, you really move fast, don't you?" quipped the young ensign. Shocked, the killer turned to face him, backing up to the wall of the tunnel. Brilly shot him an odd look. "You alright, Lieutenant? I'm sorry if I surprised you. But look, if you're wanting to watch the proceedings, there's a viewers' gallery up at the top, I can show you where it is."

Just then it was announced that the meeting was to begin, causing both of them to turn and look.

"Order. This meeting shall come to order." called out the chairman. He was a Human, a member of the Why-O's. Meanwhile, this was absolutely the worst possible moment for Brilly to appear. The killer instinctively reached back over his shoulder to activate the bomb by releasing the valve separating the two chambers. Now he was in the unfortunate position of having to get rid of his former shipmate while simultaneously counting down the crucial thirty seconds he needed for the two chemicals to mix. Not missing a beat, he reached down to his waist to grab the squeeze bulb and being priming it. Brilly would surely notice this, but he had no choice.

"Yes, my friend," he said in response. "I was coming up to see you right now, as a matter of fact and had to make a short detour to see the opening of the Tribal Assembly. Haven't been able to do that since we got back."

It was a feeble effort, so he continued talking, still trying to count down from thirty in his head. To aid this he tapped his foot rhythmically in order to keep track. Hopefully by the time he reached zero, the jovial fellow would get the hint and move on. Brilly wasn't supposed to die that day after all. The problem was in explaining it to him. New Australia would need bright young minds like his once this was over. If he lingered much longer he'd be a casualty.

"But we'll have to keep quiet now. Perhaps I'll head up to the office in a few minutes, would that be okay? See you in a few?" By that point his friend was far too curious.

"Sure, sure. I'll see you there," Brilly replied in a half-whisper. Then he looked down at the killer's waistline to see him squeezing something repeatedly. This piqued his interest. "By the way, what is all this stuff you're wearing? The backpack, I mean. Another experiment of yours? And what is that you're holding?" That's when the killer finally lost his temper.

"Nothing." he retorted, causing his voice to echo in the hallway and Brilly to eye him warily. By now the audience of delegates and nobles from fifty different tribes were settling into their seats. Some heard the argument and ventured a glance toward the west hallway. Nervous that he was nearing the point of no return, the killer made no effort to control his volume.

"Now get the hell away from me, will you? Go. You don't want to be here right now." This drew the attention of dozens more. "You hear me?"

Brilly hastened to calm his agitated friend. Reaching forward he grabbed at the man, trying to pull him back into the tunnel, even as the killer started backing away, preparing to rush the center of the arena. If Brilly was to go up in flames with all the rest, so be it. It was time to make his move. Fortunately, for hundreds who would survive that day, it was not to happen that way.

He tried turning to make his mad dash only to be collared by his colleague. Brilly dwarfed the little man; and in the ensuing struggle inadvertently grabbed the ripcord as the killer pulled away. He'd been grasping at the straps and what he pulled on instead was the trigger for the bomb. This sent the former science officer into a panic. He tried punching and kicking at the brute to free himself. In seconds half the building would be destroyed. However, if he was still trapped in that hallway at the time of the blast, the death toll would be minimal. This he could not tolerate.

"Let go of me, you stupid pig!" he screamed, prompting the good natured ensign to caution him to be quiet.

"Shhhh." he hissed. "You have to be quiet now. The meeting has been called to order." Now half the audience were aware of the scuffle currently in progress and some were craning their necks to look down at the goings on. Ironically, some began to snicker at the sight of a short-statured Human wrestling with a much bigger Suidonji who appeared to be holding onto him and preventing him from entering the arena. Precious seconds ticked by before the little man broke free and tried making a run for it. That's when Brilly called out to him by name.

"Minggatu. No." he screamed, causing his voice to reverberate throughout.

That was the last thing he'd get to say, for at the very moment those words left his mouth an enormous explosion rocked the Assembly Hall. It ripped through the metal grandstand overhead, launching bodies from their seats onto the arena floor. The immense fireball caused by the detonation singed eyebrows and scorched fur all the way across the amphitheater, causing hundreds to cower in their seats, Estrella and Slout among them. The building itself shook to the rafters. Windows shattered from the concussion. Many lost their hearing for a time; waking up to find themselves lying in heaps of rubble or covered in dust. Those who would make it out of there with the loss of an eye or a broken limb or two were the lucky ones. That's because although the hallway contained a good portion of the blast, preventing further carnage, dozens were killed. Dozens more would be critically injured. Many of these would not pull through.

CHAPTER TWELVE
A DIFFERENT FORM OF INTELLIGENCE

Word spread through the capital and quickly beyond. Citizens heading back to their homes along the side streets and boulevards froze in their tracks upon hearing the explosion. What followed was frightened screams when people realized the source of the noise. Hundreds, then thousands, turned and ran back toward the main plaza, curious to see what happened. More were to join them.

Even miles away, in the endless fields of spinach, lettuce, tomatoes, kale, carrots, and potatoes, folks stopped work to try and determine what the sound was. Some looked to the sky wondering if it was a sonic boom from yet another spaceship entering the atmosphere. Others concluded it was coming from downtown way off in the distance. Once a few of them dropped their tools and started walking in that direction, hundreds joined. Eventually it grew to tens of thousands converging upon the city center.

What greeted them when they arrived on scene was truly a horrific sight. The entire end of the building which contained the Tribal Assembly Hall appeared to be belching smoke and fire. Upon closer inspection it was clear there were no discernible flames. The windows had blown out, allowing billowing clouds of dust to escape. That indicated a bomb had gone off inside, many speculated, and they were quite correct. It was not another invasion, they reassured themselves, even as rumors of something even more sinister spread. What they could not have realized was just how lucky they'd been that day.

Fortunately, and for the sake of the planet's future, Minggatu's bomb had *not* created a deadly firestorm, a deathtrap from which no one would escape. The explosion was big enough to cause plenty of damage though. Eleven tribal delegations had been all but decimated, leaving three of them leaderless. All totaled, thirty-eight people had perished instantly or been blown to pieces, including Ensign Brilly. Hospitals would be filled to capacity, in that one hundred and seven critically wounded would be fished out of the rubble over the next several hours. That being said, more than a few survivors from the disaster were able to walk out of the building without a scratch, covered in dust but with little more than a splitting headache and ringing ears.

Estrella Mwonga was among them. She'd been at the far end of the meeting hall at the time of the blast. Sitting with the Schpleeftkorkii as an honored guest of the recently-elected chieftain, she'd invited Slout along as well. The admiral was from a different tribe but had never been a chief, shown no interest in getting involved with politics upon returning either. Besides, it wasn't that odd for a Suidonji to be seen among Schpleeftkorkii tribesmen. They were the only existing mixed-species tribe.

They'd been sitting together chatting, telling the rest of the delegation of their latest efforts to resolve disagreements between the Smilodons and Entelodonts over the saloon murder. Then, just as Henry McCarty of the Why-O's, current chairman of the Assembly, had called the meeting to order, they'd ceased their conversation upon noticing an altercation in progress on the opposite side of the arena. Next came the blast, followed by an interminable daze as they gradually came to, realizing what had happened. Minutes later they were streaming out of the building with the rest of the walking wounded, Estrella helping one of those hit by flying debris.

Yet this was to be a watershed moment for both her and

the planet she called home. What greeted her when she made it outside, with Admiral Slout right behind her, coughing and snorting from the dust, was something nearly as overawing as what had just occurred inside. She now saw looks of desperation on the faces of her countrymen. What's more they were looking only at her. Cadets from the Merchant Marine Academy had responded to the scene and were passing out breather units, blankets, bottled water, anything they could muster. Still, Estrella suddenly felt completely alone. It didn't help that the eyes of thousands of Nausties were now upon her.

If she'd had a minute or two to collect her thoughts, this might have made perfect sense. Behind her was the partially destroyed Assembly Hall. Around her were choking, wheezing tribal chiefs as well as their soot-covered nobles, making it out of the smoky interior to safety. Like her they were squinting in the bright sunlight, going from enjoying the air-conditioned confines of the auditorium to fleeing for their lives amidst carnage and death. But why were the terrified citizens of New Australia looking only at her? Why weren't they searching the crowd of survivors? Had their chieftains been among those killed? Wouldn't that be the first thing they'd want to find out? Obviously not. Perhaps it was because they now looked to Estrella Mwonga as their leader.

Within days following the brazen attempt at leveling the Tribal Assembly building with an improvised explosive device, an emergency session of the Assembly was called. This time they took over a large classroom at the Merchant Marine Academy, and with tightened security met to decide on a proper course of action. The public's reaction had been one of exasperation. This had been *an act of terrorism.* Estrella could only agree, even if she chose to keep her comments to herself.

She wouldn't need to.

Yes, she'd fully expected to be put in charge of the investigation into her parents' assassination during the Assembly meeting three days prior, if only they'd gotten to that point. The interrupted proceedings would have included a demand for a report from the Cave Lions as to their progress and this would have confirmed they'd done absolutely nothing. Sadly enough, that report would never be heard that day. However, as the emergency session was called to order, the chairman didn't seem interested in belaboring the matter. To the surprise of practically no one he moved right into a vote on whether to name Estrella Mwonga "chief inquisitor", thus granting her power to conduct the inquiry any way she saw fit, and with the full authority of the law.

There was more to it, though. By the time the session ended, and despite spirited arguments from conservatives who objected to a female being given this level of responsibility, she'd also be tasked with getting to the bottom of practically everything else that was going on as of late. The killers, the perpetrators in each and every crime committed since *Anarchy's* return, with the exception of Solomon's and Felina's murder, had been identified and were now dead. Naturally those in attendance would have had no way of knowing about Sneeeep being the primary suspect in the Mwonga Assassination. But was there a conspiracy behind all of this? That's the question she was tasked with answering.

Was Minggatu trying to kill them in order to obliterate the planet's government in a single afternoon? No question he was, any fool could see that. Plus, he was from the *Anarchy* just like the other two killers who'd, without warning, gone wild murdering people. Was this the source for the present wave of violence? Were other former crewmembers plotting something even more disastrous for the people of New Australia? If so, what could be done? Ultimately those among the gathering of aging warriors who'd objected to her appointment yielded. After all, if it had been *their* parents who'd been assassinated, wouldn't they too be expected to hunt down those responsible? *Of course they would.* Eventually she was called on to speak.

"Mr. Chairman, great chiefs of the Tribal Confederation, distinguished guests," she began. The sixteen year old stood up from her seat in the lecture hall, facing the chairman but acknowledging the other chieftains before she answered, much like her mother would have done. The gesture did not go unnoticed.

"I believe, as do many of you, that our planet is once more being threatened, only this time from within. Since the tragic death of my mother and father a month ago I've been waiting for the opportunity to bring their killer to justice. Now I've come to realize just how big a danger we're facing, not just my poor parents who died so tragically. Their lives were cut short and now more lives have been lost. This must stop. That is why I accept this charge: to weed out the madness that is at the core of all the violence. I will not rest until it is both identified and defeated. You have my word, it will be done."

The vote was close, despite her brilliant speech. Still, the measure passed. They, like Slout, had been given a taste of the teenager's innate talent for plain talk and liked what they were hearing. That being said, this was totally unprecedented. Estrella Mwonga had now been given as much power as her father had possessed in his entire lifetime.

***

"Well, well, if it isn't the great inquisitor herself, come to visit us." laughed Admiral Slout. It was the next morning and as Estrella arrived Kscheeech was already there. She'd uncharacteristically slept through the alarm on her communicator, primarily due to the session of the Assembly running late the night before. After her nomination passed she'd had to sit through an excruciatingly long debate between the Smilodons and Entelodonts, which accomplished nothing. Slout had conveniently exited by then. *He was the smart one.*

"Ran a little late did they?" he then asked, tauntingly. Estrella failed to see the humor.

"Yes, they certainly did," quipped Estrella with a smirk. "But you wouldn't know about that, would you, Admiral? By 19:00 you were already out the door."

Kscheeech sat in silence, watching the two take shots at each other. As usual Estrella was quick on the draw, lack of sleep notwithstanding. Problem was there was no time to waste on witty one-upmanship. Sensing things could degenerate, he decided to step in.

"Now stop it you two," said Kscheeech, interrupting Slout's train of thought as he was forming a wry comeback. "We've got to get to work and there's no time to lose."

This was of course a valid point. Time was of the essence. But what in the world could they do? Where should they start? Arrest the entire crew again and keep them locked up until they got to the bottom of things? That idea was already circulating. They'd heard rumors of so-called 'citizen groups' advocating such action. True, they could isolate one potential source of the problem by doing so. All three of the killers as well as the main suspect in the Mwonga assassination had been crewmen on the *Anarchy*. Minggatu was even an officer. But the million dollar question was what commonality could be found among these crimes? That's when the discussion turned to potential medical causes and mental health issues exhibited by the three killers. Had there been any patterns in their behaviors during the days leading up to their crimes? This debate resulted in a dead end. As far as anyone could tell the three perpetrators had conducted themselves normally and with no prior incidents.

Undaunted, Kscheeech suggested something else, something just as plausible. A medical condition, yes, but what if it was one they *all* shared which had caused them to lose their minds? If so, could it be identified by simply reexamining their corpses?

"I believe we still have one card left to play. We still have two of the bodies, don't we?" he queried. Estrella reacted immediately.

"Of the Suidonji who slit his own throat? Blafmer? And the other, you're talking about the Zorg who went wild in the market the other day, aren't you? Yes, I see what you mean. We can order another autopsy on the both of them. Good work Kscheeech. I didn't realize we still had access to them. Where are they?"

"At the city morgue, I believe," he replied. "No one claimed the Zorg, I know that much. His tribe wanted nothing to do with him after all that happened. Blafmer they've been keeping until the Entelodonts and Smilodons reach some agreement as to the cost of the burial ceremony. That, of course, may go on for months." This caused Slout to snort and Estrella to think deeply for a brief moment. Then she thought of something else.

"Wait, does that mean they also have the body of the Enoshi that Blafmer killed?" asked Estrella. Slout nodded as if he already knew this to be fact. "Because if they do, this will be perfect. We can use one of the corpses as the control group in order to compare with the other two, see what happened inside their brains."

"Precisely, my dear," Kscheeech replied. "That is, I believe we can, anyway. We'd have to find the right people to do it, but yes that is possible."

"Then I know just who we need for something like this," she said. Not surprisingly, Kscheeech and Slout did as well.

"Slarts," grumbled Admiral Slout. Kscheeech stated the same. No doubt about it: if they wanted answers as to what biological or neurological reasons for a test subject going insane, that's precisely who they must contact for assistance. However, this was a potential bombshell and capable of stirring up controversy in an already volatile atmosphere following the attack on the Assembly Hall. Even the mere mention of an attempt at determining whether the killers had a mental condition in common could spark demonstrations or perhaps worse. That meant the three investigators had to do this in absolute secrecy. No one outside of that room could know besides the scientists they employed. Estrella volunteered to do the recruiting.

"Exactly what I was thinking. But leave that to me, okay? I'll find who we need," she assured them. "You two keep quiet about this until we find out what they come up with." Shortly after that they went their separate ways, leaving Estrella in charge of locating scientists willing to do the job. That proved to be quite easy: the same team of Slarts who'd performed the task of reconstructing the bodies of her parents prior to their funeral.

Her next challenge was in gaining private access to the city morgue. This technically wasn't difficult in that as inquisitor she had the full authority of the law to make practically any reasonable request in order to solve crimes. The issue was in getting the bodies out of storage so they could be brought to a lab and examined thoroughly without word getting out that this was going on. *"Assume too much or too little regarding the intelligence of the masses and you'll be wrong every time,"* her father once told her. That's why she tried a rather clever tactic on the day she and the three scientists showed up at the morgue. Instead of removing the cadavers, she simply had the Slarts move all their equipment into the facility for the night. This way they could take samples and do all they needed to do without having to transport the bodies. As for the employees of the morgue? She had Admiral Slout rearrange their schedules so that all of them thought they had the night off. Once the department was secure for the evening, Estrella and her cohorts moved right in. By morning the scientists were done, and the bodies put back into storage. The only difference was they were missing their brains.

During the next twenty-four hours, Estrella awaited the results. A handful of people had seen her moving about the town with her Slart accomplices, so during that time she tried to appear busy with her investigation, interviewing Lacertilians who were the last to see her parents alive, then meeting with families of the victims from the knife attack at the town market. This provided an excellent cover. Kscheeech tagged along. It was not until the afternoon, while she was visiting with eyewitnesses to the stabbings, that she finally got the call. At the moment Kscheeech was already with her. Her next call was to Admiral Slout.

"It's done. They're ready," is about all she said to him when he answered. Other than giving him the location for the meeting in a cave laboratory far beneath the planet surface, she merely told him the time he needed to be there. "22:00 hours. Don't be late," she added. Slout grunted acknowledgment, then hung up. It would take him at least two hours to get there, meaning he'd have to leave the office shortly. It would require a very long elevator ride, not to mention trying to find the isolated location for the lab.

As for Estrella and Kscheeech, their journey was much more involved. At the time, she and Kscheeech were miles away from where the Slarts had been running their tests. They almost thought to call back Admiral Slout and ask him to order a car to pick them up. But then they thought against it. Instead they thumbed a ride on a mining vehicle that was heading in that general direction. The foul-smelling Suidonji driving it happily agreed to take them as far as he could. After that, they found others willing to help them get where they were going. They arrived with only minutes to spare, half-expecting to hear Slout already conversing with the scientists, learning of their findings. What they found when they got there was anything but that. Slout was nowhere to be seen.

The Slarts were however, what was left of them that is. Mangled and battered, it was as if they'd been attacked by wild animals. They were all three dead, yet with no discernible knife wounds or cut marks. Not from a blade, that was for sure. Nevertheless, they'd been literally ripped asunder. Estrella and Kscheeech could only look about the bloody scene with horror and confusion. Who or what could have done something like this?

At a quarter past the hour Slout finally showed, arriving in a huff, seemingly annoyed with his own tardiness. By that point Kscheeech and Estrella had already inspected the horrific mess. There were footprints everywhere, indicating the assassins had moved about the room committing the murders, occasionally slipping and sliding on the blood. The Slarts had probably been surprised by the visitors and didn't realize they were in any danger until it was too late. This did not, however, explain the ferocity of the attack. Kscheeech and Estrella had by then identified the bodies, careful not to touch anything or make additional footprints. Slout's reaction was uncharacteristic of a ship captain, not to mention a pirate ship.

"Holy hell. What happened here?" he asked, visibly shaken by the gore. Estrella ignored him, sobbing quietly as Kscheeech greeted his colleague. She couldn't help thinking that if they'd been half an hour early, it would be they too lying dead on that cave floor. This unsettled her.

"I'm afraid we were too late, Admiral," said Kscheeech. "Judging by the condition of the bodies and the fresh blood on the tables, floors, and walls, it's still moist as you can see, my guess is the killers fled only moments before we got here. They're probably still nearby, as a matter of fact." This enraged the beast.

"I see what you mean." he replied, looking around the cave and assessing the situation. "Oh my God, the blood." His response was atypical of a military commander accustomed to violent death. As far as he was concerned, the next step was to go round up whoever had done this before they got away. Instinct told him to take action, and fast. Yet he seemed panicked.

"You two stay here." he snarled, glancing over his shoulder as if to verify they were not in any immediate danger. "I'll call up some of my crewmen and we'll fan out searching for the killers. Whoever did this, they'll show signs of it, I'd wager. Probably covered in blood. Like you said, can't have gone far, I agree." That's when Estrella spun 'round to face him. This, she knew, was the absolute worst thing they could do. The proper course was to leave the cave immediately. Leave everything the way they'd found it and most of all be miles away by the time anyone else discovered what had taken place. That Slout was suggesting otherwise was enough to elicit a rather terse response from the teenager.

"No. Stay where you are Admiral." she remarked, causing her voice to echo. She then brought it down a notch or two before continuing. "Are you crazy? We're not going anywhere ... except back to your office," she then stated commandingly. Slout was coming unglued.

"What? But we have to catch them. Young Mwonga, I don't believe you're thinking clearly. There's been a homicide. We have to investigate. That's your job as inquisitor. For all we know they could be trying to make a run for it, don't you see?" Kscheeech, to the big fellow's immense frustration, agreed with Estrella.

"Actually, she's right old friend," he said coolly, hoping to head off a confrontation. Estrella had an expression on her face like she was ready to take on the big beast. Slout glared back at her with fire in his eyes. "The young lady is quite correct, I'm afraid to say. We can't be here right now, you have to understand. This was a secret meeting, or so we would have thought, and if the killers are still lurking nearby, our best bet is to make our way out while we have you to protect us." Slout seemed to struggle with this, at first storming out of the cave in disgust, then returning moments later. Upon returning he appeared as though he'd calmed down. After that he said nothing, merely gestured with his head like they were to follow him.

The three quietly left together and made their way to the freight elevator for the long ride to the surface. It would take days for anyone to discover the bodies, they could only hope, and though it pained them to be so heartless that's exactly what was needed. Once again, and for reasons they couldn't possibly fathom, their efforts in identifying the root cause of all the recent violence had been derailed. After a brief meeting at Slout's office later that night, Estrella told everyone to go home and get some sleep. As for herself, she needed some time alone to think. It wasn't just the killings of the three scientists that would occupy her thoughts that night. Slout's behavior, his actions as well as his logic, made no sense.

The following day, Estrella chose a new approach regarding her fellow detectives, starting with the hotheaded admiral. It was time to make some changes. He was one of them.

Slout's conduct when he'd arrived at the cave several minutes late for a meeting, which was highly unusual for the normally punctual ship commander, had once more raised her suspicions. Why was he late? Because he'd come a long way? Because he'd been delayed? Those would have been plausible excuses, but why was he so anxious to enlist others in chasing down the killers without taking into consideration the required secrecy for their meeting with the scientists? They'd had to remind him of this, yet they shouldn't have needed to. All had agreed beforehand there'd be no discussing their whereabouts with anyone besides each other. Nonetheless, he'd been confused and agitated when this was pointed out to him. This concerned her.

Plus, there was the truly icky part, something Estrella had noticed but did not discuss with Kscheeech or Slout. The bodies of the Slarts: *they'd been gnawed upon.* Likely strangled, their necks broken, the three defenseless creatures showed signs they'd been bitten and had parts of their faces and tentacles torn or ripped away. This had been accomplished with teeth, not with a knife or scalpel. They'd not been stabbed; they'd been mauled and there was only one species known for using a strong bite in order to disable an opponent during combat. Enoshi had teeth capable of doing such damage but didn't need to. Humans simply wouldn't. Schpleeftii preferred daggers or claws. That only left one option. A Suidonji, maybe several of them, had committed this crime.

But that begged the question: *Why assume there'd been more than one assailant?* Slarts could not defend themselves. They were far shorter than a full grown Suidonji and possessed neither the skill nor the inclination to fight. If one were attacked the other two could have scurried away, yes, but if the attack were carried out quickly the Slarts just as likely would have frozen in fear, not having the instinct to try and make a run for it. Slarts were brilliant as they were peaceful. Violence they simply could not contend with in any form. It saddened her thinking how they'd likely protested the attack and begged their killer to stop, not realizing it was no use.

"*It wasn't several; it was one. One creature did this,*" she concluded, recalling the scene she'd seen the evening before. "There was no furniture damaged. Tables and chairs weren't turned over like there'd been a brawl. Footprints were all the same size. It had to be a single killer that did it." As she showered in the morning, preparing to go meet up with Slout and Kscheeech at the Department of Naval Defense, she made her decision. The admiral, even if he did not commit the crime, could no longer be trusted.

What was she going to tell Kscheeech, though? She knew what her uncle would say. He'd tell her she was deluded. Slout would never betray the planet or his people, he'd say. He'd never have hurt her parents either. He was loyal to the core; and perhaps that was true, but Estrella had learned how to rely on her own instincts. Her mother had taught her well. Something was making otherwise normal individuals transform into marauding psychopaths. Not someone, some-*thing*. That's what made her realize what she needed to tell Kscheeech: *absolutely nothing*.

That's basically why she cancelled the meeting that day at Slout's office. She rather cowardly called in and informed the admiral she was not feeling well and was going back to bed. This he grumbled about, mumbling something inaudible toward another person who was in the room, no doubt Kscheeech himself, then replied that he understood.

"Perhaps we should all take a day off from this madness, eh?" as he put it. By that point she didn't particularly care what he said. The only thing that bothered her was what Kscheeech would think if he only knew what she was planning in his absence. That's because Estrella had no intention of going back to bed. She became a whirlwind of activity and would remain so for the next sixteen hours. Her first stop was the Merchant Marine Academy. There was someone she needed to see ... someone she should have gone to in the first place.

For there was one person she knew she could trust: Megalocyathus. He'd known her father and had advised the legendary general Archibald Hicks during the Great Rebellion. He'd known Estrella all her life as well. Best of all he was a Slartigifijian and they were incapable of lying. That's exactly what she needed right now: a *new* partner. Most of all she needed a friend; and the worst part was going to be telling the old fellow that his colleagues were dead. First task was to catch him between classes. The next task was to convince him to come with her to see for himself. This was not going to be easy.

***

He took it surprisingly well, the old fellow. Recognizing the seriousness of the situation Megalocyathus dutifully accompanied her down to the secret laboratory; pausing only briefly when he recognized his dead friends. Within moments he got to right work though, examining the corpses same as Estrella had done the night before. He too concluded it was a single attacker and that it was a Suidonji. He could even tell from close examination how hooves had been used to grip them; not claws or fingers. Estrella remained silent, watching the cave entrance and listening for anyone passing through the cavern outside. When he was done he raised up to address her, summarizing his findings.

"The killer entered quietly, I would have to conclude," said Megalocyathus, fluttering his facial tentacles as though choosing carefully what he was going to say. "No furniture was overturned. My colleagues either knew him or were not frightened by his presence. Thus, he got very close before the assault began. He then struck quickly, bit the heads, possibly in an effort to crush the skull before grasping and strangling each victim. Our friends were likely so surprised they were at a loss for what to do, poor souls. The killer, it would seem, disabled each of them using his teeth before systematically finishing them off, leaving no witnesses. That would be my theory, based on what I'm seeing. He slipped on the blood both *here* and *here*, as you can see, and that would imply he was moving fast so he could complete the task and make his escape."

He then gestured toward the entrance. "Shall we go outside

now?"

Estrella nodded in silence then exited the cave ahead of him. Apparently Megalocyathus was going to look for clues as to what the killer did next. If it was Slout, and she shuddered to think it could have been him, then he had to have hurried to clean himself before they arrived. There'd be evidence of that, she figured. Then again she didn't really want to know. That's why she stopped at the entrance. It was no longer of importance to her.

"Actually, let's not. I think I get the picture," she said, turning to face him. Megalocyathus paused while contemplating the meaning of that expression. Estrella didn't bother waiting for him to process the words. She continued with her present train of thought. What she had to ask him next was not something she looked forward to.

"Listen, I hate to say this, I really do, but I'm going to need a favor from you and you're not going to like it. Will you forgive me?" she asked. The old Slart nodded, not knowing what she was requesting he forgive. Humans were notorious for asking strange questions. It was their ability to practice deception that colored their words. He braced himself for the inevitable. She was about to ask him to tell a lie.

"You see, there was a reason those three scientists were killed, and I have a feeling we can't trust anyone else besides each other. I got you mixed up in this and I'm sorry, I really am. But you're the only one I dare confide in."

Megalocyathus could sense she had more to say. He gestured for her to continue.

"I asked your friends to examine the brains of the two killers we had in the morgue. Blafmer, a Suidonji, plus the Zorg who went crazy in the marketplace and tried stabbing people. They were both crewmen on the *Anarchy*. I've theorized that it was something biological or perhaps a temporary insanity brought on by a disease they shared. That's what those scientists set out to prove. We were meeting with them last night to hear what they discovered and someone apparently found out before we got here. That's why they were killed, I'm sure of it."

She went on to detail for him how they'd met with Blafmer only hours after the saloon murder and the affable fellow had no recollection of killing his friend. She also described how Minggatu had exhibited no behaviors which might garner suspicion prior to the Assembly Hall bombing. She then told him how they'd snuck into the city morgue and removed the brains of the Zorg and the Suidonji, plus the brain of the Enoshi who'd been murdered in the saloon. The scientists were running tests to see where there might be evidence of a neurological disorder. The old Slart listened patiently as she spoke, nodding occasionally but otherwise reserving comment.

"And that's why I need you to help me keep this all secret, the whole thing including the deaths of your colleagues. For now, anyway. I'm sorry but we can't let this get out until we've figured out what they knew before, well, before last night when they were murdered."

"I see," answered the wise old scientist. His expertise was in physics and astronomy, not neuroscience. It was going to be a hard sell. "And how do you propose we accomplish this?" he then asked. Estrella felt her scalp tingling. Her occasional mentor and old friend of the family was about to hear something she'd never have wanted to say in front of such an honest, forthright individual: *They had to hide the bodies.* No better way of putting it. She tried wording this delicately.

"Well, first of all, and I'm not the least bit excited about this, but I'm going to have to go back in there and clean up the mess. You can wait outside if you like. You can help if you want to, but I'll understand if you'd rather not." Megalocyathus once again fluttered his facial tentacles. Like all Slarts his eyes never blinked, thus it was impossible to detect emotions or even subtle changes in facial expressions.

"What about the bodies?" he then asked, causing Estrella to squirm. Her scalp now itched like she had ants in her hair. She felt herself starting to sweat. There was no use in sugar-coating it.

"Uh, yeah, I was getting to that. We're going to have to hide them. I'm so sorry, I really am. But if people find out there's been another killing, I mean if people hear that someone killed Slarts this time, there'll be, well, I just don't know anymore, Megalocyathus. I really don't know. Except for this. I need you to find me a good place to bury them. Can you do that?"

After that she waited for a serious tongue lashing which never came. Megalocyathus merely stood and looked at her in silence. She didn't dare speak at that point. He was studying her.

"Yes," was all he said. Then he proceeded to help her carry out the bodies and clean up the blood. In a couple hours they were done: buried all three in a shallow grave, said a few words, then got right to work. By 03:00 it was finished. Megalocyathus pulled away from his microscope and informed her of what he'd discovered. What he told her about next would challenge her very understanding of the natural world.

Studying the work of his colleagues, the wise old Slart determined that crewmen had been infected by microorganisms, parasites which they must have contracted during their short stay on Green Planet. This he proposed as the most likely scenario, though he had no way to prove it without further research. Nevertheless, he had a good bead on the situation, she could tell. If only she'd gone to him in the first place. Then again it may have gotten him killed, same as the others. This uncomfortable thought went through her mind once or twice as he explained his theory.

"Here, see for yourself," he said, inviting Estrella to look through the ocular at fresh tissue samples he'd taken from the brain of Blafmer the Suidonji. "Do you see the dark cells which are continuing to replicate themselves? These have invaded the subject's brain. I believe, and once again I emphasize that more research is needed, but I would venture that they *inspired* the subject, for lack of a better term, to commit acts of violence." He then went over to the computer where a document was displayed on screen. "Let me show you something else," he said.

What she could now see was text from the report filed by Admiral Slout upon returning to New Australia. The Slarts had somehow accessed the online transcript. Megalocyathus gestured for her to read it. There she learned about how the ship had made a landing, hoping to find food and provisions. What they found was a planet dominated by plants and trees with no animals to be found.

"*Not a mammal nor reptile, wherever we looked,*" it said. "*The lake we found a mile from our camp had no fish. No birds in the sky either. Only insects.*" Estrella could also see notes added to the document, not edits but actual notes inserted by the three scientists as they added their personal observations.

"Wait," she finally said. "What does he mean here, 'plants, if threatened and if possessing the ability, may attack competing beings in order to ensure survival of their species'? Bullshit. Plants can't do that, can they?"

"Ah, but you see, my colleague was talking about plant intelligence. He's indicating what may be the culprit. A different form of intelligence than we're accustomed to, I admit, but I have to respect his findings after what I've seen. *Here*, scroll down and see what he says in the next commentary." This Estrella did. She read it off to him mechanically.

"It says 'Green Planet had no mammals, birds, reptiles, or amphibians. Why might that be?' Yeah, we went over that already, so what?" Megalocyathus seemed surprised she wasn't making the connection. As bright as she was, he would have expected it to be abundantly clear. He tried explaining to the girl.

"Because the plants on Green Planet *decided* there should not be any, so to speak. Later on in the document, my colleague proposes that there may well have been great beasts living, breathing, and walking the surface at one time. There may have been any number of species, all gone extinct over the millennia, eradicated by disease, natural disasters, planetary cataclysm, no telling what. Perhaps a combination of events. But only the trees, the grass, the flowers remain, plus the insects which serve in perpetuating future generations via pollination. Now do you see?"

Unfortunately, Estrella was worn out from all she'd been through that day. She'd buried three bodies and had to clean up a bloody crime scene to boot. She'd then spent half the night assisting a brilliant scientist who, to be fair, was a bit out of his element when it came to functions of the brain. The only question she had was whether this so-called "plant intelligence" could be stopped.

"Look, I don't mean to be rude. I appreciate all you're trying to teach me about killer parasites wiping out anything on four legs back on some shithole planet I'd never heard of before. But to be honest I'm really tired right now and I just need to know if we can beat this thing. I mean I get it, I guess anyway. But the microorganism I saw in the microscope, the one that can infect brain tissue, can we kill it before it makes us destroy each other?"

To her relief, Megalocyathus was quick with a potential solution. Not only that, but to his delight, she'd effectively summarized what he and his late colleagues had proposed as a working theory on what had driven people mad with rage. If she'd scrolled down further she would have learned even more about what the scientists had suggested. The only limit to what the parasite could achieve was the creativity and intelligence of its host in devising ways to eradicate its own species. Might take generations. Might not. Either way, all competing life forms would be exterminated.

"I believe you're asking if we can develop an antidote? One which will reverse the process, save us from eventual extinction?"

"Uh, yes," she replied, feeling a tad guilty that she'd mouthed off to a Slartigifijian. "An antidote would be nice, yes. Can you make one?"

"I'll get to work on it immediately," he said. To this she heaved a deep sigh. The whole crew, starting with Admiral Slout, must be inoculated and fast. This she proceeded to explain to him, even elaborating on how she suspected Slout may too be a potential threat, though she stopped short of accusing him of killing the old fellow's colleagues. She had no proof of this and besides it was a moot point. Once inoculations were complete her countrymen would be safe.

Or would they? Megalocyathus felt compelled to inform her that the problem could indeed be more widespread than she was assuming. That is, the microorganisms very well might have found additional 'hosts' by now. To put it another way, the threat may not end with former members of *Anarchy's* crew.

"But I hasten to warn you, young Human. It's now been months since the ship returned. The crew have had, shall we say, *encounters*, liaisons if you will, with other Nausties. No telling how far the parasites may have spread."

CHAPTER THIRTEEN
OVER THE EDGE

A nd spread, it did, to those same Naustie teenagers who'd gone and 'shacked up' with former pirates whom they'd idolized as children. This had been going on for months, with it only recently becoming a major problem. Soon enough though, just as Megalocyathus foretold, it would create a controversy which would plunge the planet into chaos.

It had all begun innocently enough. Boys and girls running away from home to be with a lover wasn't that unusual. It had been going on since the dawn of time. But what had developed over the past few months was something far more sinister. Crewmen from the *Anarchy* were adults and former convicts of New Australia Planetary Prison. Many had known their victims' fathers years earlier. The only difference was they hadn't aged. That they'd seduce young Nausties to their beds was by itself quite scandalous. Then word got around about the fate of all those who felt compelled to abandon their homes to be with their "boyfriends". It'd become a cult of sorts, with doe-eyed teenagers drawn in by the allure of "spiritual enlightenment". It had all the trappings of a disaster waiting to happen.

By abandoning all of one's worldly pursuits a member would receive "true, unfettered happiness", they were told. Only this juicy bit of information wouldn't come to light until much, much later when authorities finally intervened. It was a farce of course. As it would turn out, reality was something far more predictable as well as terribly unsavory. It was just a bunch of sailors from the *Anarchy* out to have a good time at the expense of their impressionable young "initiates".

Recruits were compelled to acquire resources like food and household items via whatever means necessary. Meanwhile, the cult's leaders relied on psilocybin mushrooms in order to "connect with their spirituality", as they'd tell the young Humans, Enoshi, and Suidonji who'd left their families to join. High most of the time, cult leaders would assign their acolytes with gathering supplies. This was accomplished via raiding warehouses, pilfering stores of fresh produce, or more often than not, stealing from their parents. That's how people started to find out what was really going on ... even if information was less than forthcoming from those naïve youngsters.

The unpleasantness didn't end there. The building the former crewmen lived in with their followers was a ramshackle dormitory where the government assigned them apartments. By now it had degraded to an eyesore. Interior living conditions were deplorable with the inhabitants having hardly a care or concern for proper sanitation. Trash was tossed into alleyways, left to rot. Odors from within were so strong they could offend even from a distance. Still, youngsters flocked to the wild parties going on night after night, many of them choosing to stay permanently, despite repeated efforts by panicked families trying to rescue their wayward children.

Police responding to neighbor complaints finally raided the place, discovering the awful truth regarding just how depraved things had become. Arriving they were hit by the stench of rotting food, bile, excrement, and something else even more disturbing: dead bodies. It didn't take long to discover what had happened.

The corpses of ten former pirates from the *Anarchy* would eventually be removed from the macabre scene. All had been poisoned, many showing signs of violent reactions to whatever toxin they'd ingested. Some had induced vomiting in a vain attempt at saving themselves after no doubt seeing their fellow shipmates keeling over, grimacing in pain. This would have indicated they had some idea what it was they'd been duped into consuming. Upon further examination police would discover what it was: a simple pot of stew. What had to be determined was what their killers had added to it, as well as who they were. That proved to be even simpler. For they too were lying dead in the center of the room. It had been a murder-suicide pact executed by the cult's followers. A manifesto of sorts was left on the only unbroken table in the room.

The document described in detail how they'd been ordered by leaders of the cult to poison the planet's food supply using modified pyrethrum, which the young females had swiped from a warehouse containing fertilizer and pesticides. Fortunately, the locations of the poisoned containers were revealed within the manifesto, much to the relief of everyone present. Authorities quickly responded. *Crisis averted.* All that was left to try and digest were the sordid details of just *why* they'd done what they did. When finished reading, Estrella would have preferred they'd stopped at the locations of the tainted food bins and called it a day.

Philandering by the cult's leaders, not to mention being compelled to participate in perverse ceremonies conducted for the purpose of "releasing their spirits from emotional captivity", certainly played a part in making the teenagers resentful. That was abundantly clear. Guilt they felt for aiding in a potential mass murder is what sent them over the edge.

Detailed descriptions of bizarre sexual rituals and occasional abuse did not interest Estrella in the slightest. She urged the other policemen who'd read the manifesto not to speak about it either, even though she knew the story would leak out. Yet it was the way the followers had responded when posed with the moral quandary of poisoning their friends, family, and neighbors. Given what she already knew about the way the microorganisms worked, it deeply fascinated Estrella. By obeying their cult leaders they'd committed the unthinkable; yet they'd had second thoughts. They'd carried out orders, only to change their minds and turn on the very individuals who'd convinced them to lie, cheat, and steal. Somehow they'd drawn the line when they realized the full scope of their crime.

Even more remarkable was how they chose to deal with the resulting guilt. As a group they'd decided to be their own judge, jury, and executioner. On top of that they'd written down a full confession, along with specifics as to where the contaminated food could be found. Why didn't they simply come forward and tell authorities what they knew, threw themselves on the mercy of the court? Did the microorganisms within their brains cause them to obey an outrageous order to participate in a scheme to murder thousands of innocent people? Clearly it had. Thus, when in their minds they rebelled against what they were being told, their solution was to poison their lovers then take their own lives. Out of remorse? It would certainly seem so. Then again, maybe it was deeper than that. Maybe they simply feared public ridicule, especially that of their parents.

When they were finished at the crime scene, Estrella immediately went to find Kscheeech. There she confessed to going behind his back in order to conduct a second autopsy. Not surprisingly, he was stunned.

"You'll have to forgive me, my dear, but I simply don't understand. I've known you all your life. Since you were a child. Since you were knee high to an acrididae. I appreciate you telling me this, but I fail to see how your distrust of Admiral Slout would have anything to do with me. Perhaps you'd be kind enough to explain."

This was exactly what she'd wanted to avoid in the first place. Now she was compelled to venture an answer.

"It's only because I knew you wouldn't believe me if I told you," Estrella countered. "I'm not blaming you for that, don't get me wrong. It's just that when I've mentioned before my suspicions, I mean I've tried telling you..."

"Yes, you have," he interrupted. "He was your first suspect following your parents' assassination, remember? And what did I tell you? I said you'd never find a person more devoted to your father, and now I'll tell you why. Slout was *my* friend originally, we met while working on the ramp. You may know of this from history when it was your father who came to me looking for a captain for the *Anarchy*. I later introduced the admiral to him. Only he was nothing like you see him today. The prison had nearly broken him. He'd never tell you this, but it's true. That's why, when your father made him commander of the ship, he leapt at the chance to turn his life around. Which he did. And by the way, do you know what he did to get sent to prison? I bet you've never heard this part of the story, would you like to?"

Estrella nodded.

"He was a smuggler. Only he never hurt anyone, not in his whole life, I assure you. All that happened was he got captured by authorities, and the mobsters he was working for, well, needless to say, he didn't dare reveal their identities. The judge sent him to New Australia Planetary Prison just to be spiteful. Gave him ten years for not cooperating with the investigation. Had no choice really. They'd have killed him, those bastards. Next thing he knows he's struggling to stay alive down there in those mines, same as me, same as all of us. Then came the rebellion, then civil war, then one day Chief Mwonga of the Schpleeftkorkii makes him a captain again. You can't imagine how this renewed his spirit. His confidence returned instantly. And the rest, well, the rest we've all heard. I myself was there to see it. Well, most of it. That's why I say you can trust him the same as you can trust me."

Embarrassed, Estrella subsequently told Kscheeech what she and Megalocyathus had discovered regarding what was afflicting crewmembers from the *Anarchy*. She also told him how she'd noticed the wounds on the three scientists indicated they were made by teeth from a Suidonji. This drew an even stronger reaction.

"And you believe that proves, unequivocally and without a doubt, that it was my good friend Slout who killed the three Slarts?" taunted Kscheeech. Estrella blushed.

"No, I never said I've proved anything. You said that, I didn't.

Don't put words in my mouth, Uncle. Anyway, even if he did, it won't matter for much longer. I'm having an antidote developed right now as we speak. Once it is complete, we can mass-produce it. If we can inoculate all the crew from the *Anarchy*, and I include Admiral Slout among them, this issue will be resolved. When that's done we'll inoculate everyone else. There will be no more threat to our planet, at least not for the time being."

She next told him of the actions taken in the cave with Megalocyathus. With the three corpses carefully concealed inside a shallow grave, they'd then revisited experiments done by the scientists. Hours later they'd learned what was inducing fits of rage within the minds of the *Anarchy's* crewmen. Kscheeech was dumbfounded. He, like Estrella, had a hard time grasping how an alien intelligence turned out to be the source of all the recent violence. It sounded more like science fiction than real science.

"Goddess of the Sea. You mean to tell me those poor Slarts believed it to be plants that did all this? What kind of plant, was it a tree or a weed? A flower, maybe? How is that even possible?" he asked.

"I know, right?" quipped Estrella. "But that's what they determined from the tests they'd done. And I've got to say, Megalocyathus reviewed their research and he completely agrees. Lucky for me he explained it well. I had a hard time with it, same as you, but there it is. Some kind of plant."

"Well, which was it, a tree or a flower? Did he say?" Kscheeech again queried, hoping to clarify what exactly it was. Estrella had no answer for that.

"Could have been anything, I guess. Only thing we know for sure is that it wants us dead, all of us. That is, it wants us to kill ourselves ... as in wipe out our own species so that it can colonize our planet. All we have to go on are the protozoa we found within the brains of the two killers. Megalocyathus believes he can create an antidote which will reverse the process."

Her uncle could only shake his head as the gravity of the

situation dawned on him. Yet he could almost find a measure of comfort in knowing it had actually been the result of outside influences and not a conscious attempt at destroying the very society her father had sought to create. New Australia had come a long way since its barbarous past, a past which new generations would be better off not knowing about. Solomon and Felina had seen to this and others had assisted, Kscheeech being among them. But then another thought occurred to him: what might happen if a deranged madman took control of one of their merchant ships and staged a pirate raid on an unarmed vessel somewhere out in space? There were several crewmen from the *Anarchy* right now serving onboard two or three of them. One unprovoked attack and the IPF would retaliate with deadly force. Their world would be destroyed.

"I see," he concluded. "Then I realize what we must do, and we must do so immediately. No delay. Unfortunately, it will also mean gaining Admiral Slout's full cooperation, will you allow it? You're the chief inquisitor, after all." Estrella failed to see what that had to do with anything.

"To do what, Uncle?" she asked, eyeing him nervously. Estrella was not looking forward to facing Admiral Slout just yet, not until the antidote was ready and she could have him inoculated. No one else could know what she'd just told Kscheeech and Slout was potentially the most dangerous individual on the planet right now. The aging lizard hastily explained.

"We have to order all the ships home wherever they are. No questions asked. Slout is Admiral of the Navy. He has that authority and they will comply if the order comes from him."

Estrella stopped on the sidewalk and adjusted her breather unit. The stress was making her throat feel dry as a bone. She sighed when realizing what he was implying. *He's right. The sailors serving on our trade ships. They could, oh God, no.*

"Shit. I see what you mean, Uncle. We've got to call them back," she observed, panic in her voice. "The crewmen from the *Anarchy*, the ones out there in space right now, they could stage a mutiny."

"They wouldn't even need to, my dear. All they'd have to do is fire a missile at a passing ship. If a couple of them worked together, almost anything could happen, and then..."

"Then we'd be at war with the entire galaxy." she said, finishing his sentence. A cold chill ran up her spine.

"Exactly," Kscheeech said, stopping as well. He eyed her calmly before continuing. "So, what are you going to do? I'll support you, whatever you decide," he then added, sensing what she'd say. He was right, of course. She was just like her father.

"Department of Naval Defense," replied the teenager, not hesitating to debate the matter. It was clearly the best solution to their dilemma, so why dither? "The office might still be open. He's probably there. If we hurry, we could catch him before he leaves. Are you coming with me?"

"Of course," was his answer. "We're running out of time though. It's almost dusk." The pair then turned and headed straight for the convention hall where all government offices were located. Like it or not, she'd have to put her trust in Admiral Slout just one more time, otherwise all could be lost.

However, it may have been too little too late, and Estrella could have had no idea just how quickly their situation would deteriorate. True, within days she would receive news that Megalocyathus had completed his tests and developed an antidote. Ships were already racing back to the planet, upon Slout's order. Only problem was by that time there was a group of vigilantes forming which was bent on rounding up all former crewmen of the *Anarchy* and exacting their own form of *justice*.

CHAPTER FOURTEEN
A CHORUS OF DISCONTENT

"**I** suppose you've heard the news by now, haven't you?" asked the big Enoshi. His name was Sunda, a veteran of the war with Earth and now a farmer. At the moment he was bringing in his very last basket of potatoes for the daily trip to market and was addressing Babirusa, a Suidonji who was passing by with a wheeled cart. For years this had been their morning routine. Sunda and his tribesmen worked the fields, rotating crops during the planet's multiple growing seasons. Once finished with harvesting their potatoes they would plant cucumbers, perhaps tomatoes, alternating throughout the year. He and Babirusa had become friends over time. They had a lot in common, despite being from different tribes and species.

"What, you mean those poor youngsters who killed all them pirates the other day?" clarified Babirusa. Sunda nodded, setting his load of potatoes onto the bed of the cart, pausing to bat away flies. Babirusa's enormous pushcart was also used for transporting manure and since New Australia maintained a consistent year-round climate, crops were being planted or harvested every fifty to seventy days. "Yeah, I heard about it," replied the big-bellied teamster. "So sad. Everyone's pretty pissed off, too. By the way, do you realize what they was up to?"

"Uh-huh," said Sunda. "Rumor has it they were planning on poisoning our food supply. Police broke it up before they could pull it off. One of our tribesmen is a cop in town. Some of the lads served with him. That's how I found out. Can you believe that? They weren't going to tell us either, I bet." He then shook his head in disgust. Obviously, he was talking about the government.

"Can't blame 'em," snorted Babirusa. "Folks is scared enough as it is." The two then started making their way toward town, continuing their conversation as other farmers brought in crops from neighboring fields. Some were Enoshi, some were Humans bearing bushels of carrots to add to the day's bounty. Most had wives who ran market stalls or held jobs in town. Due to the incredible heat they'd been working since just before dawn. By midday they'd be safe inside their homes from the hot sun, not returning to their labors until right before dusk.

"They should be scared. We all should be," continued Sunda, still trying to make his point. "But that doesn't give 'em the right to keep things secret from us." He said this in a way which might invite participation from his fellow farmers now joining them for the trip into town. Enoshi were fiercely proud and stubborn by nature. Admitting fear, even for a former warrior like Sunda who was pushing forty, was next to impossible. Perhaps he was just angling for affirmation. He'd soon get his wish.

"Yes, yes, I suppose you're right," replied Babirusa. Others were more willing to express their outrage.

"More like, hell yes." remarked one of the Humans, a Why-O named Googy Corcaran. Googy had fought under General Vlad "The Impaler" years before during the Earth Invasion; now he was a middle-aged father of three. His daughter had been one of those so deeply charmed by the dashing swashbucklers from outer space. Needless to say, he and the girl's mother had been hard-pressed to reign in their star-struck teenager once she laid eyes upon all those handsome pirates. Had to keep her on a tight leash ever since. "We got families." he then added.

"That's right." exclaimed another. This time it was an Enoshi who went by Korat. His blue-gray fur was caked with mud from toiling in the potato fields. His mate lived at home with their five kittens; but that didn't lessen the danger that she and her litter could have been poisoned if it hadn't been for a timely police raid and the discovery of the girls' manifesto. That story had made it around as well and now the girls were viewed as heroes. Soon there was a small crowd of farmers gathering around the teamster's push cart as he rolled it onto the main road. The discussion became gradually more heated, the closer they got to the city.

"First one of 'em kills his own shipmate inside a saloon. Next thing we know, they're tryin' to blow up the whole goddam Assembly Hall." continued Korat. "How are we supposed to live, knowing those lunatics are out there?"

"So what are we going to do about it?" asked the aging teamster, posing the question to anyone willing to venture a guess. "Got any ideas? Myself, I don't have a clue. What of the chieftains, what are they saying? Any word from them?"

"No, not a peep," replied Sunda. "Probably in the same boat as us ... don't have the foggiest idea how to stop this. It's all gotten so crazy."

"Yeah, bonkers." declared Googy the Human. "Hell, I was buyin' the sons of bitches drinks over at the pub only months ago. Now I'm afraid one of 'em is gonna stab me in the face just for lookin' sideways at him. Had to chase 'em off once or twice when they started botherin' me wife. God knows what they'd have done if they'd gotten ahold of me daughter. Lately I'm beginnin' to think that's the least of our troubles."

"Same here." remarked Korat. "Someone's gotta do somethin', and fast."

"Like what?" pressed Babirusa. Sunda was happy to state the obvious, even if he was a bit hesitant to come right out with it. They were all thinking the same thing, he could tell.

"Well, for starters, we know we can't count on the police. They're on our side, yes, but there's only so much they can protect us from," he grumbled. This garnered a few encouraging grunts, so he continued. "Of course, we could wait on them and the government to uncover the next plot to try and murder us in our beds, but that's not gonna get us anywhere." Seeing no one was going to interrupt, he decided to suggest a solution. Simply put, they would have to band together in order to defend themselves. Nausties had always done that and besides, it would be foolish to allow crazed killers to have time to think up yet another heinous crime. "No, my friends. The best defense is a good offense. I say we round 'em up, the whole lot. Be rid of 'em once and for all."

"I agree." shouted Googy. By now the crowd of farmers had grown to twenty, with more making their way in from nearby fields. As each arrived he'd add his contribution to the cart. Babirusa would slow to allow access, then resume his pace. Meanwhile he tried playing devil's advocate.

"And how are we to do that, Sunda?" asked the burly teamster. "You're suggesting we take the law into our own hands." Googy the Human felt bold enough to address this rather sticky issue personally.

"Then that's just what we'll have to do, won't we?" he countered pugnaciously. "Right, Sunda? Once we have the numbers, of course." The old teamster wasn't fully onboard yet.

"Nonsense," scoffed Babirusa with a smirk. "We can't just deputize ourselves and in the name of the law go around arresting people. For one thing, we don't have the authority."

"*Bollocks*, we won't need it." was Googy's reply. He then looked to Sunda for direction. The big cat had clearly established himself as their leader. Googy was merely trying to show he was behind him all the way, that is until a better option presented itself. Humans were good at that.

"But we're talking about something completely illegal, here," Babirusa countered. He was sensing he'd be roped in either way but felt an urge to be the voice of reason. Sunda once more spoke up.

"That won't be a problem and it never has," blurted the big cat. "Googy's right. Once we have the numbers they won't be able to stop us. You'll see. Call it a citizen action group. Call it whatever you like."

"Vigilantism is what I call it." interrupted Babirusa, snorting and huffing on his breather unit as he pushed his cart. "They'll lock us up." He could see he was in the minority.

"No, old friend," Sunda assured him. "You've got it all wrong. If we get the numbers we need, folks'll stand aside, just as likely join us. The police'd probably love to do the same thing only they can't. See, it's Admiral Slout that's got everything under his control. All them crewmen from the *Anarchy* answer to him now, workin' for the motor pool or the Department of Naval Defense. For all we know he's been behind the whole thing all along; but my point is, we can't get to him until we first get rid o' them pirates that served on his ship. We gotta take 'em all down, Slout included. It's the only way."

Babirusa knew he was talking treason. They all were. Slout was a government official. A living legend. A military hero. Yet there was at least a kernel of wisdom tucked away in-side Sunda's twisted proposal. If they could indeed go around gathering up former members of the *Anarchy's* crew, disposing of them quickly and best of all do it in one night, perhaps, just perhaps, the police would stand aside. That being said, it was also correct what Googy and Sunda were saying about needing a sizable force to achieve such lofty objectives.

That's why, when the crowd of aging farmers reached the town market, they endeavored to do some recruiting of their own. The result? Even more would join in, and eventually all would express their concerns in a chorus of discontent over the government's failure to protect them.

"If the police can't keep our streets safe from ravenous killers, we must take the law into our own hands." was the general consensus.

Thus, by midday Sunda's vigilantes would increase their ranks to over a thousand determined souls, agreeing to gather that evening as dusk fell over the city. By dawn they hoped to be rid of the threat. Their goal was to march through the interior of the planet, then fan out within the capital itself, everywhere rounding up known members of *Anarchy's* crew. And when found? They were to be executed on the spot.

***

By midday the number of vigilantes had swelled to over five thousand. However, their plan to exact bloody vengeance was practically the worst kept secret in the city come evening time. Soon enough, news of this reached Admiral Slout as frightened employees working for him in the motor pool reported being chased by angry mobs. His response was to call Kscheeech, he in turn called Estrella. Their first move was to send out word to all remaining crewmen, wherever they might be in the capital or the planet's interior. They must abandon their homes, their beds, their girlfriends, and their possessions. They must come immediately to the shipyard where *Anarchy* was now parked awaiting refitting as a merchant ship. There they would be locked up yet again, only this time for their protection. Few were very happy about doing so.

"Don't argue, just get inside." yelled Slout. At the moment he and Estrella were standing at the top of the ramp leading into the cargo bay. Kscheeech was down at the base, gesturing for the crewmen to hurry. Despite the fact they were being hunted, many thought it ridiculous having to hide themselves away, especially now that they'd been reunited. It would be preferable to arm themselves and put up a fight. That being said, some were simply miffed at having to leave their beds at such an ungodly hour. It was currently just past 01:00. More than a few resented being pursued by aging miners and farmers, many of whom wielding little more than clubs and torches. *They were warriors, after all.*

"Is someone going to explain to me why we're doing this?" hissed one of the pirates, a Zorgolongian named Kack-urrrr. He was particularly annoyed at being roused from his leafy bed in the middle of the night. He was a miner and had finished a long work shift only hours earlier. Kscheeech knew the type. Miners were perpetually grumpy, even when well-rested. Waking up a Zorg when he'd just gotten to sleep was a good way to get clawed. Others shared his sentiments.

"Beats the hell out o' me." remarked Ellsworth Lay. He went by "Elzy" and by way of comparison he'd been in the throes of passion at the time his shipmates banged on his apartment door. Though a Human, his bed partner at the time was none other than an Enoshi female and wife of a Smilodon noble. Good that they'd found him first, as opposed to her husband. If that had happened he'd have been better off facing the vigilantes. He was not the only one unwilling to appreciate how much danger they were in.

"I don't understand." snarled Lykoi, an Enoshi marine who once served as part of the ship's security team. "Why this, Captain? Why don't we make a stand? I mean, it looks as though we're all here now, 'cept for the ones that's already dead. We can take 'em. How many are there anyway, a few hundred?" Realizing how uninformed some of them might be regarding the scope of the threat, Kscheeech tried putting things in perspective.

"More like a few thousand and there could be more," he responded. "By now, who knows? Could be ten, could be fifteen thousand. That's the way it goes with lynch mobs. They're moving toward the city center as we speak. The police won't be able to stop them, not tonight. There's too many. Our only hope is to hole up inside the ship until things settle down. Please, we don't have much time." Elzy Lay felt inclined to weigh in on the matter.

"Don't make no difference to me," he scoffed. "If they wanna fight, then shit, let's get it on. We got EIC's in this motherfucker, right? They ain't already took 'em out have they? Besides, I heard they only got clubs and pitchforks out there. We could kick their asses easy." Most seemed to feel the same.

"Well, you heard him Kscheeech," remarked Kack-urrrr. Being a Zorg he was one of the few who could pronounce the old fellow's name correctly. "The lads say they wanna make a stand. I think we could carry it off; maybe with a few squads set up in ambush. The fools will scatter once we start mowing them down with projectiles. How about it?" The retired captain of the *Chengshi* only shook his head. The last thing they needed was more bloodshed.

"Absolutely not," he replied. "It is out of the question. We certainly don't want another incident." By now Admiral Slout was aware of the debate going on down at the base of the ramp. His counterpart Estrella stood close by, primarily for her own safety. Up until then she'd remained silent, keenly aware of the glares she was getting from former pirates as they trudged past. Knowing pretty much what she'd love to say, if it weren't for the fact she was not much bigger than a Zorg and hardly able to defend herself, the admiral spoke in her place. If anyone knew how to talk sense into them, he did. He was still their commander, after all.

"Oy. You there. Stop your bickering and get on the damn ship. Leave the captain alone. He's not in charge here, *I am*. Now get a move-on. If you wanna piss and moan about the situation, do it inside. Those chieftains with the tribal council, if we cause any more trouble, they may just turn around and exile us into space. Do you want that?"

This should have been enough to quell any further argument, Estrella would have assumed. Surprisingly enough it did not.

"Exile us? They wouldn't dare." bellowed Lykoi. "If it weren't for me and the lads, they'd be buried under a pile of rubble right about now."

"That's right, Admiral, or worse." hissed Kack-urrrr. "We bore the brunt, led the IPF around the galaxy until they gave up the chase. Those ingrates out there, they owe us. They owe us plenty. Besides it isn't fair. Just because a few of our brethren went a little crazy and killed some folks, they decide they want to come after the rest of us seeking revenge. How is that justified? Ask yourself."

"Yeah, ask yourself." exclaimed Lykoi, picking up right where his shipmate left off. "Or has our brave commander now become civilized like all our old prison mates, turned into farmers and miners, forgot how to be warriors. Have you forgotten too?" Estrella braced herself when she saw the intense expression forming on Slout's enormous face. His eyes flashed with rage. She was about to see why no one should ever question *the boss*.

"Maybe you'd like to find out, then, is that what you want?" Slout roared, causing his voice to echo across the shipyard. She'd never witnessed him losing his temper and it was, to say the least, frightening. "You forget your place, sir. You served this ship once, still do. Now you dare challenge a superior officer? *Bah.* I'll have you jettisoned into space right along with the garbage, Lykoi. And that goes for the rest of you scallywags. You know me. I will not tolerate mutineers, not on this ship, not for one second, not now, not ever. Do I make myself clear?" He then stared them down, watching for anyone foolish enough to step forward. No one dared, not even the much bigger and ferocious-looking marine. Clearly their wily commander still held sway. "Now, if there are no further objections, get your asses moving before those madmen show up with their pitchforks. There will be no fighting today, you hear me? Tomorrow perhaps we'll negotiate a truce, for the time being, do as I say."

Despite a few murmurs and grumblings, this seemed to work. The pirates dutifully boarded the ship without another word. When they were all accounted for, Slout promptly ordered the ramp closed. Estrella was impressed at how they obeyed without further delay. It was only then that a very terrible thought went through her mind. They were about to find themselves *trapped*.

As the enormous door pulled shut she could see a large crowd of people beginning to congregate in the festival square off in the distance. There had to be ten thousand at least and their numbers were growing. In no time they'd surround the ship, demanding they turn over the *Anarchy's* crewmen, otherwise there'd be a riot. A cold chill shot through her like a jolt of electricity when she began to realize what must be done. There was no alternative but to confront them. This was all she could think about as Slout shouted orders at his men to find a place in the cargo hold and make themselves comfortable.

She hastily weighed her options. What if the mob tried setting fire to the ship? *Impossible*, she concluded. It was far too big and made of heat-resistant titanium alloy. However, that didn't mean those idiots might try anyway. Failing that, they'd likely lay siege to the vessel until she and the rest of those trapped inside began to starve. In fact, it wouldn't even take that long. The ship had been emptied of provisions. There was no water onboard. Come morning the heat would begin roasting them like a Christmas ham. They'd have no choice but to surrender. Might take a few days, a week at the most. After all, if the tribal chieftains and planetary police were afraid to try and stop them, not to mention if they were complicit, the crowd would only grow bolder. No telling what they'd do, given a little ingenuity and the time to devise a way in.

It was up to her to put a stop to the madness. Slout couldn't do it. They'd strike him down the moment he stepped foot outside the ship. Kscheeech couldn't hope to face them down either. He was old and frail. This was a job she had to handle by herself. Unfortunately, when Estrella explained this to Slout, he about flipped his lid.

"What? Are you insane? You can't go out there. You're practically a child." he screamed at her. Kscheeech tried pleading with the youngster as well.

"My dear, no. You can't face that rabble. They'll, well, I don't know just what they'll do, but I'm sure they won't listen. Not to you, not to anyone." he begged her. It did no good.

"Yes, they will," she replied, trying to conceal the debilitating terror she felt. "In fact, I'm the *only* one they'll listen to right about now." Slout was unmoved.

"Out of the question. We can't open that door." exclaimed the admiral. "They'll rush in and try to kill us if we do that. And you know what'll happen if they get inside, Human. My crewmen will have to fight for their lives. Hundreds will die." His former First Mate could only agree.

"Seriously, my young friend. You can't possibly hope to accomplish anything. They might hurt you. Worse, they might hold you hostage. What would we do then?" asked Kscheeech.

Only she knew exactly what she was doing, even if her co-horts would never be willing to accept her logic. Oh yes, she'd seen the way all those frightened people had looked toward her for guidance when she'd walked out of the Assembly Hall following the bombing. They were frightened and desperate, saw her as their leader that day. Nevertheless, she wasn't about to try enlightening Kscheeech and Slout on the matter. Instead she calmly asked if there was another exit besides the loading bay, one which she could utilize but difficult to access from outside once closed. There was, but Slout hesitated to reveal its location. It was the garbage hatch located on the port side about fifty feet above the surface.

"You'll have to trust me, Admiral," she said looking sternly into his eyes. "You too, Uncle. There is no one else who can persuade them to go. Their chieftains can't, or won't. The police can't either. They're outnumbered and probably in hiding. That leaves only me. They'd listen to my father if he were here, but he is not. They'd listen to my mother, but she's gone as well. It's got to be me this time, don't you see? I can't ask either of you to do it. That's why you've got to show me another way out of this crate."

"But it's up near the top of the ship, Young Mwonga," argued Slout. He then went on to explain how the garbage chamber functioned. It had to be loaded then sealed off. An outer door could then be activated, allowing the ship's refuse to be released into space. That wasn't the only challenge, however. "What's more it has to be powered by the engines in order to open." This gave Estrella an idea.

"Meaning we'll have to engage the ship's power plant, they'll hear that, won't they?" she asked. Slout cocked an eyebrow, wondering where she was headed with that train of thought.

"And?" he queried.

"Don't you see? They'll think we're about to blast off," she replied. This caused him to realize what it might lead to. The crowd would pull back, fearing they'd be vaporized by the ship's thrusters as it attempted to lift off from the surface. Nothing within fifty yards would survive. They'd have no choice but to flee the scene, thus causing disorganization. That might be all the time she needed.

"*Hmmmph*," he snorted. "I get it. So, what do you have in mind, open the garbage chute and let you climb down during the confusion?"

"Yep," she quipped. "That'll be the last thing they'd expect. And when they see it's me, they'll assume I've been released. I'll be recognized immediately. No one will harm a hair on my head, I promise. Just find me a long enough rope so I can make it down the side of the ship. Can you do that?" Slout still wasn't liking the idea. He was more inclined to just make for Frabrak 3, find an uninhabited island and lay low for a while. Unfortunately, that'd be next to impossible with no provisions on board.

"I suppose, yes. But what say you do that, and they won't listen? You'll never get them to disperse. Your father, if he were here, would agree that there's no way to communicate with a mob. Either drive them off with superior force or get the hell out of the way. That's what 'ole Solomon would tell you."

"Yes, he might," replied the youngster. "Only he's not around anymore and that means it's my decision. You have to understand, and you as well, Uncle. Our planet is in crisis. We must have leaders at a time like this. There's no one else left but me." Hearing her put it that way, he finally had to yield.

"Very well then," replied the admiral. "But for the record, I think you're out of your mind." Kscheeech for his part was speechless, even if he recognized the genius behind the idea. Seeing the daughter of Solomon Mwonga emerging from the ship would make quite an impression on all those aging villagers. Only question was whether a determined sixteen year old would have any luck changing their minds.

***

"Sunda, brother, do you hear that?" exclaimed Googy Corcaran. An enormous crowd had gathered around the base of the Anarchy, bent on killing everyone inside. By this point in time practically everyone in the city had figured out that its crew were hiding in the ship's cargo bay. All they had to do was force them out. Now it would seem Sunda's army of vigilantes had a brand new problem on their hands. "It sounds like they're leavin'." he continued frantically. "What're we gonna do?"

Ironically, given the mentality of their followers, the majority of whom were nearing forty and it was way past their bedtime, this was perhaps the best news of the night. In fact, when word spread that the pirates might beat a hasty exit, cheers arose. Sunda's reaction was immediate. He'd heard the same rumblings coming from the underbelly of the craft and in response rushed to regain control. He knew full-well that letting the ship leave with most of its crew onboard was just about the worst thing imaginable.

"Yes. I hear it. Quick, we must get their attention. We can't let those thieving picaroons off this planet. You know as well as I. They got no food, got no water. If they get away they'll raid the first ship they find. It'll start a war. All of you, fan out. Yell as loud as you can." he screamed, barely audible over the din. It had been hard enough keeping them together; *now this*. "Tell them, tell them." he commanded. They circulated through the crowd, passing the word. Korat was loudest of all.

"No, you morons. This is not what we want. Quit your celebrating. We must stop them. We can't let them go." he proclaimed. Nevertheless, many felt inclined to ignore him and back away from the vessel, fearing what would happen if they didn't clear the area in time. Having turned to farming and mining years before, most had only faint memories of how a galactic freighter functioned. This frustrated him, as well as Googy and the others who'd helped Sunda rally supporters that day. That being said, they were not in any immediate danger. It would be several minutes before the ship could activate its thrusters; a fact not lost on Babirusa, who'd in his youth served onboard the *Warthog* as a mechanic.

"My friends. Do not flee." he roared, in an attempt to aid

Korat and others now pleading with the crowd to stand their ground. "We have time. Not a lot, but plenty enough to do something. Stay where you are. We can disable the ship from the outside." Babirusa had a sterling reputation around town. Hundreds knew him. They in turn encouraged others to hear him out.

"Are you sure, brother?" yelled Sunda over the swell of voices chattering back and forth. Babirusa nodded.

"Well there you have it. We can stop the ship from taking off." he cried. It was enough to make them stop in their tracks. Those who'd started making their way home turned back to rejoin their comrades. Amazingly enough, Estrella's plan to frighten the crowd into moving away from the ship had hit a major snag. On the contrary, they were now focusing their efforts on sabotaging the vessel. This would give them confidence, making them unstoppable. It certainly wouldn't make her task any easier. Unfortunately, however, she had no idea this was going on. At the moment she was still making her way through the interior of the *Anarchy* with Admiral Slout.

When they reached the section of the ship where trash could be loaded and jettisoned into space, Slout opened up a control panel then activated the interior lighting. Next to the chamber was a utility closet and inside were found space suits for crewmen to wear during in-flight maintenance operations. In it was also a spool of cable, used as a lifeline during space walks. Slout rigged up a harness for her, then made her stand back while he engaged the mechanism which controlled the outer door. Right before he did so, he turned to ask if she was having second thoughts. Estrella was so nervous, she was ready to pee her pants.

"You still want to go through with this?" he asked. It sounded like he was taunting her. Estrella wasn't having it.

"Yes, Admiral," she replied obstinately. "You've got your job and I've got mine. Anyway, are you sure you know how to operate this thing?" Of course he did. Like any ship captain he knew every conceivable function onboard his own ship. She would have assumed that already. That's why it gave him a chuckle.

"A little rusty, maybe," he snorted. "But I'll figure it out eventually, hopefully before you hit the ground. By the way, you remember what to do when you make it down, right?"

They'd discussed the plan during the walk through the ship. She was to unhook the cable from her waist and Slout was to reel it in immediately, leaving no way for the vigilantes to climb up. After that she was on her own. Responding with an "Aye-aye," she then climbed through the now-open portal and began her descent. To her surprise there was a large crowd already waiting for her below. She was noticed instantly.

"Who is that?" she heard a voice yelling up at her. Someone identified who she was and announced their discovery to the rest. A roar arose as word spread. Like she'd predicted this had an immediate effect on the mentality of the crowd.

"It's Estrella Mwonga." cried a female-sounding voice, clearly that of a Human. Others chimed in.

"They must have captured her." yelled a Suidonji.

"Those bastards." exclaimed an Enoshi.

She could hear others reacting similarly as she clumsily repelled down the side of the craft. When she finally made it to the surface, she unhooked the harness and gave the line a tug to give Slout the all-clear sign. He promptly yanked it away before anyone could grab hold. It was hardly necessary. Everyone was far too shocked to see it was really her. Now there was no turning back.

"Are you alright, Human?" one asked, this time an individual she did not recognize. It was Babirusa. "Were you a hostage?" he continued. "Did they hurt you?" Estrella didn't answer at first, causing folks to eye her dubiously. Instead she calmly asked him to lift her up so she could be seen by the masses. When he did so the rest of the crowd cheered wildly. *So far so good*, she thought. Estrella promptly began waving for them to be quiet. It took nearly a minute for them to comply.

"Listen to me." she began. Now sitting atop Babirusa's massive shoulders, Estrella pleaded several times for them to simmer down before beginning. When she was sure they could hear her, she spoke to the crowd.

"No, I was not a hostage. You have nothing to worry about, and no, they did not hurt me. I was safe, I swear." she began. This, she knew, would sound mighty suspicious. Was she already in collusion with the pirates? She was a teenage girl, after all. They'd seen it happen before. Sunda was first to interrogate her on the matter.

"Then why did they let you go, Human? And what were you doing there in the first place?" he asked with a snarl. She'd been anticipating such a question. Estrella's relationship with Admiral Slout was commonly spoken of around the capital. She sensed that Sunda was one of their leaders. There was no choice but to answer him directly.

"Because this is where I instructed them to go, so they'd be protected." she replied. She figured that such a response would not go over well, so she paused just long enough for it to sink in, then continued. "That's right. I ordered them inside their own ship and for their commander to shut the loading bay door. I did this to save them ... from you." Sunda fumbled for words. Googy Corcoran beat him to the punch.

"And what's that supposed to mean, girl? You in cahoots with them pirates now, are ya'? Like them young folks who was gonna try 'n poison us the other day? Thought about doin' some killin' of your own, maybe? Then what? Had a change of heart, did you?" This inspired a wave of murmurs which spread like a contagion through the crowd, creating a sound much like ocean surf crashing onto a beach.

"Right." exclaimed Korat. She could see murder in his cat-like eyes, must be another one of the rabble-rousers. Meanwhile Babirusa tried looking up at her warily. She patted him on the head then continued as the crowd fell silent awaiting her answer.

"No, my friends. Nothing like that." she fired back in response, quickly gaining confidence. "As I'm sure you are aware I was selected by the Tribal Confederation as Chief Inquisitor.

They charged me with investigating all the goings-on as of late, starting with the murder of my parents. It was my job to get to the bottom of what's causing the violence, and over the past few days I've been able, with a little help from one of my childhood mentors, to identify scientific reasons why people are going crazy and killing each other."

Sunda finally mustered a comeback.

"SCIENCE?" he retorted. "Is that how you propose explaining what's been happening to us, Daughter of Solomon? *Rubbish*. There's no science to it. For years we've lived in peace. We've put our past behind us, just as your mother and father directed us. Buried it like yesterday's refuse and tried to move forward. 'Build a better society,' is what your parents taught us to do and we did. What changed all that was when those so-called heroes dropped out of the clouds one day. They're behind all of this. You know it and so do we.

Many in the crowd were now directing their attention toward Sunda. The rest had their eyes still transfixed upon the young teenager sitting atop Babirusa's ample shoulders. Estrella wasn't about to interrupt the big cat. Her parents had taught her well. She didn't have to debate the entire mob, just outwit whoever was in charge. Clearly that's who was speaking to her.

"And those murderers inside that ship, they know as well. You choose to try and protect them, why? One of those crewmen could be your parents' killers. Now, I'm sure I speak for all of us when I say how much we adored and respected your mother. Her loss was felt by every single person on this planet. And as for your father? Your father Solomon was both wise and forthright. We trusted him, we want to put our trust in you. Yet here we are and you're telling us how you're wishing to protect the very same traitors responsible for their deaths. Are we to assume that you too have turned against us?"

It was impertinent of him to speak that way. Estrella knew he'd gone too far, even by Enoshi standards. Question was, did the crowd agree? She waited for his words to marinate in the people's minds before responding. He had plenty more to say.

"We waited for the government, we waited for the police. None of them could do a bloody thing for us besides throw up their hands in confusion. And oh yes, we heard you were put in charge of the investigation. That, we figured, was a step in the right direction. Now this. You've gone over to the other side, haven't you? Betrayed your parents by siding with the enemy. That's what you did, admit it. No, there's no *science* to this. *Anarchy's* crew are a threat to our society and we're not going to stand by while they sit around thinking up new ways to kill us."

After that he seemed to have run out of gas. Now was her chance for rebuttal. Estrella could tell that the crowd was getting tired of listening to the old coot anyway. No doubt they'd been hearing the same speech all night. They wanted to hear what *she* had to say. She waited a few seconds to see what else he might have to add, then quickly put him in his place.

"Are you finished?" she asked, causing more than a few to heads to turn, first toward her, then back toward Sunda. The tactic was so typical of a teenager, it almost made people burst out laughing. Meanwhile Sunda's reaction, standing with paws on his hips looking like he had no bullets left in the chamber, made it all the more comical. Shrugging his shoulders to signify indifference was about all he could offer in terms of a comeback. Estrella let loose.

"Then first of all let me say I have NOT switched sides, as some would have you believe. I, just like the beings now holed up in this spacecraft, just like everyone else gathered here, pledge my loyalty and devotion to this planet, to its people, and to no other. And let me assure you. I, like my parents before me, represent no faction or political agenda; nor do I condone the violence that has plagued our culture since the very beginning. To that end I have no less in common with the majority of you standing here tonight."

She once again patted Babirusa on his enormous head, this time calling down to him saying, "You too, my friend." This garnered a few snickers from the audience as he looked up and returned the gesture by patting her leg.

"That, my fellow Nausties, is what I need you all to understand about me, and my intentions. But here's what I also want you to realize. When the majority of you, right along with the crewmen onboard this very ship, rose up and fought back against evil ... when you overthrew your masters and won our planet's freedom, I was not there to see it. And when you built that ramp, toiled and struggled by the sweat of your brow, working tirelessly around the clock for days on end, I was not there to lend a hand. Nor was I around when you fought each other for control of the planet in a bloody civil war. I wasn't alive when my father sent this vessel into space to capture merchant ships full of food and supplies, lest you all starve to death. But I know this much: you, and the crewmembers of the *Anarchy*, banded together to become the galaxy's most feared space pirates. As for me? I never got to see that happen either. Nor did I get to witness the raid on Star Fantasy. Yet that daring act is the reason for my existence; mine and thousands of others from the next generation of Nausties destined to follow in your footsteps."

Remarkably this inspired a smattering of applause. Though many had heard of the girl's prowess as an orator, few in that crowd of thousands had ever heard Estrella speak publicly. Her confidence and poise were mesmerizing. They were about to get their money's worth.

"I got to see most of what happened next, though. I, like all of you, bore witness to the attack by planet Earth. The devastation, the sorrow it brought. I was a small child and I saw it all through a child's eyes, but I grew up hearing the tales of bravery, valor, and sacrifice. Meanwhile the *Anarchy*, after racing across the galaxy in an effort to lead the enemy astray, was destined to be lost in space, never to be heard from again. *That* is what I was taught. We all were. Until one day, they came back."

By now the crowd was silent as a church, wondering what point she was trying to make. The temperature outside was dropping like a stone, causing people's breath to turn to vapor when they exhaled. Estrella paused to take a long drag from her breather unit before continuing.

"And then? They arrived, only to find their world had changed. Everything was different and many found it hard to adjust. But there was a problem my friends, one which we've only recently discovered, and it's not what we originally thought. They weren't just drunken wildmen roaming the streets at night assaulting our citizens, getting thrown out of bars and vandalizing businesses. Oh no, it was much more complicated and disturbing than that. Little could our returning heroes have known, but they'd all been infected with a microorganism, a parasite which is now seeking to colonize the very planet we now call home."

She waited a few moments for the audience to process what she'd just told them.

"*That*, brothers and sisters, is what has caused the recent tragedies. The one to blame for what has happened to us is not a long-lost crew of sailors from outer space. The one to blame is not a Human, not an Enoshi, not a Zorg, nor a Slart. It is not a Suidonji or a Schpleefti. What is, in fact, responsible for these horrors is a bug, a virus, invisible to the naked eye. And this tiny organism has an agenda all its own. I must tell you, what your leader told you tonight is completely correct. My parents' killers are, in all likelihood, right now hiding inside the cargo hold of the *Anarchy*."

This elicited a swirl of gasps. Estrella waited for the inevitable panicked questions from her audience. No one dared. They merely stared at her in wide-eyed disbelief.

"Only they would have no recollection of committing the act, you see? That's because the microorganism which has entered their systems attacks the brain of its host. It has infected them all, every last one of them. Each and every one of those unwitting heroes from our planet's history could transform into a ravenous killer at any moment and not remember a thing the next day. But, unfortunately, that's only the start of our troubles, my friends. Any one of us could be infected as well.

They've been among us for months, breathing the same air, drinking the same water, eating the same food. We could, any of us, be carriers. Become tomorrow's mass murderers. That's what the microorganisms are seeking. It is an alien intelligence which desires supplanting all other species with its own. We don't know much more than that and we don't know why either. But we do know it seeks to *replace* us, and that it will do so by making us go insane. Please understand when I say this, because I speak the truth: it wants us to kill each other. It wants us to exterminate ourselves. That's why I beg of you, go home to your families. Don't give in to the rage."

Finally, someone spoke up.

"But what can we do to stop this from happening?" asked Sunda. "Don't give in to the rage, you say. How will that save us from the next attack?"

Googy sounded off next. "He's right, you know? You want us to just drop our weapons and let these pirates go? Is that such a good idea, girl? Who's to say they might take off and go raiding the galaxy? They'll start another war, they will."

"You have my word, they will not." responded Estrella, looking about at all the worried faces. Babirusa was next to express his concerns. Turning his head, he asked what was on everyone's mind right about then. Namely, how could she ever hope to guarantee such a thing?

"No offense, Daughter of Solomon," he snorted. "But how can you promise that? I'm just an old ship's mechanic, I understand a little, more than some, but what you've described sounds like it can't actually be controlled, not if it affects the brain. Sounds more like we'll be right back where we left off, fearing for our lives. Forgive me if I sound insulting, but we'll need a bit more than promises at this point." Korat was already thinking the same.

"The pig's right." he bellowed. "You promise we'll be safe. How are we supposed to believe that? Is there a cure for it? As you said, what if we're *all* infected? If so then any one of us could go crazy and start killin' folks, just like them kids was gonna do over in the projects."

That was precisely what she'd hoped someone would ask.

"Yes." she yelled out over the rumbling of the crowd. "There *is* a cure. We've already developed the antidote for it in our labs." This prompted a tidal wave of excited screams as thousands of people inched toward her. Fearing being trampled, Babirusa had to move back from the advancing throng, causing Estrella to jostle from side to side. Estrella kept her cool.

"Now calm down. Calm down all of you. The danger will soon pass. At this very moment we are mass-producing a vaccine. By morning we'll be inoculating the crew of the *Anarchy*. Within weeks we'll have enough for everyone, you have my word."

Estrella sensed she had turned the tide. A silence stretched on for what seemed an eternity. Then, from somewhere in the crowd, someone started clapping. Slowly but surely it spread, soon to be replaced by cheers. Estrella could finally relax. It seemed the crisis had been averted. Even Sunda smiled with delight, prompting the young teenager to acknowledge him with a wave. When Babirusa let her down, Estrella made her way through the happy throng to give the beast a big hug. While the crowd continued to celebrate the news, he stooped down to look her in the eyes.

"I'm sorry, Daughter of Solomon," he said, as people gathered around to join him in thanking her. "You're truly just as they say. I shouldn't have doubted you." He then turned to face the crowd and immediately ordered his followers to disperse.

"Alright then." He roared. "You heard what she said. Go home to your families. She has given her word!"

CHAPTER FIFTEEN
PRETTY FLOWERS

T he next thirty days saw a dramatic turnaround for the embattled citizens of New Australia while the planet desperately sought a return to some sense of normality. Estrella's leadership and political maneuvering were crucial in accomplishing this. On the morning following the encounter with Sunda's vigilantes, Megalocyathus and his colleagues appeared at the base of the *Anarchy* bearing vials of vaccine. Only this time things were done differently. This time they were escorted by members of the Planetary Police Department.

Estrella wasn't about to take chances. The location of the secret lab was revealed at the last possible moment, and only when it was deemed necessary to send policemen down to retrieve the scientists. Even then she eliminated any risk of an attack by would-be assassins. To begin with, former pirates and their officers were "sequestered" on the ship the whole time. Perhaps a better word for it would have been "quarantined", though people involved in the operation were discouraged from using such a term.

By mid-afternoon the entire crew were vaccinated, forced to endure a rather painful injection into their deltoid or thigh, whichever the individual preferred. That, of course, would be the only choice they were given. No one was spared, starting with their commander Admiral Slout. In fact, he was first to go, wincing with pain as the needle entered his upper arm. Estrella, upon seeing him glare loathingly at the long syringe, warned him not to watch it going in. Trying to appear brave in front of the other sailors he chose to do so anyway. After seeing his reaction no one else dared to look while getting theirs.

Estrella had a lot left to accomplish if she was ever going to restore peace and security to the planet. As promised, she didn't stop with inoculating the former pirates. Within a week scientists had mass-produced the vaccine, in quantities capable of protecting the entire population.

This was accomplished by first generating an antigen which would trigger an immune response. In order to do so, cells of the parasite responsible for infecting the brains of victims were harvested from cadavers of crewmen killed during the night of the riot. Recombinant proteins subsequently were derived from these pathogens, with the antigen separated from the cells then purified. Next came the addition of an adjuvant to enhance the immune response. Stabilizers were then added to prolong storage life so that multi-dose vials could be used. Having succeeded in this, soon everyone was able to be inoculated. This took several weeks, but it was finally completed. New Australia and all her people, both young and old, were safe. The threat of self-annihilation was over.

***

It had been a month since roving gangs of vigilantes chased down and murdered former crewmen from the planet's original pirate ship. The people of New Australia sought to put the whole, ugly affair behind them. And yet this would prove to be quite easy to achieve when the entire population was invited to witness a truly memorable event: a commencement ceremony for the first graduating class of cadets from New Australia's Merchant Marine Academy.

As the last of the planet's citizens received their shots, thus ensuring no further spread of the parasites, Estrella focused her attention on the task of planning the grand affair. It was expected to draw tens of thousands. Therefore, she wanted to create something which would rival anything folks had seen before, including their annual Independence Day celebration. Her goal was to produce an experience they'd not soon forget, marshalling all her resources and talent in order to do so.

On the day of the big event, people left work early to find a good spot from which to view the ceremony. It was held in the town square and set to begin shortly after dusk. A large stage was constructed and behind that a small grandstand for dignitaries such as Captain Kscheeech and all the chieftains from the planet's tribes. Facing the stage was a large area cordoned off which included chairs for the 178 cadets. Behind that spectators would be allowed to stand and watch as one by one each student would be called forward to receive their diploma. The same PA system used in the Independence Day celebration was set up, a new lighting system was installed, and massive speakers were mounted upon platforms so that everyone for miles around could hear. In the center of the stage was a podium and next to that was a special seat reserved for Megalocyathus, dean of the school. Next to him was to be seated Admiral Slout, head of the Department of Naval Defense. And next to him was to be seated the guest of honor, Estrella Mwonga. Not surprisingly, she was to give the commencement address. The students had voted on this days prior. Naturally there was no better choice, for this was to be their special day and she was certainly a big part of it. Tomorrow they'd be officers serving in the planet's merchant fleet. They'd join crews of trade ships travelling the known galaxy.

To kick off the festivities a DJ played music to liven up the crowd. An announcer read off the names of each of the fifty chieftains as they filed in to take their seats. Some of course had only recently been *installed*, due to the many deaths resulting from the bombing of the Assembly Hall. But no one was dwelling on matters such as these on such a happy, wondrous occasion. Estrella and those helping her plan the day's ceremony had chosen to make no mention of it. This was to be the day New Australia *moved on*. It was the way of Nausties: honor the past, and by all means honor those who made possible the present. *Meanwhile, try and forget the ugly details of how it actually came to be.*

When the chieftains had seated themselves the announcer then turned to introducing the first special guest of the day, Admiral Slout. This inspired a round of applause from the gallery of dignitaries seated in the grandstand. The crowd applauded him as well. It warmed the heart to see how citizens of New Australia had chosen to once again appreciate his service to the planet. That's precisely what Estrella had hoped for. Slout mounted the steps to the stage and dutifully saluted them before seating himself. After the admiral's introduction, the announcer then turned his attention to the dean of the school.

By now all of New Australia was aware of how Megalocyathus had stepped in to aid Estrella Mwonga in developing a vaccine for the pathogen which had once threatened their world. However, no one could have predicted the emotional reception which would follow. The mere mention of his name caused the crowd to cheer wildly. Then something remarkable occurred. All fifty chieftains stood to applaud the venerated scientist as he made his way up the steps and crossed the stage to his chair. Pausing briefly to raise a tentacle toward them and then toward the audience the old Slartigifijian politely took his seat. This was followed by the entry of all 178 cadets. It took several minutes for things to settle down before the ceremony could continue; and at that point most everyone anticipated that Estrella Mwonga would be introduced. But Estrella had a surprise in store for the nearly fifty thousand citizens who'd made it out that evening. *She'd brought along some friends.*

Upon being announced as the day's keynote speaker, Estrella strode confidently onto the main stage to be greeted by yet another surge of ecstatic cheering. Before taking her seat, she waved joyfully to the crowd as they roared with delight. Then she signaled toward a large group of individuals who'd gathered nearby, beckoning them to come forward. In all the excitement they'd gone unnoticed by the tens of thousands in attendance, but soon all eyes were upon a mass of handsome, well-groomed sailors marching in formation. They were recognized immediately. It was the crew of the *Anarchy*.

They'd been given new service caps similar to those of the academy cadets seated before them, however as they crossed in front of the stage, arms swinging in unison, feet moving in lock step, people weren't terribly sure how to react. The crowd let out a gasp when they realized Estrella had decided to invite the remaining two hundred some-odd crewmembers who'd once been forced to hide out in their own ship from an angry mob. Folks who'd participated in the riot, even those who'd chased down and murdered some of their shipmates, were now witnessing something truly amazing. Estrella Mwonga wanted them to be recognized for their service to New Australia.

And yet there was so much more to it than that. She was suggesting they be welcomed once more into Naustie society. Had she gone insane? It had only been a month since gangs swept through the streets and vigilantes had hunted them in the tunnels below the surface. Hardened tribal chieftains squirmed in their seats and muttered to one another how inappropriate it was to invite them. *People need time to lick their wounds; have a chance to sort things out. It is too soon,* they opined to one another. However, they were wrong. As usual, Estrella knew exactly what she was doing. She went over to the podium and spoke into the microphone.

"Brothers and sisters, fellow Nausties, please join me, will you? Join me in welcoming the crew of our planet's most famous, most legendary ship. Let us once again welcome back our heroes."

In her booming, amplified voice, she almost dared them to reject her. Yet they did not. It took a few seconds but soon clapping could be heard. Then it grew to something more. She would not have to ask a second time.

"Welcome back." she could hear someone yelling. "Yeah. Welcome back, brothers." yelled a second. That's when the tide turned.

It started with ten, then a hundred. Soon it was ten thousand. The clapping increased, quickly evolving, ebbing and flowing, then expanding. Next came pandemonium. People cried out, expressing sincere, heartfelt passion. It was like a bomb had gone off for a second time. They wept. They waved and flailed their arms. Many proclaimed their gratitude. Some begged forgiveness. Pretty soon the class of cadets themselves stood to applaud them. Following that even the chieftains rose to their feet. It would be several minutes before Estrella attempted to regain control. When she sensed the outpouring of emotion had reached its zenith, she hastily returned to the microphone.

"Thank you." she said. "Thank you all. This, my friends, is what it means to be a Naustie. Here we honor our heroes."

This inspired even more cheers. Her timing was impeccable; even as it slowly died down, she knew she had them in the palm of her hand. It was at that moment that she gestured for Megalocyathus to begin the ceremony. The crew of the *Anarchy*, meanwhile, remained in place, facing the audience, standing proudly. Taking his cue from the spry teenager, the dean of the school shuffled over to the podium. Estrella took her seat.

"Well, my friend." he said into the microphone, pivoting slightly so as to acknowledge the youngster. "I must say, you're a tough act to follow."

This sparked a surge of laughter from the audience. Even former crewmen of the *Anarchy* chuckled in response but maintained their composure as they stood at ease. It was rare for a Slart to make a whimsical comment. Humor typically eluded them. Only difference was Megalocyathus had spent the past eighteen months working with teenagers.

"I guess I'll have to make do," he continued, pausing momentarily in order to glance at the podium. Estrella had compiled for him a list of the graduates, which was organized according to their seating assignments. All he had to do was read them off in order, right after Estrella finished her speech. But first there was a short introduction provided in the text. This he examined briefly before proceeding.

"Before we begin, let us first observe a moment of silence for those who lost their lives during the tragedies at both the tribal assembly hall as well as the town market. Let us please bow our heads and remain silent so that we may pay our respects to those who died."

In the margin, he could see where Estrella had written in parentheses: *(count down from thirty to zero)*. This he did, at first muttering to himself, then realizing he was supposed to do this in his head. When the recommended period of time had concluded, he returned to the script and thanked everyone before continuing.

"Now let us recognize some very special people in our audience here this evening. Ladies and gentlemen, if you would please, a big round of applause for the parents of this year's graduates."

The crowd let loose with a resounding wave of whoops and hollers, accompanied by enthusiastic clapping, just as the speaker requested. Estrella understood her audience well. No one would deny the cadets' parents their due on a day like this. As directed by the script, Megalocyathus waited a full minute before proceeding. It was just the right amount of time to let proud mothers and fathers enjoy their moment in the sun. That said it was in effect a metaphor for what everyone was to feel. The young cadets, waiting patiently in their seats to be called up and receive their diplomas, bedecked in pressed gray uniforms with red berets cocked to the side, were a product of the very same society which *all* Nausties were a part of. Every citizen, young and old, should feel the same sense of pride their parents enjoyed. When the prescribed sixty seconds had passed, Megalocyathus raised his tentacles. It was time to introduce the keynote speaker.

"Citizens of New Australia," announced the old Slart. "Please join me in welcoming today's speaker. Brothers and sisters, great chiefs of the tribal confederation, Nausties of all species, whether you be Enoshi, Suidonji, Schpleefti, Szorgolongian,

Human, or Slartigifigian, I present to you, New Australia's own, Estrella Mwonga."

With whatever they had left in their bodies, the crowd heaved yet another deafening roar as Estrella stood and walked over to the podium. They were looking forward to a display of her innate gift for oratory, and frankly they were in for a treat. This time she'd had several days to prepare.

"Thank you, dean Megalocyathus. Congratulations, cadets." she proclaimed, pausing to allow the crowd to quiet down.

"And to you, citizens of New Australia, let me take a moment to thank you for making it out this evening. This is indeed a very proud moment in our planet's history."

Estrella could sense they'd exhausted themselves and needed a break from screaming their lungs out. She lowered her voice before moving on.

"My fellow Nausties, this truly is a great day. One which we achieved not as a handful of individuals, but as a people. Our first graduating class from our very own merchant marine academy they indeed deserve to be celebrated. I can certainly tell you they earned it. I for one couldn't have done it, and by the way, let me tell you, few of us could. Many of you here tonight would agree, I'm sure. Especially all the parents who saw the curriculum they had to complete."

This garnered a few whoops and hollers from the masses. Mothers and fathers of the cadets were the loudest.

"They studied the sciences. They studied the functions of a galactic freighter, every facet, every protocol, everything from stem to stern. What's more they learned how to lead, and that is vital to our planet's future. They have been instilled with a level of pride in not only in themselves but in what it means to be a citizen of our world."

"They are a part of the next generation of Nausties. But what does that mean for the future of New Australia? What should we expect of them as the years pass? I'll tell you. For we are them just as much as they are us, and they know, as does every Naustie, to look upon this opportunity with deepest respect for those who made today possible."

She was briefly interrupted with applause.

"Oh yes, they have been taught to fly a space craft, operate its engines, take off and land, and most of all, command its crew with bravery and integrity. They are the best and brightest, as many have said, and I for one have seen this to be true. But there is so much more to them than meets the eye. They know our planet's history, warts and all. They know what it took, the sacrifices which had to be made, some of which are unsettling, some of which are not for the weak of heart. However, it was all necessary in order to create the society we have today and they've been made to understand this. That's why the cadets you see before you are the people who stand to inherit the mantle of leadership. View all our predecessors with reverence, not just the fallen. You, my brothers and sisters, those who fought alongside the many warriors who died in the struggle for freedom, we salute you."

This invited a much bigger response from the crowd. She gave them a few moments before addressing the cadets personally.

"Cadets of this year's inaugural class, again I congratulate you. And let me say this: remember the triumphs of the past. Most of all, understand what will be demanded of you, so to. Ensure there will always be a tomorrow for your countrymen. Make no mistake about it. Decisions will be made, some of them difficult. Sacrifices will be expected, some of them barely conceivable at the beginning of the day. Rest assured that you, just like your parents before you, just like our heroes who gave their lives, will someday find yourselves facing challenges that will test your very souls. Believe me, I know."

Estrella eyed a few of the cadets in the front row who'd known her growing up. Her words made them nod and snicker knowingly. She quickly returned her attention to the rest of the graduating class.

"I was lucky. I had two great teachers, Solomon and Felina. But let's be honest. All that my mother and father tried teaching me would have done me no good if it hadn't been for people like Megalocyathus, guiding me every step of the way. He was my mentor, just as he is now yours. When I needed him, he was there to help save the planet from danger. As was captain Kscheeech and admiral Slout. I learned a lot from them. I'm sure they will always be there for me, should I need them again. And that's why you too must seek wisdom, wherever and whenever it may be offered. Fear not, my friends... there will always be those you can count on. For it is the way of our people. We support each other. We are family.

"In conclusion, let me leave you with some sound advice: Following tragedy, seek always to forge ahead. Never look back. Overcome the inevitable challenges which life presents you and yes, act morally and with fairness toward all. That is what sets us apart as intelligent beings. In fact, that's what sets us apart as a people and a culture of many cultures melded into one. For it is our differences that not only make us unique, they but make us stronger than our foes. That is why no one, no planet, no species shall ever destroy us. Those who have sought to defeat us have failed. Even alien microorganisms bent on causing our extermination has been weeded out, identified, isolated, and eliminated. Perhaps they should have taken a lesson from our enemies from Earth.

"My point is this. *By whatever means necessary*, remember those words. New Australia can and will survive. Your task is to see to it. And that is the charge you will be given today when you cross this stage to receive your diploma. You must see to it that our planet society lives on."

The audience erupted. Over the din of cheering, Estrella thanked the audience once more. This prompted a standing ovation from the chieftains seated in the gallery behind her. On cue, the sound engineer played some inspiring music while Estrella yielded the podium to the dean of the academy. Megalocyathus happily rose to resume his duties while the crowd continued to cheer wildly. The celebration would continue for several minutes as Estrella smiled from her seat and waved back at the audience. The old Slart didn't wait for them to calm down this time. He launched right into reading off the names of the graduates, calling them up to the stage to receive their diplomas. The crowd continued clapping and cheering throughout, applauding every cadet as their name was announced. It seemed as though the celebration would never end. Even the dignitaries seated onstage wanted to be a part of the joy and pride being expressed.

All except for one, that is. For there was one person among them, one particular individual who had long since lost interest in the jubilation and outpouring of patriotic fervor. It was Admiral Slout, and despite his position as head honcho for the Department of Naval Defense, despite the fact his crewmen had been honored and recognized, and despite the fact he'd been specifically mentioned in Estrella's wondrous speech, his thoughts had drifted about like a rudderless ship.

Sure, he'd sat through the emotion-packed commencement address and listened to Estrella's words of bravery and dedication to duty. He'd nodded politely, applauded whenever he heard others doing so, however his mind was somewhere else. It wasn't the parasites inside his brain this time. Those had thankfully been eradicated.

And it wasn't due to side effects caused by the vaccine. His nights were no longer filled with horrific images which compelled him to bolt upright in bed remembering things he could not bear thinking about; trying desperately to believe he was not capable of such acts yet knowing in his heart they'd occurred. Like others within his crew he'd struggled through the withdrawals, clinging to words of encouragement from friends like Kscheeech who would always reassure him that whatever he'd done, it was not his fault. That, with time, had been enough to get him through those first few days after being vaccinated. A gallon or two of ale at night didn't hurt either, even if Slart scientists had warned him not to over-indulge. There were some days he simply couldn't shake it off and get on with his life. Other days he tried rationalizing that he might only be imagining things that didn't really happen. Now, for some reason, it was starting again.

As the crowd of thousands continued to applaud, as an endless queue of cadets passed by to receive their diplomas, the bad dreams returned. Slout tried blocking them out. Fought against them entering his mind and told himself, "It's a lie. Stop it, stop thinking those things. I was never there, couldn't have been." This eventually succeeded, just as it always did. To complete the process, he simply needed to focus his attention on something which might distract him: something attractive, something appealing. He looked around for a minute or two, but initially made no progress. Seeing nothing within the sea of bright young faces, eager to hear their names called, Slout ultimately looked away, out toward a big field where his old ship was parked. He stared at the massive freighter-turned pirate ship-turned freighter once more. Then something else caught his eye.

Though some distance from him, he noticed a clump of flowers growing near the vessel's landing gear. They were quite beautiful, with purplish-colored petals sprouting from long stems of green. It was enough to keep his mind occupied. He studied the plants for a few moments, focusing his attention just long enough so that the flashbacks would pass. Meanwhile the lavender and white sprouts made him remember something more pleasant: his time walking through the forests of Green Planet. The budding plants made him recall hordes of giant flowers he'd seen growing in a clearing between the trees. There'd been thousands of them, and in the next clearing thousands more, perhaps millions. Clouds of pollen eventually caused him to retreat to the ship on that lovely day; but thoughts of this somehow put his mind at ease. He finally cracked a smile.

However, there was something else that captured his attention. He started to notice how there was a long trail of them growing along a dirt road leading away from the *Anarchy*. It almost looked like someone had taken the time to arrange them, perhaps in an effort to make it more aesthetically pleasing. That was unlikely. Who would have had the time to do such a thing? Nevertheless, it appeared as though someone had. Slout chuckled as his eyes followed the line of lavender buds as they led away from the ship, out toward a gigantic mound of iron ore. This had been piled up by mining engineers in anticipation of being loaded onto ships bound for the steel mills of Suidonj, as well as it's colonies on Frabrak 3. Within days they'd be departing. The admiral continued to smile as he viewed thousands of tiny lavender petals barely visible as they seemed to make their way toward the mountain of ore.

"Pretty flowers," Slout mumbled.

He failed to make the connection.

BEFORE YOU GO

Thank you for reading Return of Anarachy: The Fall of New Australia by King Everett Medlin. If you enjoyed the book, please do us a solid and leave a review. A few sentences about what you liked goes a long way. We really appreciate it.

You can learn more about Chandra Press, our books, and our authors by visiting our website www.chandrapress.com

If you like free books, exclusive deals, and more, join our awesome newsletter: www.chandrapress.com/newsletter.